Pa

'You're not quite as icy as you'd like to be, are you?' Stuart said to Claire.

She felt a hot wave sweep over her and tried to move away from the exquisite torture of Stuart's hands, but he merely clasped her closer to him. She threw back her head and stifled a moan. He smiled at her flushed features and pained expression.

'Tell me exactly what you want me to do – and none of that coy "sleep together" business.'

Claire was torn. She didn't want to submit to the sweet, swelling ache between her legs and yet she felt she would die of frustration if she didn't.

Palazzo

JAN SMITH

BLACK
lace

Black Lace novels are sexual fantasies.
In real life, make sure you practise safe sex.

First published in 1997 by
Black Lace
332 Ladbroke Grove
London W10 5AH

Typeset by CentraCet, Cambridge
Printed and bound by Mackays of Chatham PLC

ISBN 0 352 33156 9

Chapter One

Claire Savage switched her lamp off with a snap and turned to check the shadowy office. The silhouettes of her desk, filing cabinets and leather sofa were the same as usual; only her new tropical fish tank stood out gleaming and unfamiliar in the half-light, the gemstone colours of the fish twisting and circling. She smiled. The tank was a luxury, she knew, but one she felt entitled to as managing director. And, heaven knows, she had worked hard enough for it; after just five years, Barker and Savage was one of the most successful advertising agencies in the UK, with a turnover that would make Croesus blush.

She walked past her desk to turn the tank lights off, and hesitated as something caught her eye from under a pile of papers. She pulled the photograph frame from its hiding place and stared at the face that smiled back at her. Sean. In spite of everything that had happened between them, Claire still felt her stomach twist. She traced the high-cheekboned face with its lopsided, dangerous smile and sighed. The agency's success had had its price; that price had

1

been her marriage. If she hadn't been so caught up in her work she might have spotted the warning signs: his late nights in the studio, the clients who needed entertaining at weekends; the unexpected gifts of flowers, no doubt to ease a guilty conscience. As it was, she had had no idea that Sean was seeing somebody else until the woman herself had called to tell her so, and then Claire's pride had left her no alternative but to tell him to leave. She knew she was giving the woman exactly what she wanted, but couldn't help herself. The hurt and sense of betrayal went too deep. And so her marriage of ten years had been shattered, with one simple slam of a door.

Claire dropped the photo into a drawer and turned the fish tank lights off. As she made her way to the ladies toilet, she wondered wearily how she was going to last until the following morning. She had booked a week in Venice more out of defiance than anything else, and hadn't been looking forward to going on her own. Then her friend Cherry had offered to go with her, and suddenly the prospect seemed much more attractive. In fact, now she could hardly wait to get away. Bold, brash and big-hearted, Cherry could always be counted on to help Claire put her personal problems into perspective.

Claire slipped into one of the brightly lit cubicles, and as she did so she heard the door open.

'. . . so I told her to write her own bloody report.'

'You didn't!'

'You bet I did, silly cow.'

Claire recognised the voices straightaway. They belonged to two of her senior executives, who obviously didn't realise there was someone in one of the cubicles – least of all that it was their managing director.

'Have you seen the toyboy that's just joined Felicity's group?'

'The new graduate? What's he called again?'

'Nick Fisher.'

'Oh yes, Nick. *Very* nice. But a bit young and wholesome for me, my dear.'

Susan giggled. 'Young, yes, but maybe not as wholesome as you think.'

'What do you mean?'

'He caught me pulling my stockings up in the corridor. Poor love nearly died blushing. I thought his flies were going to pop!'

Deborah's voice grew wistful. 'What he needs is an older woman, to show him the ropes.'

'I know precisely what kind of ropes *you'd* show him.' Susan giggled again.

'Given half a chance, Susie,' sighed Deborah. 'He'd probably run a mile if I made a move on him, poor lamb.'

'He would if he saw you like that – you've got lipstick all over your teeth.'

'Where?'

'There. That's better. Now, where to? Fancy a spritzer in the Trout?'

The women's voices grew fainter as they went out of the toilet and disappeared down the corridor. Claire found she was gripping the lock of the door so tight her knuckles were white. Sean's photograph and the salacious talk about young Nick Fisher had got to her; her panties were damp. Furious with herself for being so easily aroused, she straightened her clothes and went to wash her hands.

Her eyes met her reflection in the mirror. The woman who stared back was undeniably attractive, with a sleek black bob, smooth skin and eyes that had an almost oriental air. But the determined set of the mouth in the flushed face warned the world she was not a woman to trifle with. Claire sighed and blinked away tears of frustration. Just three months without a

3

man, and she was having to fight off the urge to masturbate in the office toilet! She had never thought of herself as highly sexed before. In fact, she suspected her lack of enthusiasm in the bedroom had been the main reason Sean had found someone else. She combed her hair and carefully re-applied her lipstick, although she didn't know why she was bothering. There was no-one waiting at home to appreciate it.

It was dark and raining when Claire reached the car park. She turned her collar up against the drizzle and ran over to her Mercedes, tottering a little in her high-heeled court shoes. She plipped the alarm off and swung herself thankfully into the leather interior. She turned the key in the ignition. The engine turned over and then died. She tried the key again. A cough and then nothing. Damnation! Claire slammed her hand on the wheel. After waiting a few moments, she tried the ignition a third time, but with the same result. Seething with irritation, she climbed out of the car and lifted the bonnet, staring at the regiment of mechanical parts as the rain lashed down at her. Why was she doing this? She didn't know one end of a crank shaft from the other. She shrugged and climbed back into the car to find her mobile phone.

The breakdown number was engaged. It gave Claire no comfort to know she wasn't the only driver stranded in the rain, but filled her instead with frustration – even if she managed to get through, it was likely to be ages before they could reach her. She tried the number again. This time it rang. As she waited for someone to answer, tapping her nails on the dashboard, she saw the door to the agency open and the figure of a man emerge. He walked quickly towards the gates, hunched against the rain, and was halfway across the car park when he spotted Claire's Mercedes with its bonnet up. He hesitated, as if debating with himself, and then changed direction towards her. She sent up a silent prayer of thanks and wound the window down.

'Do you want a hand?' he asked.

Claire almost laughed as she recognised Nick Fisher. From what she had heard in the ladies toilet it was him that needed the hand, not her. She forced herself to look into his serious eyes. 'I'm trying to get through to the AA, but I'm not having much luck.'

Nick wiped the rain from his face. 'I'll have a look at it if you like. You can always try the AA again later, if I can't get it going.'

'OK. Thanks.' Claire watched him as he bent over the bonnet. There was something about the arrogant way he held his body that reminded her of Sean. However, the graduate was nowhere near as tall, with blue eyes rather than green, and he wore his hair shorter than Sean. Still, she had to admit, he was very, very horny. After a few minutes, he came back to the window.

'I think your points are wet. Do you have something I can wipe them with?'

Claire shook her head. She didn't allow so much as a duster to clutter the interior of her precious car.

'Never mind.' Nick shrugged. 'I'll use my sleeve.' He returned to the front of the car.

Then Claire had a brainwave. She bent down and wriggled out of her panties, sliding them down and over her feet. She knocked on the window, and Nick reappeared.

'Will these do?' She handed him the bundle.

He took them, and, realising what they were, blushed furiously. 'Probably.' He didn't look at Claire, and bent over the bonnet once more. After a minute he signalled to her to try ignition again. She turned the key and held her breath. To her disappointment, the engine stuttered once and then purred into life. Nick gave her the thumbs up and slammed the bonnet down.

'Here.' He passed Claire's panties back to her through the window. As their fingers touched, he jerked his hand back as if it had been burned.

'Can I give you a lift somewhere?' she asked.

He hesitated.

'Go on, it's the least I can do,' urged Claire, watching the uncertainty flicker across his face, and knowing she shouldn't be putting herself so blatantly in the path of temptation. It had always been one of her most unbreakable rules not to fraternise with employees.

When Nick finally nodded and made his way round to the passenger door, Claire was surprised by the flash of triumph she felt. She knew then that she was going to seduce him. For a moment, she suffered a stab of guilt – he was ten years younger than she was. But what the hell! Hadn't she always put her career before her sex life in the past? It was time she started being a bit more selfish. He climbed into the car and she watched him fasten his seatbelt.

'Where to?'

'Tottenham Court Road.'

'Good. That's not far from me.' She punched the buttons on the CD and Chris Isaak's 'Wicked Game' filled the interior. As she drove, she became aware that her skirt was sliding up her thighs, and resisted the urge to pull it down. Her legs had always been one of her best features, and she guessed that her passenger might think so too. She was right. Nick couldn't tear his gaze from the flex of her thigh as she drove, nor from the shadow of her crotch, doubly alluring because she had no underwear on. He shifted in his seat. A drop of rain fell off Claire's hair to snake down the long line of her throat, illuminated suddenly by the headlights of a passing car.

'Are you all right, Nick?'

'What?'

'You're very quiet.'

'Oh, yes, sorry. Just a bit wet, that's all.'

'How are you enjoying life at the agency?'

'It's great. Felicity's keeping me busy.'

'I bet she is.' Claire gave a throaty chuckle. 'She's a bloody good account director. No regrets, though?'

He met her bold glance and shivered. 'No. No regrets.'

'Are you cold?'

'A bit.'

'What you need is a cup of coffee. We're only a few minutes away from my place. Can I offer you one?'

'Well – '

'Please. I'll feel awful if I drop you home like this.'

'OK. Thanks very much.'

Five minutes later, the Mercedes slipped into the parking space on the street below Claire's maisonette. She found herself shaking as she killed the engine, suddenly unsure how to proceed. It had been ten years since she had slept with anyone but Sean, and here she was, about to seduce a twenty-one year old. She must be out of her mind! Nick got out of the car, and she followed, locking the doors and running through the rain to join him under the porch. She fumbled in her briefcase for her keys, and pulled them out, only to drop them again on the pavement. She and Nick both bent down to pick them up, and then stopped, staring into each other's eyes as they reached for the keys together. Neither of them could mistake the need they saw there.

Claire grabbed the keys and straightened up. 'I think I've made a mistake. I'll run you home.'

Nick gazed into her green eyes, and then shook himself. 'Whatever you say.' He walked back to the car and she followed him slowly, oblivious to the slanting rain and cursing herself for being a tease and a coward. She had really blown it now. Miserably she plipped the alarm off again and they both climbed back into car.

'Where did you say you lived?'

'Tottenham Court Road.'

Claire went to put the key in the ignition, but to her surprise, Nick reached across and stopped her.

'Are you OK?'

'Of course.' Claire looked down at his hand where it rested on hers, and felt recklessness sweep over her. In response to his question, she lifted his hand. She brushed his palm with her lips and then slowly took his index finger into the heat of her mouth. She took it in as far as it would go, and then withdrew it luxuriously, tasting the salt of his skin and faint tang of engine oil. Nick sucked in his breath as she moved on to his middle finger and gave it the same lavish attention.

'Oh, God,' Nick sighed.

Claire was surprised to see that he was leaning against the headrest, his eyes closed. His coat had slipped, and she could tell by the bulge in his trousers that her mouth was having a definite effect. Slowly she pulled the finger out again.

'Do you want me to stop?'

'No! Please, no.' Nick opened his eyes and stared into hers. Then doubt flickered across them. 'That is, unless you want to?'

Claire reached for his other hand and placed it on her breast. He could feel the taut weight of it in his palm, and the dampness of her blouse where it was sticking to her flesh. He shuddered and made a clumsy attempt to put his mouth to the clinging material.

'No.' She pushed him back. 'Wait.' She glanced at the windows to check they were steamed up and then

8

wriggled out of the driving seat, swivelling round to sit astride Nick on his seat. He stared at her, his eyes wide and questioning. She bent down and kissed him, putting the full weight of her thirty-one years into that kiss, ripe with the promise of fulfilment. Nick groaned under her lips and moved his hands to explore her body, but she caught them in her own and pinned them down. Once she was certain they were still, Claire released Nick's hands and unloosened his tie. She pulled it out of his collar and then used it to bind his hands together.

'Claire?'

'Shhh.' She pulled his arms over his head and tied his hands firmly to the headrest. 'Is that comfortable?'

'Yes, but . . .'

Claire silenced him with another kiss, this time even deeper than before. He returned it frantically. She could tell he was very, very turned on and the knowledge caused an answering rush of moisture between her legs. She leant back and looked at him. His chest rose and fell as she began to undo the buttons of his shirt.

'Oh God!'

'Shh.' She opened the shirt to reveal his chest, smooth but manly, the nipples puckered and desperate for her touch. She obliged, tracing her nails over them at first, and then nipping them playfully with her teeth. Nick groaned and Claire captured his face in her hands and kissed him again. He thrust his tongue into her mouth and she sucked on it knowingly for a moment, before leaning back again. Nick bit his lip and stared into Claire's hypnotic eyes, his gaze widening as hers dropped to his crotch. He shifted slightly under her and blushed. She reached for his zip and pulled it down, releasing him gently from the confines of his boxer shorts. He sighed as he felt the kiss of air on the fevered flesh. Claire leant back against the dashboard and watched him. He looked almost beautiful, and achingly vulnerable. She felt an intoxicating rush of power, that made her heart pound and body melt. She caressed the weeping tip of Nick's cock with one manicured fingernail. He could see the shadow between her legs and opened his own a little wider, to spread hers wider too. Claire followed his stare and smiled. She hitched her skirt up until the dark triangle of her sex was fully exposed. Never taking her eyes off him, she slipped a finger inside herself. As she expected, she was very wet. She sighed her satisfaction. Nick's cock leapt, his eyes rivetted by the movement of her hand. He tried to arch up to touch her and strained against his bonds. But they were too tight.

He watched Claire's flushed face. She had thrown her head back, eyes closed as she surrendered herself to the rub of her finger against her clitoris. She bit her lip. Heat thrilled and tingled through her, making her moan. She took her time, bringing herself to the very brink of climax, then pausing for a moment before bringing herself even closer still. Finally, she could hold it back no longer. She gave one last, urgent thrust and pleasure flooded through her as she came, shuddering on her finger.

'Please.' Nick groaned. 'Oh please!'

Claire opened her eyes and fixed them on Nick's face; she had almost forgotten him in the depth of her own pleasure. She smiled, placing her salty finger on his lips. He sucked at it greedily, and then nipped it with his teeth in his frustration. Surprised, she cried out and slapped him. The blow wasn't hard, but forceful enough to make him glare at her with sudden animosity. She reeled under the glance, and then laughed.

'Nick. I'm sorry.' She stroked his face and then ran a fingernail from his mouth, over his chin and throat

10

and down over his chest to his stomach. It stopped perilously close to his throbbing cock. His previous antagonism forgotten, he arched under her.

'Please!'

She leant towards him and took his bottom lip in her teeth, realising she had to take pity on him. Gently she wrapped her fingers around the shaft of his cock, and then lowered herself on to it. He shuddered and closed his eyes, his ecstatic face illuminated by the street light through the window. She clenched her muscles and felt him jerk under her, his cock gripped by the silken steel of her sex. For a moment she didn't move, simply savouring the feel of a man inside her again. Then she began to rock slowly, her knees on the seat, grasping the headrest where his hands were still tied. She reached down and reclined the seat, moving sensuously all the while on top of Nick, who was by now practically sobbing as she kissed him. With all her skill, Claire concentrated on wringing every drop of erotic pleasure from the boy beneath her. She moved as if underwater, never allowing his frantic gasps or thrusts to hurry her, until she felt him tense and give one last convulsive heave. He cried out with the force of his orgasm and then slumped on to the seat. The fact that Claire had not reached satisfaction herself this time didn't worry her. That hadn't been her objective.

'OK. It's a wrap, lovey.'

Cherry Sinclair slipped off the stool and reached for the dressing gown, pulling it on over the peephole corset and suspenders. She was so chilled her nipples felt as if they would tear the terry towelling to pieces.

'Why do you have to have it so bloody cold in here, Gerry?'

The photographer leered at her breasts. 'It has its uses.'

11

'Most people use a fan,' said Cherry. Gerry Fitz-Gerald might be one of the UK's leading glamour photographers, but he wasn't known for splashing his money around. 'You're just too tight-fisted!'

The photographer laughed, his raddled face wrinkling even more. 'A fair cop, my dusky beauty.'

Cherry grimaced. He often called her that. He had once told her that she reminded him of one of Gaugin's South Sea maidens, with her cloud of hair and melting brown eyes. Coming from anyone else she would have been flattered, but Gerry's compliments made her skin crawl. During his long career he had earnt a reputation for taking advantage of some of the younger models' eagerness to please.

Cherry disappeared behind the Japanese screen in the corner. 'It's a bit dark in here. I can't see a thing.'

'Hang on, lovey.' He flicked a switch and an uplighter winked on behind the screen.

'That's better, thanks.' Cherry guessed that the light had thrown her silhouette on to the parchment, and shrugged. It wasn't as if Gerry hadn't seen her naked before, as she strutted and posed for the top men's magazines. And besides, she had better things to think about.

As Cherry bent down to open her holdall and pull out her jeans and sweater, her mind went back to the date she'd had the night before. When she met Alex at the restaurant, she was relieved to find that he was just as attractive as she had remembered – maybe even more so. They chatted through the courses, and the electricity that crackled between them could have lit a power station. Then, just after the brandy had been brought to their table, he leant towards her, his Irish voice as melodious as an underground stream.

'Let's not pretend any more. Tell me, Cherry. Do you want me as much as I want you?'

Cherry had nodded slowly, her brown eyes widening under his. Then, to her surprise, he had slipped off his chair and disappeared under the table. The table cloth fell to the floor and hid him completely. Cherry looked anxiously at the waiters to see if they had spotted the movement, but they were going about their business as usual. She was quickly distracted from her worries, however, by the flutter of fingers on her ankles. Their touch as soft as a butterfly's wing, they drifted lazily up her legs, pausing to caress the sensitive skin at the back of her knees before continuing their journey to the top of her stockings. Cherry gasped as Alex's fingers found flesh.

'Is there anything else I can get you, madame?' The waiter bent over Cherry, who gasped then giggled.

'No thank you. I'm completely fine.' Puzzled, the waiter nodded and went away. Cherry took a gulp of brandy. The liquid warmed her throat and stomach, setting them aglow almost as much as her sex, which was beginning to throb under Alex's slowly circling thumbs. After he had stroked the pouting lips through the lace for a few moments, she felt him reach up and tug her pants off. There was a pause, and then her knees were pushed apart. She had almost sobbed as she felt the melting, unmistakable touch of a tongue on her clitoris.

'Are you all right in there, lovey?' Gerry's voice cut through Cherry's daydream. She shook herself and looked at her watch. Quarter past seven. She was going to be late to meet Claire.

'Yeah, fine.' To her annoyance, she couldn't reach the buttons at the top of her dress. 'Can you give me a hand with these?' She stepped out from behind the screen and turned her back to Gerry.

'Sure.' The photographer fastened the buttons deliberately slowly, pressing himself against Cherry's buttocks and letting his fingers linger on the skin of her shoulders and back. She laughed and turned towards him, then grabbed his bulging crotch.

'Ta very much.' Cherry grinned up into his saucering eyes. Her grip tightened. She hadn't managed to claw her way up in the business without learning how to deal with testosterone-riddled toads like Gerry FitzGerald. 'You're a dab hand with buttons, Gerry. And a great photographer.' The man's eyes were watering now. 'But I don't like your sneaky lighting effects, and I really don't fancy fucking you.' Cherry gave the rapidly softening cock a wrench. 'Not tonight. Not ever.' She picked up her holdall and the suitcase beside it and smiled brightly at the gasping photographer. 'Is that OK, *lovey*?'

'Anything you say . . .'

'Smashing! Ta ta, then. See you when I get back from my hols.'

Claire laughed when Cherry told her the story, with embellishments, a couple of hours later.

Cherry chuckled with her, and then sobered as she eyed the pile of clothes on Claire's bed. 'You can't possibly need this lot. We're only going for a fortnight.'

'I want to look my best.'

Cherry looked into her friend's still-smiling face. 'You *are* feeling better, aren't you?'

'A bit.' Claire grinned as she picked up a pair of bikini bottoms.

'So come on then. Spit it out.' Cherry's dark eyes were shining with curiosity. 'Who is he?'

Claire feigned surprise. 'I don't know what you mean.'

'You can't tell me that a man hasn't had a hand in this transformation.'

'No.' Claire smiled at the memory of Nick's grateful

14

expression when she had dropped him home. 'At least, not really.'

'You have slept with someone, though?'

Claire held up a very short pair of shorts. 'What do you think of these?'

'Very nice.' Cherry knew that her friend could make a sack look sexy, but had to admit that the shorts would show her legs to perfection. 'Stop trying to change the subject.'

Claire shrugged. 'I suppose I just got some of my self-confidence back.' That was putting it mildly. Her uninhibited response to Nick had really shocked her. But it had also given her a taste for adventure. Excitement curled in her belly at the prospect of finding out what else she was capable of.

'Well it's about time. I could wring Sean's neck for what he did to you.'

Claire frowned. She felt that way too, but didn't like to hear Cherry say it. 'And what about the new man in *your* life? Alex, isn't it?'

'He's nice enough. But just a one night stand, really. To tell you the truth, I've had enough of smooth-talkers and flash Harrys.' She sprawled on the bed and idly picked up the packet of condoms that Claire had tucked into a side pocket. 'In fact, I've come to a decision.'

'Oh? What's that?' In spite of herself, Claire blushed to see that Cherry had discovered the condoms. She could never be casual about things like that – even with her oldest friend.

'From now on,' said Cherry, 'I'm looking for Mr Right.'

Claire raised an eyebrow. 'Oh yes? The question is, will your Mr Right succeed in fighting off all your Mr Right Nows?'

'Ha, ha, very funny. But I'm serious. No more one night stands for me.'

Claire smiled to herself. Their trip was going to be even more entertaining than she thought. Here she was, footloose and fancy free after ten years, and Cherry had turned into Mother Teresa! She caught sight of her watch as she reached for a beach towel, and gasped. 'Oh Lord! You'd better give me a hand with this lot, or you'll not get the chance to put your resolution to the test in Italy. We're going to miss the plane!'

Chapter Two

'Now that,' sighed Cherry, 'is a thing of beauty. What do you think?'

Claire pushed her sunglasses on to the top of her head and looked at the boot her friend had placed on the café table. It was made of the softest beige suede, beautifully styled, and trimmed with indigo leather. Before Claire could deliver her opinion, however, the waiter arrived with their order and Cherry put the boot hurriedly back in its bag among all the others under the table.

The boot had been replaced with a new object for Cherry's adoration: a bowl of pistachio and vanilla *gelato*, scattered with dark curls of chocolate. Claire watched her friend dive into it with her spoon, wondering how on earth she managed to keep her spectacular figure – she always seemed to be eating. Smiling, she replaced her sunglasses, and leant back to enjoy the late summer sunshine on her shoulders. As always, the famous Piazza San Marco was teeming not only with sightseers but with pigeons too, that hopped about under the carts of street vendors, looking for crumbs. But their search was mainly in vain: the carts sold only sun hats, postcards and magazines, of no use to anyone but the tourists. She let the hubbub of voices wash over her and watched the scene through half-closed eyes. Even though it was September, she was glad of her sunglasses. The incredibly clear Venetian light seemed to bounce off every surface – the pale buildings and pavements, the sparkling water of the lagoon, and, most spectacularly, the gold leaf that gilded the Basilica's arched doorway, and the starry clock tower with its winged lion that loomed above them. For once, the clock tower and basilica were free of scaffolding, but the same couldn't be said of the other buildings around the square. Many were festooned in the ubiquitous plastic sheeting that had become as much a part of Venice as the green water of its canals. But Claire didn't mind. The city was a city of contrasts, and never failed to enchant her.

She sipped her espresso and slipped off her shoes to stretch her toes under the table. She and Cherry had spent the morning combing the lanes of the *mercerie* – the glitzy shopping streets that wound around the heart of the city. They had lingered enviously over silk shirts, Prada bags and perfume, both spending more than they could really afford, before eventually tiring of the crush of tourists and making their way back towards the hotel.

Oblivious to the stares of passers by, Cherry licked the last traces of ice cream from her bowl and leant back in her chair, a look of bliss on her face.

'That was lovely,' she said, closing her eyes. 'Now I could just have a little snooze.'

'Why don't you?' Claire leant forward to wipe a smear of ice cream from her friend's chin. 'You might as well. The whole city will be shutting down for siesta in half an hour or so.'

'What, even the shops?'

'Most of them.'

Cherry grimaced. 'I suppose if I can't shop, I might as well have forty winks. What about you?'

'I was thinking of having a wander around.'

'Bloody hell!' Cherry had picked up the bill, and was staring at it, her eyes wide with shock.

'Don't blame me.' Claire laughed wryly. 'It was you that insisted on plonking yourself down here, rather than waiting until we got back to the hotel. These cafés are notoriously expensive.'

'Now you tell me!' Cherry pulled a face, but handed her lire to the supercilious waiter anyway. She stood up and began to gather all their bags together. 'You run along. I'll take this lot back to the hotel.'

'Are you sure you can manage them?'

Cherry nodded. 'I'm as strong as an ox, me.' Then she tottered off across the square on her high-heeled sandals. Her friend watched her progress for a moment, noting with a smile how many masculine heads also turned to stare.

Back in the streets of the *mercerie*, many of the shopkeepers had already put up their shutters, and the crowds were beginning to thin. Claire made for the quieter streets of the *dorsoduro* – literally the 'hard back' of the city – which was made of tougher clay, and had encouraged the Venetians to build some of their finest palaces and churches on it. She paused for a few minutes on the bridge to gaze down the Grand Canal towards the Santa Maria della Salute. It was a sight that always made her catch her breath: the white domed cathedral rose from the buildings around it like something from a fairy tale, its white and grey stone shimmering in the light and reflecting in the murky waters of the waterway. Then she headed west, towards the quays of the *Stazione Marittima*. It was not a direction most people would take; the

19

quarter's narrow streets were unspectacular and even down-at-heel in parts, but Claire always thought of it as the real Venice, free of the mask it usually wore for tourists. The shops here sold practical things like vegetables and screwdrivers, rather than the frothy glass and plastic gondolas that were scattered over the rest of the city like a rash. As she expected, the crowds soon dwindled to almost nothing. She wandered down the alleyways with their faded pink and brown houses, looking up at the washing that was slung between the top stories, their reds, white and greens flapping gaudily against the sky.

Claire finally found herself alone in a tiny *campo*, or square, that was so small it didn't even have a name plaque. There was a single tree in the middle, beside a newspaper kiosk which had been boarded up for the siesta, and was flanked on one side by a canal, and on two others by a palazzo. She shielded her eyes against the sun and looked up at the elegant building, noting that it was in unusually good condition for that part of the city. Painted in shades of cream and beige, with white moorish plaster work edging the windows, it reminded of her of an elaborate ice cream. Like the rest of the houses in the quarter, its windows were shuttered against the midday sun, its balconies deserted.

Claire sat on the crumbling edge of the canal. She could have been the only person alive in the world. No sounds came from the alleyway or the palazzo, and there was nothing moving on the water: no boats, no cargo barges, not even a piece of litter to disturb the smooth surface. She closed her eyes. The sun was hot on her skin, and she could feel the stone simmering through her skirt to her thighs and buttocks. She shifted her legs against each other, feeling the skin stick and part reluctantly. She opened her eyes and was about to stand up and move towards the shade

20

of the tree, when she stopped. Someone had beaten her to it.

A man was already lying there, his skin dappled by the pattern of leaves above him. He was dressed in coarse blue trousers, with a striped shirt that was pulled out of his waistband and left open to reveal a tangle of hair. He was lying with his hands behind his head, perfectly relaxed. Claire guessed that he was a workman of some kind, taking advantage of the siesta to escape the heat. Not wanting to disturb his sleep, she stood up, with the intention of tiptoeing back to the alleyway. But then she froze. His eyes were open and watching her. She put her hand to her throat, feeling suddenly very alone and vulnerable. But then she relaxed a little. She was being silly. The deserted air of the *campo* was only an illusion, she knew. It was surrounded by houses, and she only had to call out and someone – probably dozens of people – would hear her. As if sensing her renewed confidence, the man smiled, his teeth white in the shadows. Claire looked more closely at him and found herself answering his smile with one of her own. He was a thick-set man, with a broad nose and short, tightly curled black hair. Not her usual type at all. And yet she was strongly drawn to him. He lifted his hand and beckoned slowly to her. In normal circumstances, his arrogance would have infuriated her, but the heat of the sun and their isolation in the square seemed to have cast them adrift from real life. She was curious in an odd, detached way.

She pushed her glossy black hair out of her eyes, aware of a trickle of sweat that was snaking down between her breasts, making her blouse stick to her skin. The man beckoned again. This time she moved towards him like a sleepwalker. She sank down on to the ground beside him, careful not to let her skirt or legs make contact, and returned his scrutiny with her own. His eyes were not what she had expected; they were not brown, but a dark, fathomless blue. And he was not as young as she had thought either; there were many grey hairs scattered among the black. But his body was hard and well-muscled in a way that spoke of hours of manual work, rather than of sessions in the gym. Claire saw something gleam out of the corner of her eye, and dropped her gaze to the medallion that lay among the curls on his chest. She recognised the universal symbol of St Christopher, the patron saint of travellers. The corners of her mouth tugged upwards, and, taking her smile as encouragement, the man reached for her hand. She resisted him slightly as he pulled it towards him, but then relaxed when he merely pressed it to his chest. His skin was warm, and slightly damp, and she could feel the tickle of hair on her palm. She let her hand rest there, motionless, while he never took his eyes off her face. His expression was neutral. Claire realised that it was up to her what – if anything – would happen next. She couldn't help herself. She felt the pulse beat in her throat as, almost of its own accord, her hand slid beneath the cotton shirt to seek out his nipple. She stroked her thumb across it. He frowned and smiled at the same time, a curiously questioning expression that made him look much younger, and even a little vulnerable. She flinched as he lifted his own arm to cup her left breast in his palm, but made no move to pull away. His hand looked very big and very dark where it rested against the white cotton of her blouse. Claire knew he had discovered that she was not wearing a bra, and felt her nipple tighten in anticipation. Her heart was thudding against her ribs, as if she had been running, and she wondered whether he could feel that too. Her skin grew damp under his palm as he circled her nipple with his thumb, teasing the sensitive flesh

22

through the material until it was stiff. He reached for the top button of the blouse, and slid it out of the button hole, then his eyes flickered up to meet hers in an unspoken question. She did not move, smile, or even breathe in response. Taking that as his answer, he moved down to the next button, and then the next, tugging the blouse out of her skirt and drawing it carefully back to expose her upper body to his gaze.

Claire closed her eyes and felt the sweat cool on her skin. She was proud of her breasts; they were not particularly large, but firm, with the last traces of her summer tan still gilding the skin and her apricot-coloured nipples. It seemed an age before the man touched her. When he did, his hands were cool, and she could feel the callouses on his palms as he cupped her breasts and then pinched first one and then the other nipple between his thumb and forefinger. The effect was electric. Claire moaned and arched herself up towards him. In reply he pulled her on to his lap, so that she was facing him, with her skirt bunched up around her thighs.

He bent his head to take one of her nipples in his mouth, and she grasped his wiry hair with her fingers. The subtle, spicy scent that rose from him made her head swim as he sucked on her, taking as much of her flesh into his mouth as he could. He reached up to curl his hand around the nape of her neck, as if to prevent her from pulling away. She didn't want to. The heat that had flushed between her legs had become an ache, and she was pressing herself more and more urgently against the rigid length of his cock beneath his trousers. He moved to the other breast, his stubble grazing the sensitive flesh. He polished it with his tongue, spiralling it over and over the nipple until she thought she would explode with tension. She ground herself against his cock. Then, suddenly, he stood up and pulled her to her feet. He led her to the kiosk and pressed her up against it.

She saw the wisdom of his move. They were less exposed in its shadow than they had been under the tree, hidden from anyone passing on the canal, and also protected from the sun. Their new position was only overlooked by the palazzo, but its windows were shuttered, and it looked deserted. Claire forgot her anxiety about being seen, as her lover urgently kissed her throat, and moved lower to imprison both her breasts in his hands, driven now by his own need. He roughly caressed her breasts, and dropped his mouth to snake his tongue into her bellybutton. Claire writhed with pleasure, pleasure that increased as he slid his hands under her skirt, and ran them up her thighs to the junction between. He pushed her skirt up and ground his palm against the drenched cotton of her pants.

'Yes,' she moaned. Then, remembering herself, '*Si, per favore.*'

He needed no further urging, but quickly wriggled his fingers beneath the elasticated rim and plunged them into her. She stiffened and pressed herself into the wooden wall of the kiosk, surprised by the onslaught of sensations that shook her. His fingers twisted in the slippery channel, revelling in her heat and the juice of her arousal. There was little finesse in his approach, but it still had the desired effect. Claire felt heat build in her as his fingers probed deeper. His thumb found the nub of her clitoris and began to rub it purposefully, almost roughly. Claire bit his shoulder to stop herself from crying out. She was used to her lovers taking their time with her, bringing her gradually to fulfilment. But this man was in a hurry. In spite of that, or perhaps even because of it, the pressure quickly built into a raw, urgent pulse that she'd never experienced before. The first spasm of her climax seized her, stiffening her limbs as he continued to probe relentlessly into her, his thumb almost punishing her clitoris with pleasure, until, shaking and sweating, she cried out her release. When it was over she fell back against the wood and opened her eyes.

Her lover was not looking at her, but tugging at his belt and the zip of his trousers to release his penis. Claire stared at it, detached. It reminded her of him: not long, but thick-set, and standing up proudly from the nest of black curls. She was so exhausted by her climax she felt almost no curiosity about what was going to happen next. The man dug in his pocket and brought out a packet; it was only when she heard the sound of tearing foil that she realised it was a condom. She made no effort to help him put it on, but merely watched as he slid it over his cock, groaning at the contact of his own hands and squeezing his eyes shut. When he opened them to stare at her again, the desire she could read in their navy depths sent heat shimmering through her once more. She bent down to remove her pants and kicked them to one side. Wasting no time, he gripped her buttocks under her skirt, kneading the flesh, and lifted her so that her toes of her sandals were only just brushing the ground. Then he pressed himself against her. She wriggled higher so that the lips of her sex were open and she could rub her clitoris directly on the shaft of his cock, and entwined her arms around his neck to kiss him. He returned her kiss fiercely, thrusting his tongue against hers, plundering the softest parts of her mouth. He had lifted her entirely off her feet now, and held her poised above his cock, his fingers spreading her buttocks so that her sex was open and aching for him. She felt the tip of something hard and silky nudge against her labia, seeking entrance, and for a second, she panicked. What was she doing?

25

What if someone saw them? But it was too late: the man pushed into her decisively. She was so wet he slid in easily, banishing all her thoughts of flight, reluctance and even shame. There was nothing left but lust. Claire's innermost flesh cleaved to the rod that pierced her and she moaned and pushed herself further on to it. There was no going back now. He raised and lowered her on himself, slowly at first and then with increasing urgency, until the kiosk was shaking with the force of his thrusts, and Claire was moaning aloud, with no thought of anything except her own release.

'Come and see this, my friend.' The man standing at the window beckoned to his companion, who paused, then put his pen down on the desk and went to join him. It took a moment or two for his eyes to adjust to the sunlight in the square outside, and even then he almost missed what the other man was looking at. But, suddenly, he saw the couple in the shadow of the kiosk.

The two men watched in breathless silence as, oblivious to their stare, the woman twined her legs around the waist of her lover, her limbs pale and shapely against the dark material of his trousers. Her skirt was pushed up around her waist, her blouse open to reveal her breasts, sheened with sweat and dancing to the rhythm of the man's thrusts. Her lips were parted with pleasure, her head thrown back, the long column of her neck exposed.

'*Che bellezza*,' murmured the first man, his face intent and greedy.

His companion had seen that look before. 'You want me to follow her?'

'*Naturalmente*. But of course.'

* * *

She felt the man stiffen inside her and pulse his release, even as she trembled on the brink of her own climax. This time, however, satisfaction slipped away from her. Her lover was too shaken by his own pleasure to sense her need; he collapsed against her and closed his eyes.

They stood like that for several moments, Claire's legs still wrapped around the man's waist, his weight pressing her into the wall. Finally, however, he withdrew and lowered her to the ground. She leant against the wall to steady herself for a moment, then tugged her skirt down and began to fasten the buttons of her blouse. In spite of the fact she had not reached orgasm a second time, her limbs were heavy and slow to obey her commands. She started with surprise as a black and white dog trotted out from the alleyway, and someone called out a greeting to someone else on the other side of the canal. The city was waking up. The man swiftly fastened his shirt, tucked it into his trousers and then lifted her hand to his lips.

'*Grazie, signorina,*' he said. He kissed her palm, and went to recover his haversack which still lay under the tree. Then he slung it over his shoulder, gave her one final wave, and disappeared down the alley.

Claire smoothed her hair. She could hardly believe what she had just done. It was as if the episode had happened to someone else. Was it possible that losing Sean had unhinged her, and turned her into a nymphomaniac? She grinned at the thought. She had only been nineteen when she met him, and not particularly experienced. Her recent adventures were probably just a biological urge to catch up on some of the things she had missed. She saw her pants lying in the dust by her feet, and quickly kicked them under the kiosk.

The streets were beginning to stream with people again as she made her way back to the hotel. Claire was certain that they must be able to see her recent activity written all over her: her skin was glowing, her limbs tingling, and she felt as if sex was oozing from every pore. She crossed the bridge back to the main quarter and lingered there for a few minutes, watching the sleek *motoscafi* and the slower *vaporetti* unloading their passengers for the Guggenheim museum and the Accademia. She didn't feel like going back to the hotel just yet. In fact, she needed a drink.

On a whim, she made for the Calle Vallaresso, and less than five minutes later found herself standing in front of Harry's Bar. She hesitated a moment, eyeing the gleaming motorboats tied at the quay, then shrugged and went inside. As she remembered, the interior of the famous watering hole was not particularly elegant nor interesting – in fact it was quite plain, with its wooden bar and round marble-topped tables. Most of the tables were taken, not by film stars, but by American tourists, all bellowing at each other and sipping on cocktails. There were a few suited businessmen sitting at the bar, and a well-groomed woman who couldn't be anything but Italian, enveloped as she was in mink, despite the weather.

Claire paused just inside the door, before spotting an empty table and claiming it. As she sat down, her view of the bar was blocked by a group of Japanese tourists who streamed in, aiming their cameras in every direction. She tried to catch the barman's eye over the flashes, but without success. Then a thought struck her. Panic-stricken, she fumbled in her skirt pocket. Miraculously, her money was still there, although the notes were terribly crumpled. More people came in, and she saw through the crush that the barman had started to serve the Japanese group. She felt a prickle of irritation. Hadn't he seen her?

28

She realised she wasn't looking her best, and thought longingly of the smart Joseph suit she had left hanging up at home.

Just then, a strange sensation crept through her. Without knowing what made her do it, she turned, and saw a man she hadn't spotted before. He was sitting at the bar, dressed casually in a black turtleneck and black Chinos, holding a gin and tonic. Had he been staring at her, or was paranoia beginning to settle in? If it was, it was hardly surprising. Her gaze slid hopelessly back to the barman, who was refilling some of the Americans' glasses. Claire blushed, then sneaked another look at the man in black. He was definitely not staring at her now – his profile was etched against the tiles like a Roman coin. She took the opportunity to examine him properly. He was good-looking in an exotic, very Mediterranean way, with a high forehead and olive skin, and medium-length black hair swept back off his face. He was not heavily built, but held himself with a casual grace that reminded her of a panther, or some other big cat. As Claire watched, he picked up his glass and took a swig of gin, then turned his head to look straight at her. Their eyes locked for a second. She averted her gaze hastily, but not quickly enough to miss the smile he gave her. Out of the corner of her eye, she saw him signal to the barman, and then murmur something in his ear. Both men looked in her direction. She pretended to examine the cocktail list in front of her, but felt her blush deepen into crimson. Then, to her horror, the barman came straight to her table.

'What can I get you, *signorina*?' He spoke in English.

Was she so obviously Anglo Saxon, Claire wondered? '*Una birra, per favore.*' She answered him in Italian, piqued that he had taken her for granted. He nodded and left. The man at the bar caught Claire's glance, picked up his glass and approached her table.

'May I?' He pointed to the empty seat next to her. 'I saw you were having a wee bit of trouble catching Giancarlo's eye. I hope you don't mind?'

Claire had to stop herself from gaping in surprise. His accent was as Scottish as shortbread and whisky. Just in time, she remembered her manners. 'Not at all. I was beginning to think I was invisible.'

The man smiled. 'Far from it.'

Close up, he was even more attractive than she had first thought. His eyes under the heavy brows were dark and intelligent, glinting with humour. But it was his mouth that really held Claire's attention. The lips were full, and sensuously moulded, without being the least bit feminine. She was filled with an insane urge to kiss them. He smiled again, unaware of her struggle.

'Stuart MacIntosh.' He held out his hand.

She took it. 'Claire Savage. Pleased to meet you.' His skin was smooth and warm against hers. 'Forgive me if I sounded surprised. I thought you were Italian.'

'I am.' He grinned at her doubting expression 'Well, half Italian, anyway. I was brought up in Paisley.'

'Ah, that explains it.'

Giancarlo arrived with Claire's beer, and she gratefully took a draught of the foaming liquid. She saw her companion's gaze rest on the line of bubbles on her top lip, and wiped it quickly away. 'Are you here on business, Mr MacIntosh, or pleasure?'

'Business.' He took a drink from his own glass. 'Please, call me Stuart. What about you?'

'Pleasure.'

'You're here on your own?'

'With a friend.'

He stared into her eyes as if trying to read something there. 'Is this your first trip to Venice?'

'No.' She shook her head. 'I've been quite a few times before.'

'That's a pity. You can't beat the excitement of a first visit.'

Claire fell silent as pain welled up unexpectedly from the place she thought she had buried it. Her honeymoon had been her first visit. Stuart was watching her, his gaze sharp, and she was glad when the barman arrived with his bill.

'*Grazie*, Giancarlo.'

It occurred to Claire that Stuart must be something of a celebrity, to warrant such prompt attention from the supercilious barman, and she said so.

When Stuart laughed, it transformed him – crinkling up his eyes, and softening the severe lines of his face. 'Hardly! But I do spend quite a bit of time here. He just knows me, that's all. Tell me – ' he said, his face suddenly serious. 'This friend of yours. The one you're on holiday with. Is it a he or a she?'

Claire flushed, surprised at the question. She had not really been listening to what he was saying, but had lost herself instead in the melodious burr of his voice. 'A she. Why?'

'I was wondering if you'd like to come to the opera with me tomorrow night. That is, unless you have someone in your life just now?' He picked up her hand and traced his thumb across the faint white line where her wedding ring used to be. The gesture was intimate, and caused a thump of heat between Claire's thighs. She pulled her hand away.

'– I don't know.'

His intense expression melted into a smile. 'Don't worry. It was only a thought. If you have other plans, or if you think your friend would object . . .'

'It's not that,' interrupted Claire. 'Cherry would be delighted to get rid of me for the night. Its just . . .' She paused. She had enjoyed her sexual encounters with Nick Fisher and the anonymous Italian, but didn't think she was ready to see anyone seriously

31

yet. Sean had hurt her too much. But, of course, she couldn't begin to explain all that to Stuart.

He watched her, his eyes never leaving her face.

She shrugged suddenly, all resistance flooding away. 'I'd love to come to the opera with you.' She lifted her glass to finish her beer, and, as she did so, looked at her watch. 'Heavens! I didn't realise it was so late. Cherry'll think I've been kidnapped.' She took some money from her pocket and put it next to her bill. Both she and her companion eyed it where it lay, crumpled, on the saucer. Claire looked up to meet his hot brown gaze, and it suddenly struck her, with absolute certainty, that he knew why the banknote was in such a state. She flushed. He couldn't possibly.

'Where are you staying?' he asked. There was nothing in his voice but polite curiosity. She was being ridiculous.

'The Metropole.'

'Shall I pick you up at half-six, tomorrow night? We can eat after, if you like.'

Claire stood up awkwardly. 'Fine. I'll see you then.'

She left him with a wave. Back out on the Calle Vallaresso, she began to breathe more easily. Stuart MacIntosh had made her feel like a teenager again – uncertain and gauche. And she wasn't sure she liked the feeling.

Chapter Three

*A*t the same moment that Claire stepped back into the afternoon sunlight of the Calle Vallaresso, Cherry was sitting glumly on a bollard by the edge of another canal, staring at a wall on the opposite bank. Far from worrying where Claire had got to, she was more concerned about herself. She was hopelessly lost. She frowned at the high wall with its crumbling pink bricks. On the other side lay the port she had discovered an hour or so earlier, but having wandered away from it, she couldn't find her way back in – it was as if the entrance had mysteriously disappeared, like something in a fairytale. To make matters worse, the sun was sinking lower, her high-heeled sandals were hurting, and the smell of cooking from the windows of the shabby tenement behind her was making her stomach growl. There was nobody around to ask directions from. She wished she'd stayed in the hotel after waking from her nap, or at least had brought her guidebook with her. She stood up and straightened her shoulders. There had to be a way to get back in to the port – all she had to do was to follow the wall. She set off again in the direction she had been walking, hobbling a little on the dusty pavement.

As she rounded the next bend in the wall, her spirits lifted: there was a man sitting on the edge of the canal, his feet dangling just above the water. The sunlight formed a halo around his cropped blonde head, which was bent over a sketchbook. His whole body was rigid with concentration. He didn't look up as she approached him, although she guessed that he must have heard her heels. Cherry stood for a moment, uncertain what to do.

'Ahem.'

He looked up at last, shielding his eyes against the sinking sun. In the shadow of his hand, his gaze was as frank and fathomless as a child's. He stared at her, but said nothing.

'I was wondering – could you tell me how to get back to the port?'

'The port?'

Inwardly, Cherry gave a little sigh of relief that he spoke English, although there was a distinctly un-British drawl to his words. 'Yes. The place with the boats, and the statues of lions.'

'You mean the arsenal?' He was still looking at her as if she was a curious insect he had found. She flushed. He might not have been trying to irritate her, but he was succeeding.

'If you say so.'

The American looked back down at his book. Over his shoulder Cherry could see that he had sketched in the tenements, with their tumbledown brickwork and lines of washing. Even from a distance she could tell it was very good. He frowned and deepened the shadows under the balconies with his pencil. Cherry shuffled her feet and he looked up again, surprised to see her still there. He gestured vaguely in the direction she had come.

'That way, I guess.'

It was a moment before Cherry realised she'd been dismissed. 'Well, ta very much for your help, I'm sure.' She stomped away from him, back towards the bend in the wall, and before she disappeared around it she made a point of tossing him a disgruntled glare. But she needn't have bothered. He was hunched over his sketchbook again, and had obviously already forgotten her. 'Bloody Yanks!' she muttered to herself as she flounced out of sight. She wasn't used to people being off-hand with her – particularly men – and found the American's attitude intensely irritating. Then, catching herself in her mood, she chuckled. Would she have been so irritated by the man if he hadn't been attractive? She recalled his tanned, clean-cut features and lazy grey eyes and shrugged. He was probably gay, she decided. All the best-looking men were. Half of her male colleagues in the modelling business had jealous boyfriends at home.

She walked resolutely on, trying to keep the wall of the arsenal on her left-hand side, until she found that her way forward along the canal was blocked. Seeing no other option, she cut through an archway underneath a tenement block, which led into a courtyard. The rattle of cutlery and crockery drifted down to her from the open windows, making her stomach growl again. She was starving. She quickened her step through the courtyard, and emerged on the other side. Bewildered, she looked to her right and left, but couldn't see the wall of the arsenal anywhere. Where had it gone? Was she still tucked up in her bed at the hotel, dreaming? With a cry of triumph, she spotted an alleyway that cut to her left, and went down it. It quickly transformed itself into a cul-de-sac, and she found her path blocked yet again, this time by a canal that smelled of rotting vegetables. Grumbling, she retraced her steps, until she found herself back in the courtyard.

'You look lost.'

Cherry jumped, and turned to see that the American was standing behind her. She scowled. It was just like the man to add to his rudeness earlier by deliberately creeping up on her. 'That's hardly surprising.'

He lifted an eyebrow. 'Where're you headed?'

As if he didn't know. 'The arsenal, I suppose.' Cherry gave the word particular emphasis, but the man just quirked his eyebrow again. Sarcasm was obviously too subtle for him. She made to push past him, but he caught her wrist.

'You're going the wrong way. That's where I'm headed, if you want to tag along.'

She tugged her arm away, and glared up at him. She didn't want to accept his help, but had to admit she needed it. At the rate she was going, she wouldn't get back to the hotel before dark, and the thought of being alone in such a run-down part of the city gave her the shivers.

She nodded ungraciously. 'OK.'

She felt a stab of guilt at his answering grin, but smothered it when she remembered his earlier offhand manner. So what if she was being rude? He deserved it. As the American strode off across the courtyard and through a side gate she hadn't noticed before, she fell awkwardly into step beside him. They didn't speak as they marched along, and it was only a few minutes before Cherry regretted accepting his offer of help. Her sandals had started to murder her in earnest, and even though she was practically skipping along at his side, he didn't slow his long-limbed pace.

Finally, she couldn't take any more. 'Are you doing this on purpose?' she puffed.

36

He stopped so abruptly that she bumped into him. 'Doing what?' he asked, grey eyes innocent.

'Walking so bloody fast. Is it your idea of a joke?' She dabbed at her perspiring forehead. 'Because if it is, it isn't funny.'

He frowned. 'You should have said sooner that I was going too fast for you.' They set off again, this time the American ambling at a ridiculously leisurely pace, that Cherry found almost as hard to match. She threw a sideways glare at him, and their eyes met for a moment. She could have sworn she read amusement there, but he looked away before she could be sure. Turning into a busy thoroughfare, she began to recognise some of the shops. Then they took another turn and they emerged into a familiar large square, with a mausoleum-like gate and assortment of marble lions guarding it.

'There you are. The arsenal.' The American's expression was guarded as he looked down at Cherry.

She was in a decidedly bad humour now. Rather than thanking him, she started to walk away.

'Hold on there a moment.' His voice stopped her in her tracks. 'It seems to me that you could do with a lesson in manners.'

She was speechless, but only for a moment. 'Me?' she spluttered. 'You've got to be kidding. Talk about the pot calling the kettle black!' She whirled away from him again, but as she did so, turned clumsily on her ankle. 'Ow! Now look what you've made me do!'

The American's unsympathetic gaze dropped to her feet. 'You're bleeding.'

Cherry saw that it was true. The strap of her sandal had broken the skin, streaking her foot with crimson. 'That's your fault!'

'Really?' The man's grey eyes, so serene before, had storm clouds gathering in them now. 'Perhaps you can tell me how you figure that out?'

She ignored him, and hobbled to sit on the steps of the Arsenal. She felt stupidly close to tears. To her surprise the man followed, and knelt to examine her foot. He unfastened the sandal and slipped it off, probing the damaged skin gently. Their eyes met again, and this time she definitely saw the amusement in them: a silver lining in the clouds. He grinned at the sandal that was dangling flimsily from his finger. 'You should wear something a mite more suitable for sightseeing.'

At that, Cherry's patience snapped completely. 'Who do you think you are! I'd have been perfectly OK, if you hadn't sent me round in circles!'

His amusement evaporated. 'What the devil's name are you talking about?'

She leapt up and snatched the sandal from his hand. 'As if you don't know!'

'Hi. What's going on here?'

Cherry rounded on the newcomer to tell him to mind his own business, and stopped. After a moment she realised that her mouth was hanging unattractively open, and she snapped it shut. When the American turned to the man who was standing beside him, he could have been grinning into a mirror.

His reflection's smile was more hesitant, however. 'I see you found your way OK,' it said.

As she glanced from one man to the other, she couldn't think what to say. They had the same grey eyes and halo of short blonde hair. One of them was dressed in a blue shirt and was carrying a sketchbook under his arm, while the other was wearing a jumper in same shade of blue, and an expression of dawning realisation.

'I guess we'd better introduce ourselves,' he said. 'I'm Quaid, and this is my twin brother Harper. I take it you've met.'

The other man blushed like a teenager. 'I'm sorry if

I was off-hand with you.' He pointed apologetically up at the sky. 'I wanted to catch the light. It can be unpredictable.'

Not wanting to look into the four disconcerting grey eyes another moment, Cherry bent to replace her sandal. She felt like a prize idiot. If her foot hadn't been stinging so much, she'd might have laughed at herself.

Quaid – she thought it was Quaid – said: 'I'm real sorry. I didn't know your foot was bleeding. If I had, I'd never have walked so fast.'

She straightened up and winced. 'Don't worry, it's nothing.'

'It doesn't look like nothing to me' The other man looked down at her bloody sandal. 'Can you walk OK?'

'I'll manage.'

He held out his arm. 'I'll help you back to your hotel, if you like.'

'No way,' interrupted the other twin. 'The least I can do is take her there, seeing as it was me who walked too fast.'

His brother glared at him.

'Look! I'm perfectly all right.' Cherry's embarrassment made her curt. 'I can manage quite all right by myself, thank you very much.' She tossed her hair over her shoulder and walked away with as much dignity as she could muster, trying not to favour her stinging foot. When she reached the corner, she couldn't resist sneaking a glance back. The Americans were still standing where she'd left them, staring after her, like matching statues in blue.

Chapter Four

Claire had had enough of the sunshine. It bore down on the beach, only partly relieved by the breeze that was snapping the canvas of her sunshade. Two children ran shrieking past, their bodies glistening with water and good health, bellies sticking out unselfconsciously as they pattered over the pebbles. Claire smiled behind the sanctuary of her sunglasses at her own ingratitude, remembering how she'd have given anything to escape her office less than 48 hours before. Now here she was on the beach at the lido, her skin turning to the delicate shade of *cafe con latte*, feeling more than a little fidgety. She suspected that it wasn't just the inactivity that was making her restless: try as she might, she couldn't shake off the memory of a pair of intense brown eyes.

'Do me a favour, will you Claire? I need more cream on my back.' Cherry spoke with difficulty as she was lying flat on her face, with her mouth pressed into her towel. Claire sat up and rummaged in the beach bag for the bottle. As Claire smoothed Factor 15 into her friend's hot skin, Cherry lifted her heavy plait out of her way and turned her head to look at her.

'You've been very quiet this morning.'

'Have I?' Claire's tone was noncommittal.

Cherry grinned. 'Could it be anything to do with your mysterious Scotsman?' She laughed. 'You are a dark horse.'

'What do you mean?'

'You know what I'm talking about. We've been here less than two days and you've already copped off. Well, it just goes to show, you can't keep a good woman down. *I will survive, as long as I know how to love, I know I'll stay alive...*' She launched into a tuneless rendition of Gloria Gaynor's anthem for dumped lovers everywhere.

'Shhh, people are looking.' Claire flushed. 'I think "copping off", as you so charmingly put it, is an exaggeration. I'm only going to the opera with him.'

'Rather you than me. Opera! Yuk.'

'Philistine.' Claire slapped her friend's shoulder, anxious to change the subject. 'There. That's you greased up again.'

But Cherry wasn't going to be easily distracted. 'You still haven't told me what he looks like. Is he horny?'

Claire gave her a quelling look. 'I'm sure I don't know. He's slim. Dark. Quite good-looking, I suppose.' She wasn't being deliberately evasive: she couldn't remember exactly what Stuart MacIntosh looked like. All she could recall were the compelling details: his eyes; his hands, and the sensuous mouth she'd been so tempted to kiss. But when she tried to put the snapshots together to make a whole picture, she couldn't do it. It was probably an indication of how much her encounter with him had unsettled her. She blushed. She couldn't deny that there had been an instant physical connection between them – a

41

current that crackled like static – but she felt ambiguous about their date. Waking up that morning, her first reaction had been to call it off. She had even picked up the phone to do it, before remembering that she had no idea how to get in touch with him.

'You're off into your little dream world again,' warned Cherry. 'Is he that gorgeous?'

'Don't be silly. It's just the sun making me sleepy.' Claire eyed the unforgiving Mediterranean light that bounced off Cherry's back and shoulders. 'You'd better be careful. You don't want to burn.'

'Why is it that whenever we get on to an interesting subject, you always change it?'

'You can talk.' Claire decided that attack was the best form of defence. 'You still haven't told me what made you late for dinner last night.'

'Yes I did. I got lost.'

'Oh? Then why was there such a suspicious glow to your cheeks?'

Cherry groaned and pressed her face back into the towel. 'It's true. I did get lost. But then I was found again.'

'By a man?'

'Two, if you must know.'

'Attractive?'

'Very.'

'And you're still keeping your resolution about casual flings?'

'Yes, worse luck.'

'I'm impressed.'

'Well I'm not. I'm bloody frustrated.'

Grinning, Claire pushed the sun cream back into her bag and leant back on her towel with a little sigh. After a few drowsy minutes, the sunlight that filtered through her eyelids seemed to grow kinder, more soothing, and she felt herself drift off into limbo. She listened to the whisper of the waves on the beach and then heard Cherry's sun lounger creak as she sat up to put a shirt on.

'Bloody hell!'

Claire's eyes snapped open, to see that Cherry had dropped flat on to her towel again like a commando.

'What is it?'

'One of the blokes I met last night, over there, by the green umbrella. Don't look!'

Claire couldn't resist.

'I said don't look! He'll see us.' She tried to shrink further into her lounger.

Claire frowned at her friend. 'What on earth's got into you? You're acting like a teenager.' She paused and cast another interested glance in the forbidden direction. 'Anyway, you're too late. He's coming over.'

'He's not!'

'See for yourself.'

'Morning ladies. Mind if I join you?' At Claire's intrigued nod, the American sat on the bottom of her lounger and crossed his long legs. His swimming trunks showed off his toned body, and his smooth, tanned skin. He took off his sunglasses and turned to Cherry. 'I was hoping I would bump into you again, I wanted to apologise.'

'For what?' Cherry sat up reluctantly, clutching her towel to her bosom. Claire grinned at the coy gesture. No one would think her friend made her living taking her clothes off.

'For not realising sooner that we were talking at cross purposes yesterday. I had you down as plain rude. Guess I was wrong. I'm sorry.'

Cherry tried and failed to hide the pleasure in her eyes. The American turned to Claire and lifted a questioning eyebrow.

'This is my friend, Claire Savage,' said Cherry.

'And this is . . .' she paused, embarrassed. 'I'm sorry, I don't know which one you are.'

'Quaid, Quaid Albright, at your service.' He saw Claire's puzzled expression. 'My brother and I are twins.'

'Really?'

'It's caused some confusion in its time, I can tell you.' He threw Cherry a loaded glance. 'Yesterday, for example.'

Realising she had no option, Cherry explained to Claire what had happened at the arsenal.

'It's no wonder you didn't want to tell me about it,' laughed Claire. Her amusement was so infectious that the American was grinning broadly, and even Cherry wore a shamefaced smile.

'I felt like a real idiot,' she confessed.

'No. It was my fault. I should've realised you'd bumped into Harper. That kind of thing happens all the time.' He hesitated. 'I'd feel a lot better if you'd let me apologise to you properly.'

'Oh?' Cherry was immediately suspicious.

'Can I take you out for dinner tonight?'

To Claire's delight, her friend actually blushed. 'I don't know . . .'

Claire jumped in. 'I'm going to the opera, remember. You get out – enjoy yourself.'

Cherry threw her a despairing look.

'That's settled then.' Quaid languidly uncrossed his legs and stood up. The movement brought his swimming trunks to eye level with the two women, who tried hard not to stare at the impressive bulge it held. They just about succeeded. Quaid was entirely unaware of the effect he was having. 'I'll pick you up at eight, shall I? Where are you staying?'

'The Metropole.' Claire answered for Cherry, who seemed to be speechless.

44

'Fine. I'll see you then.' He winked at Claire. 'A pleasure to meet you.'

When he had sauntered out of sight, Cherry scowled at Claire. 'What on earth did you do that for?'

'You can't tell me you don't like him.'

Cherry kept a mutinous silence.

'He's absolutely gorgeous,' Claire said. 'Those eyes! And that marvellous...' she paused deliberately, '... smile. Go on, admit it. You fancy him like mad.'

'OK. I do admit it. You know me too well. But I'm looking for Mr Right, remember, not some cheap holiday romance.' Cherry groaned and fell back on to the lounger. 'Just when I was managing to keep my resolution, you had to go and spoil it all!'

The sky lay like a band of mother of pearl over the lagoon, throwing the distant silhouette of Santa Maria della Salute into dramatic relief. It had been raining, and the pavements caught the last slanting rays of the sun. It was a scene of contrasts, all black and gold, the pedestrians reduced to anonymous shadows, moving against the glistening stones and the luminous water of the lagoon. The old-fashioned street lamps on the edge of the quay began to glow with feeble light. In less than quarter of an hour it would be dark. From her vantage point in the porch of the Metropole, Claire could hear the slap of water against the quayside, and the knock of wood as moored gondolas bumped against each other. She shivered and pulled her stole closer around her.

She had worried all day about what to wear, and had settled at last for one of the most formal dresses she had brought with her. It was a snugly fitting sheath of creamy satin, that left her shoulders bare and fastened at the back with a row of tiny buttons. The buttons were so difficult to reach she had had to ask Cherry to help her with them. As expected, her sharp-eyed friend had remarked on her lack of underwear. Claire had protested that it was because the dress was so tightfitting, not because she had any amorous designs on Stuart MacIntosh.

Claire coloured at the half-truth and tried to push the thought of Stuart aside. She peered instead at the passing pedestrians, who drifted in and out of the Metropole's pool of light like exotic fish. She had been worried that she was over-dressed, but she needn't have been: the passing men and women were effortlessly glamorous. Reassured, she shivered again. The breeze from the lagoon was stiffening her nipples, making her aware of them sliding against the satin of her dress. She looked at her watch to distract herself and was surprised to see that Stuart was late. He hadn't seemed like the type to keep anyone waiting. Perhaps he wasn't coming? The thought provoked a mixture of relief and disappointment in Claire. It would be the first time she'd been stood up since she was a teenager, but, in spite of the humiliation, it might be for the best. Stuart MacIntosh had a disturbing effect on her, and she wasn't sure she was ready to be disturbed yet.

'*Signorina?*'

Claire turned at the voice behind her and saw it was Guiseppe, the head porter. 'Signor MacIntosh is here for you, Signorina Savage.'

Claire frowned, but Guiseppe merely beamed at her, his round face splitting with delight when he realised she didn't understand. 'Your *barca a motore* is here. If you please to follow me?'

Guiseppe led her back into the hotel, past the bar to a side door she had not noticed before. It opened on to a tiny jetty, edged with scarlet poles and lit by single lamp. Stuart MacIntosh straightened as he saw her coming towards him, and flicked his cigarette

46

into the water beside the motorboat that was moored there. Claire flushed, feeling as if she had been wrong-footed already. Stuart was taller than she remembered, and more exotic looking. If she was honest, she hardly recognised him at all, dressed as he was in cream, rather than black as he had been the day before. But when he spoke, she felt a jolt of familiarity.

'You look lovely.' His softly accented voice caressed her as he took her hand to help her step into the boat. The deck rocked a little beneath her high heels, and she had to lean against him to keep her balance. He steadied her elbow with his hand, and settled her on a seat at the stern. She saw with some relief that they were not alone: there was a man standing to attention at the helm, on the other side of the cabin.

'Are you all right?' asked Stuart.

Claire realised that she hadn't said anything, and smiled at her companion. 'Sorry. I hadn't realised that you'd be arriving by water.'

He grimaced. 'Yes, I'm sorry about that. It is a wee bit ostentatious, isn't it? But Vittorio insisted I use his boat for the evening.'

'Vittorio?'

'Giacomo Vittorio. My client.' He paused and shrugged. The gesture owed nothing to his Scottish roots; it was one hundred percent Italian. 'Actually, he's more of a family friend. That's the way it goes over here, we're always mixing business with pleasure.'

Stuart cast off the mooring rope and the silent chauffeur throttled the boat out into the canal system, away from the lagoon. Claire took advantage of the activity to look around her surreptitiously. The boat was obviously expensive – all polished wood and brass – and she could see through the curtains of the

47

cabin that it was upholstered inside with raspberry-coloured velvet. She sneaked a glance at Stuart and his eyes met hers, as dark as melting chocolate. The lashes that veiled them were luxuriant, almost feminine, but the message in them was entirely male. Claire felt an answering stir in her belly, and moved her leg a little further away from his, so that she could no longer feel the warmth of his thigh through her dress. To cover her awkwardness she made a show of looking at the scenery as they slid along the water from one pool of light to another. The bridges that criss-crossed over their heads held the usual traffic of pleasure-seekers and tourists, some of whom stared down at them as they passed. Delicious aromas drifted from the open windows of canal-side restaurants, accompanied by laughter and the tinkle of glasses and cutlery. Claire sighed: the city at night was both romantic and eerie.

'It's so beautiful,' she said dreamily.

'Aye, it is.'

Something about the tone of Stuart's voice made her turn her head, to see that his gaze was still locked on her face. She blushed and looked away again. Stuart leant back to enjoy the breeze across the water, resting one arm carelessly across the back of the seat. She felt it brush her shoulder, and sat up to avoid the contact.

Their journey took them under the marble balustraded bridge of the Fondamenta de la Fenice, and as Claire saw the blank windows of *La Fenice*, the famous opera house, she could not suppress a cry of dismay. Once so elegant, the phoenix was now blackened and degraded, and its bricks held the faint smell of charring.

'It's hard to believe it could happen in a city full of water, isn't it?' said Stuart, his voice heavy with regret.

48

'It looks so different. Dead, almost.'

'Of course, I was forgetting that you know the city. When did you say your first visit was?'

'I thought you said we were going to the opera?' Claire clumsily changed the subject.

'We are.' Stuart laughed. 'Surely you don't think the Venetians could do without their favourite national pastime? They've set up a marquee by the railway station, but I don't like it much. It's too big. Tonight I'm taking you to one of the smaller theatres that sometimes put on performances.'

Relieved to be back on a safe conversational footing, Claire plunged in with a question. 'Do you go to the opera much?'

'I do when I'm in Venice. But at home I'm normally too busy.' He stretched his beautiful lips into a rueful grin. 'You know what it's like in London. So many things to do, but never any time to do them.'

'You don't live in Scotland, then?'

He shook his head. 'I moved years ago. Small town Scottish life got a wee bit...' he paused while he searched for the right word, 'claustrophobic.' His wry tone made Claire think there was another, more compelling reason for the move, but she was distracted by his next question. 'Where do you live?'

'Near Covent Garden.'

'Do you work?'

Claire wrinkled her nose. The hot-house atmosphere of Barker and Savage seemed a million miles away, and she preferred to keep it that way. 'I'd rather not talk about it, if you don't mind. I'm on holiday, remember.'

'Fair enough.' Stuart was unruffled by her request. 'We'll do a deal, shall we? No talking about work.' He held out his hand playfully to Claire, who shook it after a momentary hesitation. It was warm and reassuring, and as he released her hand she felt a

49

pang of regret. He leant back on his seat again, and watched her through hooded eyes. His smile had gone, and for a moment, Claire felt a frisson of unease. Was she imagining it, or was he looking at her the way a cat might watch a mouse? His abrupt change from playful to serious was disconcerting, and wasn't helped by the fact that she could only partly make out his features in the sliding shadows.

'Of course, we could make a proper game of it.' His tone was deliberately light. 'If you wanted, we could pretend we were someone else entirely. Who would you like to be? Greta Garbo? Madonna?'

She gave a nervous laugh. 'I don't think so.'

'Don't you like to play games, Claire?' The question was asked with a smile, but his eyes were intense, almost predatory.

She shook her head. 'No.'

'What? Not at all?'

'I've always felt uncomfortable with that kind of thing.' She smiled and shrugged uncertainly. 'Perhaps I'm too honest.'

'That's a pity. We all need to forget ourselves sometimes.'

Claire frowned. 'You might be right. Life hasn't been a bed of roses lately.'

Stuart's gaze dropped to her lap, where she saw she had subconsciously covered her naked wedding ring finger with her other hand. 'I'm sorry to hear that,' he murmured.

Claire was thankful when she realised the boat was slowing down, heading for a small jetty and a doorway that blazed with light.

'Here we are,' said Stuart. He looked at his watch. 'We're late.'

The boat bumped alongside the striped poles, and the chauffeur jumped out. Stuart waited until he had secured the rope before he helped Claire out. They

50

went inside. The interior of the theatre, with its rich velvet hangings, gold leaf and glittering crystal reminded her of the inside of a jewellery box. She didn't have much time to admire it, however, for Stuart placed an urgent hand on the small of her back to guide her across the deserted foyer.

'We'll have to hurry. If we don't make it before the prelude starts they won't let us in until the interval.'

They climbed the marble staircase, moving from light into gloom. An usher appeared from the shadows to show the couple to their seats. Claire was surprised when he pushed aside a curtain and opened a door for them, and she found herself in the womb-like seclusion of a box. They were only just in time: as soon as they were seated, the house lights went down. Claire leant forward on to the padded balcony as the first wistful notes of Verdi's *La Traviata* drifted into the auditorium. At first, she was distracted by the conductor, who was wearing a disastrous wig, but by the time the curtains opened on Violetta's ball, she was hypnotised by the swirling music and had drifted off into turbulent, bitter-sweet memories.

The last time she had seen *La Traviata* had been with Sean, to celebrate her birthday. He had taken her to a Chinese restaurant, where they had eaten too much dim sum, washed down with too much saki, and he had given her her present, a pair of antique amethyst earrings. After the opera and another bottle of wine, they had weaved the two hundred yards across Covent Garden, thankful that home was so close. Sean had pounced on her almost as soon as they were in the house. He stripped her of everything except her new jewellery, and pressed her backwards on to the stairs. Claire flushed and throbbed with remembered sweetness, recalling the movement of his blonde head between her legs, and the muscles of his back under her fingers when he penetrated her

51

afterwards. Her blush deepened when she remembered how bitterly she had complained the next day about the carpet burns on her buttocks. Was it any wonder he had left her for somebody else?

Caroline Westwood was not the kind of woman to complain about a few carpet burns, or anything else, if the rumours were true. Less than a month after Claire's birthday she had come to see her, to lay claim to Sean. Claire had been so incensed by the other woman's casual possessiveness, so humiliated by her cool demeanour, that she had never given Sean the chance to put his side of the story, or even to ask forgiveness. She sighed and rubbed her empty ring finger. Had she been too hasty? She missed Sean a lot: missed his lean, hot body in her bed, and his mouth against hers. She even missed the things she used to find annoying, like the way he banged the toilet seat down, and left his muddy football socks in the sink.

It had taken her three months to come to terms with the simple fact that Sean had been bored with her. After ten years together, their love life had been satisfying, but hardly adventurous.

'O mio rimorso . . .'

Claire started, surprised by how much of the performance she had missed. She turned to see that Stuart was not looking at the performers, but at her. He leant forward and whispered in her ear.

'Are you OK? You seem like you're in a different world.' His breath was warm, yet raised goosebumps all over her skin. She shivered. Seeing her reaction, he hesitated a moment, then pressed his lips to the pulse that was leaping just below her ear. The kiss, and the brush of his fingertips on the nape of her neck was electrifying. Her stole fell to the floor. She bent to retrieve it, but Stuart stopped her with gentle pressure on the back of her neck.

'Leave it.' His whisper was authoritative. She felt strangely boneless, and unable to resist as he reached for her and pulled her on to his knee.

'But, the opera.'

'Watch it. Enjoy it.'

Claire succumbed to his hypnotic voice and turned back towards the stage again. His fingers continued to stroke the smooth flesh of her back and shoulders almost absent-mindedly as they both watched the singers. She sighed, and drifted off into the music again, until she felt the caress of cooler air on the hollow of her back. She tensed as Stuart undid another half dozen buttons.

'Relax.' He murmured and slipped his arm around her inside her dress. She flinched at the chill of his cufflinks against her skin, and fought her immediate instinct, which was to jump up. Gradually, however, the music, the warmth of his body against hers and the scent of aftershave began to work on her senses, lulling them into acquiescence. Claire glanced around the auditorium and saw that the audience was engrossed by the performance on the stage. Even if someone had lifted curious eyes to their box, Stuart's arm and hand were hidden by her dress. Neither she nor Stuart took their eyes from the singers as he slowly started to caress the curving flesh of her belly and found the dimple of her bellybutton. His fingers dallied there a moment, then moved higher, to tease the hardening bud of Claire's left nipple.

'Dammi tu forza, o cielo . . .'

Claire gasped. Through the satin of her skirt, she could feel that Stuart was aroused, and shifted slightly to lessen the pressure on the rigid flesh. He groaned under his breath, which in turn caused a rush of heat between Claire's legs. His hand suddenly left her breast and slid down between the sensuous material and the skin of her ribs and stomach to her groin. Alarmed, she tried to pull away, but was caught in an unrelenting grasp.

'Chegli diro? Chimendara il corragio?'

Stuart's questing fingers hesitated when they met the v between her legs, and Claire guessed that he was surprised to find she wasn't wearing pants. She held her breath, and tried to quieten her heart, which was hammering in her ribcage. He tweaked the curls. Claire moaned involuntarily. Encouraged, he stroked a finger teasingly along the lips of her sex. She squirmed, and he took advantage of the movement to slip his fingertip just inside her. Claire knew he had found her wet, and turned to glance at him out of the corner of her eye. He was still facing the stage, but his eyes were unfocussed, as if he was staring at some distant object, and his face was flushed and frowning with concentration. At the sight of his obvious desire, a tiny bubble of moisture burst inside Claire and trickled on to his hand. In response, he pushed his finger up into her as far as it would go.

Sitting there, impaled on Stuart's finger in front of dozens of people, Claire felt as if she was going to melt. Her very bones were softening with desire. Her arousal was proved by the heat that gripped him and was soaking through her dress to his trousers. But still she didn't turn her face from the singers on the stage.

'Tu m'ami, Alfredo, tu m'ami, none vero?'

Claire was already close to orgasm. Stuart pushed two more fingers deep inside her. She felt the fire build, and grasped the edge of the balcony. The frustration was causing tiny beads of perspiration to break out on her top lip and between her breasts. She forced herself to remain absolutely still. He did the same, keeping his fingers motionless, savouring her pulsing, slippery warmth.

'Saro la, tra quei fior, presso a te sempre, sempre, sempre

presso a te . . .' As Violetta begged Alfredo desperately on the stage, every taut centimetre of Claire's body yearned for the release that only Stuart could give. Sensing her need, he began slowly, very slowly, to move his fingers inside her, grasping, toying, playing with her deepest, most secret flesh.

'Amami, Alfredo, amami quant'io t'amo amami, Alfredo quant'io t'amo, quant'io t'amo . . . Addio!'

Wave after wave of pleasure washed over Claire, swelling with the music to an unbearable crescendo, until she finally shuddered her release, still staring at the stage. Stuart held her gently against his shoulder. Then, before the spasm had completely died away, he slipped his hand out of her dress and fastened it up again.

They watched the finale of the second act in silence, with Claire only moving back to her own chair as the house lights went up. She hardly had time to compose herself before there was a knock at the door and a waiter came in with champagne. She watched as the glasses were filled, not able to bring herself to look at her companion. In spite of her recent adventures with Nick and the Italian workman, it was not like her to rush into things sexually. She had known Stuart MacIntosh less than three hours in total. What must he think of her? The waiter left the box. The silence stretched out, but Claire didn't know how to break it, for any subject would seem absurd after the intimate act they had shared. Instead she looked down at the crowd in the auditorium, some making their way to the toilets or the bar, others reading their programmes and commenting on the performance so far. She realised that most of voices she could hear were Italian.

'There doesn't seem to be any foreigners here,' she said.

'No,' agreed Stuart. 'This place is something of a

local secret. It's not in many of the guide books.' He paused. 'Why won't you look at me, Claire?

Reluctantly, she raised her huge green eyes to him.

'Are you embarrassed?' he asked.

'I suppose so.'

'There's no need.' He smiled at her, a warm intimate smile that resurrected the throb between her legs. 'It's strange, but I had you down as a woman who knows how to enjoy pleasure, not one that would be ashamed of it.'

She was stung. After the thoughts she'd just been having about Caroline Westwood, that was the last thing she wanted to hear from him. 'Well, perhaps you were wrong.'

'Perhaps.' Stuart was unperturbed by her cutting tone. 'But I doubt it.'

She turned away to hide her irritation and discomfort, and looked out over the auditorium. Who the hell did he think he was? When the bell eventually rang for the end of the interval, she offered up a prayer of thanks. She couldn't wait for the evening to end.

'Here we are.'

'Thanks for walking me home,' said Cherry. 'I've had a nice evening.' Her cheeks were glowing from the Chianti she had shared with Quaid over their seafood *tagliatelli*, and the air was making her more than a little dizzy.

'That good, huh? Can I see you again?'

'Perhaps.'

Quaid hesitated, then realised that he would have to be satisfied with that.

'Goodnight.' Cherry moved towards the porch of the hotel.

He caught her hand, his square, handsome face

56

disappointed. 'Aren't you going to invite me in for a coffee?'

She shook her head, but wobbled as she was doing so. Quaid steadied her by putting his arm around her waist. She resisted the urge to snuggle against him. 'I'm tired.'

'You do look a mite sleepy, at that.' He grinned at her. 'Goodnight.' He bent towards her, but Cherry, anticipating the kiss, moved her head at the last moment so that his lips slid harmlessly past her cheek.

'No you don't!' She wagged a finger at him, her eyelids drooping. 'I know you men. You're only after one thing.'

'And what might that be?' He was still smiling, but his grey eyes had taken on a steely edge.

'What do you think?' She drew herself up. 'Well, Mr American, I'm not that type. Not any more.' She turned on her heel, meaning to whirl impressively away, but stumbled on the low step of the porch. She would have fallen if Quaid hadn't jumped forward to grasp her elbow.

'Whoops!' She struggled to right herself, and frowned. 'That's strange – wine doesn't normally have such an effect on me.'

He looked at her sceptically 'Is that so? What's your room number?'

Cherry scowled at him.

'Don't be a fool. I only want to see you upstairs. Unless you'd rather one of these handsome Italian porters put you to bed?'

She gave in. 'It's number 35.'

'Try to look sober, we don't want to get stopped on the way up.'

Cherry giggled. 'That'd be funny.'

'You mightn't think so in the morning.'

She allowed Quaid to guide her up the stairs to her

room. When they reached it, she hunted for the key in her bag, then dropped it, and stifled a giggle. She leant against the wall while Quaid retrieved it from the carpet and opened the door. Inside the room the covers of her bed were turned down invitingly.

'There you go,' said Quaid.

Cherry looked up at him through the tendrils of hair that had fallen over her face. 'Do you still want to come in for coffee?'

He could hardly have mistaken the proposition in her eyes, but his own expression was cool. 'I don't think so.'

Piqued, she moved towards him. 'Are you sure?' She stood on tiptoe to bring her mouth to his, and felt his lips yield, smooth and hot, under her own. He politely returned her kiss, but no more. Her blood fired, she pressed herself against him and ran her hand down his chest, savouring the heat of his skin through his shirt, until she reached the waistband of his trousers. Before she could move any lower to discover whether he was aroused or not, he gently caught her wrists and held her at arm's length.

'You're wasting your time, darling. I wouldn't want you to think I'm only after one thing, like all your English beaux. To tell the truth, it's not my style to take advantage of a lady that doesn't know what she's doing.' He turned Cherry around, and gave her a pat on the behind. 'Now go, and get a good night's sleep.' Then he pushed her into the room and closed the door.

As the American left the Metropole's front entrance, Claire and Stuart were arriving at the jetty. Stuart helped Claire to climb out, then stood awkwardly for a moment beside her. She had refused his offer of dinner, and now her lovely face was impenetrable as he looked down at her.

'Have I upset you? If I have, I'm sorry.'

Claire shook her head and gave him her best advertising industry smile. 'You haven't. I've had a lovely evening. Honestly.'

'Can I see you to your room?'

'No. There's no need.'

'Then can I see you again tomorrow, maybe for lunch?'

'I don't think so.' She met his eyes directly for the first time since they had left the box at the theatre. Her own were brimming with a mixture of embarrassment and steely resolution. 'I don't think that would be a good idea.'

'Why not?'

'I'm not looking for a relationship just now.'

Stuart gave her his most charming smile. 'If I've taken things too fast, I apologise. The impetuous Italian in me sometimes gets the better of the cautious Scot. Can't we start again?'

'You haven't done anything wrong. Honestly. I just don't want to get involved.'

'Then at least take my phone number, in case you change your mind.'

Realising it would be churlish to refuse, Claire waited while he scribbled his number on the back of a card, then took it from him.

'Good night,' she said formally, resolving never to contact him.

He made no move to stop her as she walked away into the hotel. Watching the taut swing of her buttocks he felt himself grow hard. Claire Savage was a puzzling woman. He couldn't have mistaken the power of her response in the theatre. In fact he had rarely known a woman to orgasm so easily. Her body would be easy to conquer. But her mind. Her mind was something else. He felt a shiver of anticipation.

59

He took out a cigarette and lit it, drawing the smoke deep into his lungs as he stared after her. If Claire Savage thought she was going to brush him off that easily, she was in for a surprise.

Chapter Five

The phone woke Claire the next morning, trilling insistently into her ears. She was still half asleep when she picked it up.

'Hello?'

'Hello, Claire?'

'Jess, is that you?' She was disorientated to hear the voice of her personal assistant at Barker and Savage, thinking for a moment that she was back at home.

'It is. Listen – I'm really sorry to disturb you on your holidays, but we've had a bit of an emergency at this end.'

'Emergency? What kind of emergency?' Claire struggled to sound awake.

'You know the Amore perfume shoot? Well, we'd arranged to do it in Rome, and we had everything lined up there – models, photographer, location – everything. But the Vatican's changed its mind at the last minute about letting us use one of their apartments. They say we can't have it now, which leaves us with nowhere to shoot the ad.'

'Isn't that Felicity's account?' Irritation flashed through Claire. 'It's her problem, not mine. Really,

Jess, you know better than to disturb me on holiday. I get few enough of them as it is.'

'I know.' The other woman cleared her throat. 'But Felicity's gone down with a mysterious virus. She's at home chucking her guts up.'

'You mean to tell me I have an agency full of people, and not one of them can solve this? What am I paying you all for, for heaven's sake?'

'Well, we just thought – or rather, Felicity thought – that as you were actually on the spot, in Italy, you might be able to source another location for us.'

Claire saw the logic behind that and her anger ebbed a little. 'What exactly are you looking for?'

Jess brightened. 'It's got to be somewhere grand, with a room big enough to take a fair size catwalk. And it needs to have a lot of natural light – big windows – oh, and preferably some frescoes too.'

'You're not asking for much, are you?' Claire frowned. 'I've no idea if there's anything like that in Venice. But I'll try. In the meantime, why not get on to Universal Film Locations and see whether they can find anything. It's a long shot, but someone might be making a film or a TV special we could piggy-back on.' She scribbled some notes on the pad by her bed. 'When do you need the new location by?'

'Ah, that's the other problem.' Some of the nervousness crept back into Jess's voice. 'The photographer, stylist and the models are already at Heathrow. We could have done with it yesterday, I'm afraid.'

Claire knocked on Cherry's door.

'Go away.'

She ignored her friend's instruction and walked in. The curtains were still drawn, and the only sign of Cherry was a hump in the middle of the bed. A groan rose from it. She put down the tray she was carrying and whisked the curtains open.

'Come on, get up. I've brought you some breakfast. It's almost eleven o'clock. What's the matter with you?'

Cherry poked her head reluctantly over the covers and squinted against the sunlight.

Claire eyed her critically. 'Don't bother, I can guess. Let me pour you a coffee.'

Cherry struggled to sit up against the pillows as Claire filled two cups of scalding black liquid. 'Do I look bad?' she asked.

'Terrible. Here, get some of this down you.'

'What's that bloody racket?'

'Church bells. It's Sunday, remember.'

'Bloody hell! That's all I need.'

Claire looked at the clothes that were strewn over the floor. 'I can see you and Quaid had fun last night.'

'Oh, Claire,' Cherry wailed, 'I've made a complete idiot of myself.'

'How?'

'I threw myself at him.'

'And?'

'And he turned me down. He must think I'm a slut. So much for my resolution.'

Claire raised her eyebrows and sipped her coffee. 'If it makes you feel any better, I didn't enjoy myself either.' That wasn't strictly true: she remembered Stuart's probing fingers and coloured. 'I won't be seeing Mr MacIntosh again.'

They both stared into their coffee cups, wrapped in their own thoughts, until Cherry broke the silence. 'What shall we do today? How about some sightseeing?' she grimaced. 'I don't think I'm up to the beach.'

'Oh Cherry, I'm sorry. Jess called me this morning, and the agency want me to find a shoot location for them. I'm going to have to work, I'm afraid.' Claire nodded at the tray she had brought in. 'That's my peace offering.'

63

'Don't worry. I'm sure I'll find something to occupy myself.' Cherry's glum expression belied her words.

Claire stood up. 'I have to go, I've a lot of phone calls to make. But I'll catch you later this afternoon, shall I?'

'OK. Don't work too hard.'

When Claire had gone, Cherry slumped back on to her pillows and closed her eyes. If only she hadn't had so much to drink last night. She had really enjoyed Quaid's company, but then her rampant libido had had to go and spoil it, as usual.

Then she must have dropped off again, for the next thing she knew, the ringing of her phone woke her. She picked it up.

'Morning. Or should I say afternoon?' The voice was unmistakeable. 'Harper and I thought you might like a bite of lunch.'

Cherry was so surprised, she couldn't reply.

'Unless you've got something better to do?'

'No!' She blushed at the eagerness in her voice and tried to moderate it. 'Where shall I meet you?'

'We're down in the lobby right now.'

'Give me twenty minutes.'

Claire slammed the receiver down with a cry of irritation. Although she had been on the phone for hours, she had drawn a complete blank. Not one of the public buildings in Venice, it seemed, was suitable for the Amore shoot. Or, if they were suitable, they were out of bounds for commercial purposes. Italian bureaucracy must surely be the most efficient in the world, she decided; it was certainly pushing both her patience and her knowledge of Italian to the limits.

If all the public buildings were ruled out, she was

going to have to find a private one. But where should she start?

What she needed was the help of someone who knew the city well. Someone who could speak Italian fluently, and had connections with the local people. She frowned and flung herself down on the bed, trying not to think of the one man who sprang to mind.

An hour later she swallowed her pride and picked up the phone again.

'I was surprised to hear from you again. Very surprised,' said Stuart.

'I know. I suppose I over-reacted last night.' Claire smoothed down her skirt and reached for one of the biscuits on the porcelain plate. In an attempt to keep the meeting on a business footing, she had deliberately dressed formally, in a calf-length skirt and silk blouse – the sort of thing she might have worn to the office. Stuart was also dressed for work, in a dark grey Versace suit, white shirt and a Gucci tie. He wore it well, with a carelessness that showed he was used to expensive clothes. Claire found it hard not to stare at him. In spite of the tension between them, or maybe even because of it, she found him more attractive than ever. With his neat, exotic features and lean body, he reminded her of a big cat. A leopard perhaps, or a panther. Distracted, she looked at their surroundings. They were sitting on a large covered balcony, the metallic blue of the Venetian sky framed by icing-sugar Moorish plasterwork.

'I had no idea your friend Vittorio lived in a palace,' she said, to put the conversation on neutral ground. 'Although I might have guessed, after seeing his boat.'

Stuart shrugged, unsmiling. 'This is just one of his

houses. He has quite a few, including a flat in Mayfair.'

She looked enviously at the ottoman divans they were sitting on, and at the Persian rugs scattered on the tiled floor. 'It must cost him a fortune to furnish them all.'

'It does. That's where I come in. Antiques is my business. I source them for Vittorio.' Stuart stood up. 'If you've finished your coffee, I'll show you round. We'll start in the ballroom. That's the biggest room, so it's probably the best bet for your shoot.'

Claire followed him out of the balcony, intensely aware of the distance he was keeping between them. His face had been carefully blank throughout their conversation so far. Remembering how easy his smile had been the night before, she felt a pang of regret. They walked down a long corridor, and then down a curving flight of stairs, with Stuart always keeping a couple of paces in front of her, like a tour guide. At the bottom of the stairs he opened a massive pair of carved double doors. She followed him into the ballroom, her high heels echoing on the parquet. Stuart opened the shutters, letting light stream in through the windows.

'Vittorio likes to keep this room dark, because of the ceiling.'

Claire looked up, and gasped. A melee of flesh, water and leaves was tumbling towards her, pinning her to the spot. She only began to breathe again when the jumble resolved itself into a woodland scene. Diana was easy to recognise, by her discarded bow and quiver of arrows. She was naked in the forest pool, her nipples puckered and skin flushed by the chill water, surrounded by a bevy of giggling nymphs. And in the foreground stood Acteon, in mid-transformation from man to stag. The expression of pure agony on the face beneath the sprouting horns made Claire wince: he had suffered a harsh punishment for disturbing the Goddess of the Hunt at her bath. By the quality of the painting it was clear the scene had been created by a master – maybe even Titian himself. Although the patina of the paint showed that it was very old, the colours were still vibrant. She almost expected to feel poor Acteon's tortured breath on her face.

'I can see why he doesn't want the colours to fade,' she murmured. 'It would be a tragedy.'

The rest of the room was almost as impressive. Painted an ethereal shade of blue, the walls were laced with a complex tracery of plaster, twined with vines and fig leaves. Two crystal chandeliers hung from the ceiling and caught the sunlight, winking rainbows around the walls and across the honey-coloured parquet.

'What do you think?' asked Stuart.

'Its lovely. Almost perfect for the shoot, except it would have been better if the fresco was on the walls, rather than on the ceiling.'

He raised an eyebrow.

She gave a nervous laugh. 'I'm sorry. It really is very beautiful.'

'Would you like to see the other rooms, just in case?'

Unable to restrain her curiosity, Claire nodded.

She waited for Stuart to close the shutters again, noting how stiff his movements were, and lifted her chin. If he was going to be prickly with her, she could be just as prickly in return. As he led her out of the ballroom, she resolved not to be so obviously impressed with the other rooms he showed her.

Her determination was swiftly melted, however, by the beauty of the Palazzo Giardino. As Stuart marched her through room after ravishing room, the seductive atmosphere of the building began to have its effect on her, until she was sighing with admiration and envy. No expense had been spared on furnishing the rooms, and yet there was nothing gaudy about them. Persian and Aubusson rugs lay on floors of intricate mosaics, polished wood, and marble. The furniture had also been chosen with care, and was mainly Louis Quinze, although there were a few Art Deco pieces. For the most part, the walls needed no adornment, but what paintings there were were of the highest quality. She recognised a Canaletto, a Picasso and two by Velasquez, and wondered whether Stuart had found them for Vittorio: if he had, it was no wonder he could afford to wear Versace.

Gradually, however, she began to realise that as beautiful as the palazzo was, there was something missing. It was not a home. There were no signs of everyday living: no TVs, no pets, no books, other than the antique leather volumes that lined the walls of the library.

'You did say that Vittorio *lives* here?'

Stuart was quick to catch her meaning. 'He stays in what used to be the servant's wing, through there.' He pointed to a studded door, then bent to open the one next to it. 'This is the last of the public rooms.'

Claire walked inside. The room was smaller than any of the others she had seen. The walls and a divan were upholstered in the same raspberry-coloured velvet as the cabin of the motorboat. She smiled to herself: it seemed that Vittorio's restrained taste did occasionally desert him. There was one window, narrow and heavily shuttered, and on the wall opposite glittered two huge Venetian pier glasses. Looking up, she saw that the ceiling was mirrored too, with dark antique glass that cast back her own foreshortened reflection. Why had Stuart brought her there? It was patently too small for the photoshoot. Claire guessed that the room was close to the balcony where they had drunk coffee, and moved to the window to see if her guess was right. The scene below, sectioned by the slats of the shutters, was immediately familiar: there was a small *campo* with a newspaper kiosk, doing a hectic trade. A black and white dog snuffled in the gutter. She made the connection. The Palazzo Giardino was the palazzo she had admired on her first day in Venice, the same one that overlooked the *campo* where she had had sex with the Italian workman. Because the entrance was on the other side of the building, she hadn't realised it when she arrived. She coloured.

'Can I ask you something?' said Stuart. He had moved silently to stand beside her.

'Of course.'

'If you hadn't had this emergency to deal with, would you have called me?'

Her eyes slid away from his. 'I don't know.'

'You wouldn't have, would you?' There was a beat of silence. 'I really don't like being used, Claire.'

Her emerald eyes flashed up at him, but she relaxed a little when she saw he was smiling. 'I didn't mean . . .'

He silenced her with a wave of his hand. 'I know how it is. If you have a job to do, you do it, and make use of any connections you might have. But I must admit, I'm hurt.'

Claire put her hand on his arm. 'Stuart, please.'

He took her wrist and turned it to look down at the delicate tracing of the veins on the inside. He stroked his thumb across the skin, sending shivers down her body. She closed her eyes, but opened them again immediately when she heard a snap and felt the chill of metal on her wrist. Then, before she realized what was happening, he imprisoned her other arm too. Uncomprehending, she frowned down at the metal that bound her wrists together.

'What on earth!'

'Shh.' He smiled at her. 'I really enjoyed the opera last night.' He reached up to stroke her cheek. 'I enjoyed you. You feel so good, Claire.'

She shivered at his intimate words. Seeing her shiver, he laughed under his breath. 'I couldn't believe it when you sent me away. I know you better than you think. You want me, don't you?'

She ignored his question and, struggling to conquer the sensations that were thrilling up and down her body, thrust her hands imperiously towards him. 'Get me out of these, right now.'

Stuart shook his head, a glint in his eyes.

'I'm not in the mood for jokes,' she snapped.

'I'm not joking.'

Claire drew a deep breath.

'If you're thinking of screaming,' he said, 'go ahead. Vittorio's had this room soundproofed. You'll only be wasting your time.'

Claire snapped her mouth shut again and stared at him. Was he completely mad? She realised how little she really knew about him, and felt the first stirring of fear. She eyed the door behind him, and then launched herself towards it, jinking in an attempt to evade him. She needn't have bothered. He caught her easily, and pulled her against his hard body.

'Are you really so afraid of me?' he whispered, bending to push the dark silky hair out of her eyes. 'Or is it yourself you're afraid of?' Then he kissed her, with an urgency that sent white hot rivulets of desire coursing through her body, and left her weak and trembling. She closed her eyes. 'Trust me. Trust yourself. We can find pleasure you never dreamt possible.' His Scottish burr was so soothing, so hypnotic, that she wanted to listen to it forever.

She hardly noticed as he steered her to another part

of the room, and gently pulled her arms over her head. Moments later, however, she felt herself drawn up straight – so straight, in fact, that she had to stand on her toes to keep her balance. She tipped her head back, to see that her wrists were now fastened to some kind of pulley in the ceiling. Stuart stood back and looked down into her eyes, which were cloudy with desire and confusion. He grabbed a chair from the side of the room and sat astride it, facing her. She bit her lip.

'What do you want from me?' she asked.

'That's a good question.' There was a slight frown between his brows as he stared at her. 'One that's perhaps not as easy to answer as you'd think.' Then he stood up abruptly and walked away, leaving her to dangle while he first took off his tie and then his jacket. Claire tried not to stare at the way his shirt clung to the muscles of his back and chest. Why was she so powerfully attracted to him? Her sex tingled with anticipation, but when he turned back to her, she stared at his chest, determined not to give him the satisfaction of looking at him.

'Will you kiss me, Claire?'

She shook her head: she had never felt so powerless in her life. Yet it wasn't her bonds that left her vulnerable, but her own treacherous body.

Seeing her answer, he kissed her. In spite of her protestations, she found herself responding, opening to his demanding tongue, yielding to his lips, until she was kissing him back as fiercely as he was kissing her. When his mouth finally left hers, she just stared dazedly at him. His own gaze dropped, and he began to undo the buttons of her blouse, one by one. She made no move to try to prevent him. More to the point, she didn't want him to stop. A dark, delicious thrill was running in her blood. In a matter of moments, her pretty blue and white bra had been revealed. He stared for a moment at the agitated swell of flesh above the lacy cups, but didn't try to touch her.

'Stuart,' she murmured. 'There's no need to do it like this.' She moistened her lips with her tongue. 'I want you. I want us . . .' Her voice died away.

'Say it.'

'I want us to sleep together.'

He kissed her again, and this time she could sense the triumph running through him. Then, he took something out of his pocket and she heard a click. She shrieked when she saw what he held.

'Don't worry. I'm not going to hurt you. Stand still.' He reached up with the knife to cut Claire's blouse away from her arms. It drifted to the floor.

'Stuart!' she squeaked. 'That cost a fortune!'

But he ignored her, gently running the edge of the blade up from the waistband of her skirt to her bra. He was breathing hard, his features dark and unreadable. Claire shivered with delight as his eyes travelled over her exposed skin. He unzipped her skirt and tugged it off her, then swung her round to face the mirror on the wall. They both stared at the unsettling reflection. Stuart, in particular, drank in every detail: the thrust of breast above her bra; the raised arms; the hollow of her belly and ribs, and, last of all her sex, an enticing mound hidden by her pants, framed by the suspender belt and stockings that encased her legs, down to her high-heeled shoes.

He moved to stand even closer behind her. Then, painfully slowly, he brought one hand round to cup her right breast. Claire's eyes widened. He put his other arm around her and gripped her chin, forcing her to look in the mirror. Her nipple stood to attention as he stroked it through the cotton of her bra.

'Don't you think we make a lovely couple?'

She had to admit it was true. Both slender and

72

dark, they matched each other perfectly, almost like brother and sister, the brown silhouette of Claire's upper body etched against the whiteness of his shirt. Claire felt again the prickle of heat between her legs as he bent to kiss the pulse below her ear. She closed her eyes, only to open them with a gasp as he pinched her nipple playfully.

'I want you to watch.'

She flinched as Stuart's brown hand insinuated itself under her bra to capture her breast. His other hand dropped from her chin and did the same, imprisoning her other breast, flesh against flesh. He closed his own eyes, breathing hard. Claire could feel his cock pressing against her buttocks through his trousers. She wriggled to avoid the contact, but only succeeded in making him groan. He opened his eyes again and pushed her bra up to reveal her breasts. He rolled the button-hard nipples between his fingers and thumbs.

'Oh God,' Claire gasped.

He grasped her chin again and forced her head up. His other hand left her breast and tentatively touched the curve of her mouth. Claire felt his cock leap against her as he pushed the tip of his finger between her lips, and a streak of perversity made her clench her teeth, denying him access. Unperturbed, he let the finger drop to her collarbone. It trailed a slow line of fire down between her breasts to the dimple of her belly button, where it rested for a moment. Stuart watched her face closely in the mirror and raised an eyebrow.

Claire arched against him, but he just held her closer and tightened his grip on her chin. The finger began to travel lower, until it rested on the top of her pants. His breath stirred her hair as his reflection stared into hers. Then he deliberately dropped his gaze and slipped his finger under the material. She held her breath as the questing finger twined luxuriously in her pubic hair before moving lower still. She wriggled again, only to be stilled by Stuart's steely grip. She knew that he would find her wet and ready for him, as he had the night before. He shifted his weight slightly and pressed his thigh between her legs, lifting her bottom up and her toes almost off the ground. She felt her labia gape open and closed her eyes in ecstasy as his finger slid inside. Stuart groaned, and then, seeing Claire's eyes were closed again, started slowly to agitate his finger in her heat. It had the desired effect. Her eyes flew open to meet his warm, amused ones in the mirror.

'You see?' His finger continued to move tormentingly inside her. 'You're not quite as icy as you'd like to be, are you?' His other hand released her chin to tease her swollen, painfully erect nipples. She felt a hot wave sweep over her and tried to move away from the exquisite torture of Stuart's hands. But he merely clasped her closer to him. She threw her head back and stifled a moan. He smiled at her flushed features and pained expression.

'Please,' she gasped.

'Please what?' whispered Stuart, increasing the friction of his finger on the swollen bud of her clitoris. 'Tell me exactly what you want me to do – and none of that coy "sleep together" business.' Claire was torn. She didn't want to submit to the sweet, swelling ache between her legs, and yet felt that she would die of frustration if she didn't get some release. It seemed to her that Stuart's demand had become academic as the spasms of her orgasm began to shake her. Suddenly, however, he withdrew his finger, robbing her of satisfaction. She sobbed at the loss and slumped shivering on to the pulley.

He released her from her bonds, picked her up in one easy motion, and carried her over to the divan where he sat her down. Still reeling from the sensations he had aroused in her, she barely noticed. He frowned down at her as she rubbed her wrists, the dark curtain of hair hiding her face. He lifted her chin and stared into her eyes, brimming at once with frustrated desire and confusion. She hesitated, then moved to kiss him, but he stopped her.

'Don't you trust me, Claire?

She nodded uncertainly.

He sighed. 'We'll see. I suppose it should be enough for now that you want me. You do want me, don't you?'

'Yes,' she whispered.

'Say it properly. Tell me what you want me to do to you.'

'I want you to fuck me, Stuart.' She could hardly believe she'd said it.

He pushed her back and fastened her wrists again, this time to the legs of the divan with strips of silk. Claire wanted to prove to him that she trusted him. Driven by that desire and the terrible frustration that had built between her legs, she allowed him to do it, and gave only a tiny murmur of protest when he moved to tie her ankles too, drawing her legs wide apart. Using his knife, he cut her bra and pants off her, leaving only her stockings and suspender belt. Then he left her and went to a part of the room where she couldn't see him.

Claire opened her eyes to find herself looking at her reflection once more, this time staring down at her from the ceiling. All her worst fears were realised. She was utterly exposed except for her stockings and shoes, her tanned body forming a provocative X on the divan, the white skin of her panty line with its tangle of pubic hair looking almost laughably vulnerable against the raspberry velvet. A trembling wave of shame and lust swept through her.

Her heart thumped as Stuart re-appeared next to the divan, completely naked. Her eyes ran from the neck and chest, down over the taut muscles of his stomach, to rest at last on his manhood. It was as leanly elegant as the rest of him, but long too, and heavy, like a cosh. She moaned with desire and closed her eyes. A moment later she flinched at the silky stroke of skin on her cheek, and guessed that it wasn't a finger. She turned her head away quickly, only to have her chin pulled back again.

'Open your eyes, Claire.' She obeyed, to see Stuart's engorged penis just centimetres from her face. 'Kiss it.' His face was dark with desire. Again, she obeyed. The tip trembled and oozed a single pearly drop.

He bent down and produced another strip of silk scarf, which he wound tightly round Claire's mouth. Ignoring her furious glare, he returned to the bottom of the chaise and knelt between her legs. She knew from the reflection above her that the intimate folds and shadows of her sex were pulled open and revealed in all their glory. As Stuart stared into her, Claire felt herself throb beneath his gaze, and even more moisture formed on the sensitive skin.

'Beautiful.' He groaned. 'So beautiful.'

She squeezed her eyes shut. She couldn't remember ever having been so turned on, not even with Sean in the early days. Stuart grasped her bottom and lifted it to place a cushion beneath it, so that she was raised up, her clitoris thrust forward, begging for release. He moved closer, until she could feel his breath on her, then, with almost religious reverence, he spread her labia even wider. Claire moaned as he placed a long, burning kiss between them. He laughed and looked up at Claire's eyes where they glinted like emeralds above her gag. Then he turned his attention back to her sex, which was pouting now, like a ripe fruit bursting with juice. He ran a finger tip around the edge of the outer lips, tweaking the hairs softly and making her shift against her bonds. He dropped his finger lower to caress the puckered flesh of her arsehole, dark and rosy in the cleft of her buttocks. Her body thrilled gently in spite of itself, and Stuart suppressed a smile. He went back to her clitoris. It was darkly flushed and engorged with blood, proving the strength of Claire's arousal. He flicked it experimentally, and she leapt against her bonds. Satisfied, he dropped his head and, deliberately slowly, ran the tip of his tongue around the swollen nub. If she hadn't been gagged she would have howled. The lust that had been building inside her swept up to meet the melting caress, and she felt her sex swell with an answering rush of moisture. She trembled all over as he lazily circled her clitoris several times with his tongue. Then he drew back and knelt down, looking for something he had placed under the divan earlier. A low buzzing sound filled the room. Claire lifted her head and gaped at the vibrator. It was bigger than anything she'd had inside her before. She shook her head urgently.

'No?' Stuart's rich voice was amused. 'I've told you. You have to trust me.' He applied the dildo to the sensitive sole of Claire's foot. She arched and bucked against her bonds. The vibrating tip ran up the inside of her leg, over her knee to her inner thigh. He knelt between her legs and once more spread her labia as wide as they would go. Then he pressed the tip of the vibrator to her clitoris. She leapt as if she had received an electric current, flashes of heat licking up from her belly, and stiffening her limbs. She thought she might shatter with the force of the sensation. Her lover continued to rub the vibrator rhythmically over the tortured nub of flesh. Her panicked breathing gradually deepened, and Stuart began to probe the depths of her vagina with his

77

fingers, inserting and withdrawing them with the same relentless rhythm as the vibrator, twisting, searching, teasing. She felt her bones melt and curve under the throbbing pleasure. She had never guessed she could feel such overwhelming sensations, not only confined to her vagina but rippling and shaking the whole of her body.

At just the right moment Stuart took the tip of the vibrator off her clitoris and carefully inserted it into the vagina itself, just a centimetre or two to start with, replacing the pressure on her clitoris with the slower rub of his own fingers. She moaned and clutched at the velvet upholstery. Pushing her to the very brink of orgasm with his fingers, he continued to slide the apparatus into her, centimetre by throbbing centimetre, until it was about halfway in and the delicate mouth of Claire's sex was fully stretched to accommodate it. She opened her eyes and stared at her writhing reflection on the ceiling. She could see the vibrator sticking out of her, and Stuart's dark head bent to his task. The sight almost pushed her over the edge and she closed her eyes again, hardly noticing as he climbed on to the divan to straddle her. He pressed his cock between her breasts, kneading the ripe globes against his skin, and then stroked it against her cheek.

She opened her eyes and stared unseeingly at him. She was writhing like a madwoman, snarling at him through her gag to give her release. He leant back and, reaching behind him, turned the vibrator up to its highest speed. With one last aching leap of his cock, he thrust the vibrator into her, right up to the hilt. Claire arched her back and screamed her ecstasy into the silk as Stuart's semen splattered over her face and breasts.

After several drowsy minutes, she opened her eyes again. Stuart had slumped against her, the weight of

78

one leg pressing her into the divan. She looked up into the mirror and saw the startlingly erotic sight of him laid full-length beside her, his face flushed and surprisingly vulnerable in the aftermath of his orgasm. The vibrator was almost completely buried inside her now, and Claire shifted uneasily. Stuart opened his eyes and, seeing the reason for her discomfort, turned the apparatus off and withdrew it. Then he untied her gag. She shivered and looked at his face only inches from her own, deeply unsettled by the intimacy of his gaze and the power of the orgasm he had given her. His eyes dropped to her mouth, and he moved to kiss her semen-smeared lips. She stopped him.

'Thank you,' she whispered.

As soon as she got back to her hotel room, she put a call through to Jess.

'Hi, it's Claire. I think I've found what you're looking for.'

'That was quick!'

'It's called the Palazzo Giardino. I'll fax the details to you. The only frescoes are on the ceiling, I'm afraid, but I have the name of a local artist who might be able to help us knock some up for the walls.'

'Great.' Jess hesitated. 'Are you OK? You sound a bit strange.'

'I'm fine. I'm just worn out, running around after you lot. You can tell the photographer and his crew to get on the first plane here. Find them a hotel. But do me a favour – don't book them in here. I want some privacy.'

'Sure.' There was another pause, a longer one this time. 'Erm – I probably should have mentioned this earlier – you know Felicity, she always wants the best, and she didn't think you were going to get involved in this project at all.'

'So?'

'Well, what I'm trying to tell you is – ' Jess took a deep breath. 'The photographer – it's Sean, Claire. I'm sorry.'

Chapter Six

Claire slowly replaced the receiver. Sean, of all people, was coming to Venice. There was no way she was going to be able to avoid him, as, in Felicity's absence, she would have to co-ordinate the shoot. Her holiday – the peaceful break she had been so looking forward to – had turned into a farce. All she had wanted to do when she got off the plane was to laze on the beach, do some sightseeing, visit a few galleries and spend time with Cherry. She had been looking forward to a pleasant, idle fortnight, with no complications.

But then she had met Stuart; there was no doubt in Claire's mind that Stuart MacIntosh was a major complication. The afternoon she had just spent with him in the palazzo already seemed hazy, even surreal. Her cheeks scalded at the thought that she had not only let him tie her up, but that she had also submitted herself to him completely, and had taken the most intense pleasure in it. That pleasure had been heightened by a strange thrill of power, which on the surface had seemed at odds with the humiliating position she had been in. The afternoon had unearthed new aspects of her character that shocked and disturbed her, and yet she was already looking forward to their next encounter. In fact, she could hardly wait. What did that make her, she wondered? A slut? A masochist? She didn't know.

And now Sean was coming. If she hadn't met Stuart, she might be looking forward to seeing Sean again, maybe even trying to mend some of the bridges they had burnt. But as it was, the situation was impossible.

To make matters worse, she had hardly seen Cherry at all. Guiltily, Claire picked up the phone again and dialled her friend's room. She let it ring for a while, but there was no answer. She smiled with relief. So Cherry had found something to occupy her? Claire wondered whether it could be the tall American. In spite of Cherry's despair that morning, Claire didn't think the man would be able to keep his hands off her for long – not if he had a drop of red blood in his veins.

At that moment Quaid Albright was thinking almost exactly the same thing, as he watched the dark cloud of Cherry's head bent towards his brother's blonde one.

'I think I like that one best,' she said. 'What do you think, Quaid?' As she pushed the sketchbook over the table towards him, he tried not to notice how the neckline of her dress dipped to reveal the uppermost swell of her right breast. He shifted in his seat to ease the pressure on his groin, and examined the drawing.

'It's real good. But I prefer the one of the tenements.'

'Well I think they're all brilliant.' Cherry sipped her wine. 'I wish I had your talent, Harper.'

The other twin blushed like a girl. 'It's nothing more than a hobby.'

'What do you both do, for a living?' The girl turned her melting brown eyes on Quaid. She had already learnt that he did most of the talking for the brothers.

'Our pa left us the family ranch in Montana. We work it together, raising cattle, mainly.'

'You mean you're real live cowboys!' Cherry's eyes grew round.

Quaid grinned. 'In the flesh.'

She made a show of finishing her tart, licking the cream from her fingers, not looking at either of them. 'I suppose you've both got wives, or girlfriends at least, back home on the ranch.'

Quaid shook his head. 'Nope. I guess we've been too busy to look for the right girl. This trip to Europe might do the trick, though. We thought it was about time to take us a break, see some of the world.' He flashed a grin at his brother, but it froze on his face when he saw how Harper was gazing at Cherry. All of his life he had protected his younger twin, but right at that moment what he wanted to do, more than anything, was smash his fist into his jaw. Instead, he made the effort to smile at Cherry.

'What about you?' he asked. 'Do you work?'

'Me?' Cherry looked flustered. 'Oh, I do a bit of this and that . . .' she hesitated. 'Mainly in the fashion business.'

'Sounds glamorous.'

'It isn't. Most of the time it's dull, and it's always knackering. But tell me more about your ranch. Is it big?

'It isn't much, as ranches go, but it's enough to keep us happy. Most days, when the weather's good, you can see nothing but sky, and you feel as if you could float clear to heaven.' Quaid's lazy grey eyes had taken on an evangelical gleam. 'Isn't that right, Harper?'

'Mmm?' His brother's pencil paused in its flight over the paper. 'Oh, sure is.'

Cherry rested her chin on her hand. 'You know, I always dreamt of living on a farm,' she said wistfully. 'Where I grew up, in Stepney, there were eight of us in a flat no bigger than a shoebox.'

'Why didn't you move to the country when you got older?'

'Oh, it was just a dream. I'm a townie through and through.' She laughed. 'I wouldn't know one end of a cow from the other. And besides, I need to be in the city to work.'

'You could always find something else to do.'

She shook her head. 'It's a nice thought, but . . .' Before either of the brothers could pursue the conversation further, she stood up. 'I really have to be going. Ta for a lovely lunch.'

'Can I walk you back to the hotel?' Quaid was quick to offer his help.

'We can both walk you back.' Harper also got to his feet.

His brother gave him a quelling look. 'The lady doesn't need two escorts. You stay here and order another beer. I won't be long.'

Harper scowled at him, but sat down again, while Quaid took Cherry's hand.

As they walked through the sleepy city without talking, Quaid was intensely aware of Cherry's fingers resting in his, delicate and warm, like a bird. He risked a sidelong glance at her. With her long brown legs and tight sundress only barely restraining her curves, she drew the eyes of every male that passed. And yet she seemed unaware of it. In spite of her blatant sex appeal, there was something innocent about her that swelled him with the urge to protect and defend. Disturbed by the power of that unfamiliar emotion, he was finally goaded to break the silence.

'Are you OK?' he asked. 'You're real quiet.'

'I'm sorry. It's just that I feel such a fool about last night. I was drunk. I really am sorry.'

'What exactly are you apologising for?'

A blush crept over her cheeks, turning the olive skin tawny. 'Do you want me to spell it out?'

Quaid grinned. 'I think you're going to have to.'

'OK. I'm sorry for propositioning you. You must have thought I was sex-mad.'

The American threw his head back and laughed, long and loud. 'Darling, you are truly priceless. The only thing that was stopping me from jumping all over you last night was the fact we'd both had too much to drink. In my experience that never makes for a satisfying time, for anyone involved.'

'So you do like me?'

He pulled her to him. 'You have no idea how much.' He took her face in both his hands and kissed her, bruising her lips against his, not releasing her again until she was breathless.

'We both drank wine at lunchtime,' she gasped in a small voice.

'Ah, but nowhere near as much, I reckon.' The meaning in his words was clear. He dropped his voice. 'Can I come up for coffee now?'

Cherry stared at him, her face flushed, 'I – I don't know.'

'Then let me make your mind up for you.' He took her hand and tugged her into an alleyway that led off the quayside. It was cool there, and deserted. He pushed her into the shadow of a doorway and placed a big hand on either side of her head. Then he bent down and kissed her again, more gently this time, teasing her lips, then trailing his mouth over her chin, her neck and her throat. He reached down to cup her breast through the cotton of her dress. She wasn't wearing a bra, and he tested the weight of it in his palm, rubbing his big thumb over the stiffening button of her nipple as he did so. His face was tight with desire.

'You surely are the finest thing.' He dropped his head to suckle her breast through her dress. She gasped and arched against him, scalded by the heat of his mouth. After a moment, he slipped the dress off her shoulder, and slid his hand under the neckline to find the bare flesh beneath. He cupped her breast possessively, then pushed her dress down with both hands, until her breasts were completely revealed. He looked at the smooth globes with their dark areolas puckering in the air of the alley. He groaned and took one in his mouth, flicking his tongue over it, tasting it, savouring the rubbery feel of it between his teeth. Cherry slumped weakly against the door. He moved on to her other breast and gave it the same lavish attention. Her arms were restricted by her dress, but she still managed to reach up and rake her fingers through his cropped hair. It was surprisingly soft to the touch. Quaid cupped her buttocks in both hands, pulling her against the bulge in his trousers. He pressed his thigh between her legs, lifting her off her feet, and, still grasping her with one hand, slid his other hand up over her knee, skimming her thigh until he reached the hem of her dress.

'Can I, darling?' he murmured against her lips. 'You're so sweet.'

Cherry nodded. He pushed her dress up and when his hand found her pants, he insinuated a fingertip under the elastic where it stretched over the tautened muscle of her thigh, then ran it round, towards the junction between her legs and the thicket of pubic hair. He eased her a little higher against the door to give easier access to his finger and watched her face as he slid his first knuckle between the damp lips of her sex. She squirmed and closed her eyes. Encouraged, he pushed his finger deeper into her.

'Oh, Quaid,' she groaned.

That was the only cue he needed. But he was just about to unzip his trousers, when he froze. There was someone coming down the alleyway. He lowered a surprised Cherry back on to the ground, and, as there was no time to pull her dress up, leant forward to shield her with his body.

'*Buon giorno.*' The old man gave him a delighted, toothy grin, and craned his neck to see more of Cherry as he passed.

'*Buon giorno,*' Quaid mumbled back. He watched until the old man had safely left the alleyway. 'We can't do it here,' he groaned.

'You're right.' Cherry pulled her dress up to cover her breasts, her face flaming. 'We can't. I don't know what I was thinking of.'

Quaid followed her back on to the quayside, and fell into step beside her as she marched towards the Metropole, walking with some difficulty because the bulge in his trousers hadn't had time to subside. Cherry turned towards him as they reached the porch of the hotel.

'I'm sorry,' she said. 'I'm not going to invite you up. I'm not in the mood now. Maybe tomorrow.'

He stood, perplexed, as she vanished into the hotel, leaving him alone on the pavement. What the devil had he done wrong? It wasn't his fault the old man had come along. He made his way back to his own hotel in a haze of frustration, completely forgetting that Harper was still waiting for him at the cafe.

Claire had arranged to meet Stuart for a drink at Harry's Bar. He was already there when she arrived, sitting at the same table they had shared before.

'Hello,' he said, his tone intimate. He stood up to greet her with a kiss on the cheek, and drew her down to sit beside him. 'What can I get you to drink? A beer?'

'Not this time. A martini, please.'

'Giancarlo! *Due martini, per favore.*'

'*Si, signore* MacIntosh.'

Stuart turned to her. 'You look tired.'

She grimaced. 'I've been on the phone solidly since this afternoon. I called your friend Pietro, and he's agreed to do some frescoes for us.'

'I'm glad he could help you out.'

Claire glanced across at him through her lashes. 'I don't know what I'd have done without you. First you help us with the palazzo, then the frescoes.'

He shrugged, and gave her a half-smile. 'It's all in a day's work.'

'Are you sure your client's happy about us using his palazzo?'

'He's delighted.' He took her hand, turned it over and carefully kissed the palm.

She smiled. 'What an old- fashioned thing to do.'

'Is it? I suppose I must be an old-fashioned kind of man.'

Claire tingled, remembering how they had spent their afternoon in the raspberry velvet room. 'I wouldn't say that.'

He rubbed his thumb across her wrist, where the handcuffs had bound them. The look he gave her, hot and level, made the blood cartwheel in her veins.

'*Due martini.*'

Claire jumped as the barman put their glasses on the table.

'*Grazie,*' said Stuart. He dropped his hand, that was still holding hers, beneath the table.

'The service is certainly quicker than the last time I was here,' laughed Claire.

'So it is,' he murmured. His eyes fell to her lips as he pulled her hand towards his crotch under the table and pressed it to his erection. Claire flushed, flattered that she had such an effect on him, but nervous that others might see. She scanned the room, then relaxed a little when she saw that no-one was taking any notice of them. He ground her palm harder against him. Trying to act nonchalant, she took a sip of her martini.

'I don't know what you've done to me,' murmured Stuart, 'but I haven't been able to think straight since this afternoon.'

'Perhaps it's the weather. It's very warm.'

He laughed, and released her hand. 'You're right, it is. Do you mind if I smoke?'

Claire shook her head. He lit a cigarette, and she watched his lips curl sensuously around it.

'Don't look at me like that,' he said, under his breath, without taking his eyes from his cigarette.

'Like what?' She knew what he meant, but was embarrassed to admit he had caught her in the act.

'Like this.' He did look at her then. The desire was so stark in his eyes, that she felt her mouth go dry. She licked her lips. Then, under the table, the tips of his fingers brushed her bare knee beneath her skirt. He continued to smoke, and to watch her. His fingers moved higher.

'Don't,' she breathed.

'Don't?' His hand paused.

'Not here.'

'Where then?' His voice was urgent.

Claire's confusion struck her dumb: she didn't want to take him to her hotel in broad daylight.

'Will you come back to the palazzo again with me?'

'What about Vittorio?'

'He's not back until tomorrow.' Stuart stubbed his

cigarette out decisively in the ashtray and pulled her to her feet. 'Come on.'

Vittorio's boat was waiting at the quay, with the same chauffeur who had taken them to the opera. In the cabin, Stuart pulled her to him, his hands and mouth demanding. The journey lasted no more than a few minutes, but it was enough to reduce Claire to a heap of nerve endings. She felt as if her skin had been flayed, leaving her raw and pulsing.

When they arrived at the quay of the Palazzo Giardino, Stuart led the way up through the lower floor. There was no noise, no sign of anybody else in the building, as he guided her once more through the studded doorway into the raspberry-lined room. He closed the door behind them, locked it, and pressed her against the padded velvet. His hands roved possessively over her body through her cotton dress. He rubbed his palms up the inside of her thighs, stroking upwards to stoke the fire between her legs.

'I hate these,' he said, frowning down at her pants that had impeded the progress of his hands. Seizing the flimsy lace in his hand, he ripped it off her. The violence of the act was so shocking, so unexpected, that she flinched. But then she melted against him again as his palms resumed their ascent, kneading her thighs, spreading them wider. When his fingers dipped into her, they both groaned.

'Are you always this wet?'

She shook her head dumbly at his frank question, her embarrassment battling with the lust that was pouring through her.

'Tell me you want me,' he whispered. 'I need to hear you say it.'

'I want you,' groaned Claire.

'Say it again.'

'I want you.'

Anticipation thrilled through her as Stuart growled

and swept her off her feet. He carried her to the high padded stool she had noticed earlier, and pushed her face down over it. Keeping her pressed down on the velvet with one hand, Stuart pushed Claire's skirt up to reveal her buttocks, and stroked them lovingly.

'Can I tie you again?' he asked, his voice dark with lust.

Wordlessly, Claire nodded. She watched as he bent to the feet of the stool and fastened her wrists and ankles with soft leather straps that hung there. It went through her mind that the stool must have been built exactly for that purpose, and wondered how many other times Stuart had used it. An unexpected wave of jealousy swept over her. But then all thoughts were driven out of her head, as he lifted his hand and brought it down, hard, on her exposed rump. She shrieked and struggled to rise, but the straps kept her pulled flat to the stool. Stuart pressed her further into the velvet and swiped her again, his palm cracking against the smooth skin in the silence of the room. Claire writhed, feeling hot and humiliated. Why was he doing this to her? Again and again, Stuart's hand rose and fell. It didn't hurt exactly, but stung maddeningly, making her cheeks pepper hot. Then something else began to build in her toes, and trembled up her legs towards her sex. With the next flurry of blows, he let his hand fall a little lower, on to the more tender part at the top of her thighs. Her sex tingled with the impact and she began to gasp, not with pain but with frustration, as the pressure between her legs built up unbearably.

The one-way filter of the pier glass lent a silvery glamour to the scene that was taking place in the raspberry-lined room. Giacomo Vittorio leant back in his seat, breathing heavily, secure in the knowledge that although he could see the couple, they could not see him. The English woman was very beautiful, even more than he had thought when he had first seen her in the *campo* outside. She was positioned over the stool so he could enjoy her to the full, and could see the reddened cheeks of her buttocks quivering under the blows that rained down on them.

He had been disappointed the previous evening when Stuart had told him he had missed their first encounter. The woman had apparently phoned him unexpectedly, and so it was unavoidable. He really couldn't blame the boy for seizing the opportunity. He would have done the same.

Stuart stopped belabouring the woman, and began to stroke her buttocks, murmuring soothingly. Thanks to a hidden microphone, Vittorio could hear the proceedings as well as see them. He held his breath as his protégé crouched down to spread the lips of the woman's sex from behind. Vittorio was so close that he could see juice of her arousal glistening on the delicate, inflamed membranes, although the sight of her clitoris was denied to him as it was pressed into the stool. Stuart slowly pushed two fingers into that enticing orifice. Vittorio sat up and, moving closer to the window, curled his fingers around the shaft of his cock that jutted from his greying pubic hair.

Her face still pressed into the velvet upholstery, Claire was almost beside herself with frenzied desire. She wriggled to rub her clitoris on the stool, then froze as Stuart's fingers spread her sex wide and she felt his breath on the very centre of her. He began to lap her with his tongue, rough, rapid strokes, and then to dart it in and out of her. She was close to orgasm now, but he was determined not to give her release just yet. Feeling the muscles of the channel begin to clench, he withdrew his tongue and flickered it teasingly up the crack of her buttocks towards her anus. Claire squirmed, rebelling at the thought of any invasion there. But resistance was futile. Knowing it, Stuart groaned and gently bit her buttocks. She felt his finger bury itself deep inside her vagina and then withdraw to rub her juice on the puckered entrance higher up.

'No, please,' she gasped.

'No?' He teased the virgin orifice, running his fingertip around it slowly. 'Are you sure?'

'I –'

He plunged his other hand into her vagina, sliding his fingers forward between the lips until he found the centre of her pleasure. As soon as they brushed it, Claire was galvanised, and bucked her hips involuntarily. Stuart took advantage of the movement to push the tip of his finger into the tight entrance of her arse.

'Aahh!' She couldn't hold back a shuddering moan as her excitement increased, feeling the sensitive skin stretch to accommodate his finger. Stuart drew in his breath sharply and released it in a loud groan, then both of his hands abruptly left her.

Claire sobbed as she heard the zip of Stuart's flies, and the crackle of a condom wrapper, then moaned as he pressed the inflamed tip of his cock against her sex, rubbing it up and down in the moisture that had gathered there. She felt something push into her anus again, and guessed by the increased pressure that it was his thumb this time. Pure pleasure thrilled through her, pushing her towards the brink of an orgasm that promised to be her most powerful ever. She held back from it, half-afraid, and not wanting to lose herself so completely. She stiffened as Stuart withdrew his thumb and moved the tip of his cock to nudge against the oiled orifice.

'No – I can't –' she murmured brokenly, shaking her head.

With a groan, he quickly slid the tip of his cock downwards and plunged the length of it deep into her sex. Claire screamed and writhed in ecstasy. The hard flesh filled her completely, stretching her so much she thought she might explode. He pulled out a little and then slid into her once more, this time even deeper than before. Claire's orgasm exploded blackly out of nowhere, a split second before Stuart arched backwards with his own, tumultuous release.

Claire was still reeling under the impact of her orgasm when she felt him withdraw. He zipped up his chinos and bent to unfasten the straps that bound her. Trembling, Claire lowered herself off the stool and pulled down her skirt. Her legs were shaking so much she could hardly stand, and she had to clutch the velvet to stop herself from sinking to the ground. She could tell by the flush of Stuart's face that she wasn't the only one suffering from the after-effects of lust. She looked more closely at him: there was some other emotion on his face too.

'Come on,' he muttered, not meeting her eyes. 'Let's get out of here.'

He took her to a cafe on the Grand Canal, beside the Rialto Bridge. It was growing dark, but the waterway was still thronged with boats. They watched the comings and goings in silence, until their drinks arrived. Claire picked up her glass and looked at him over the rim, noting how the lines of his face had fallen into a stern expression. It was as if she was seeing him for the first time, and her heart did a little somersault. She put down her glass.

'Have I upset you in some way?' she asked.

'Good God, no!' He took her hand and squeezed it.

'It's just that you seem distant, almost angry.'

'I'm sorry.' He rubbed her knuckles with his

thumb, then looked up and smiled at her. 'If you must know, I'm jealous.'

'Jealous?'

'I can't bear the thought of you with another man. For a moment back there, I wished there had been nobody but me.'

Claire shifted in her seat, not knowing how to respond to his confession. In one way she was flattered by it, and in another it made her uncomfortable; possessiveness was one of the least attractive of Italian traits.

'Tell me about your other lovers,' he urged.

The request surprised her, and she was going to refuse when she saw his face. His expression was intense, and strangely vulnerable. She shrugged. 'There's nothing much to tell really. I've had one or two casual flings, but I've only been in love once. With my husband. We were married ten years.'

'What happened?'

She sipped her martini. 'The usual sordid story. He had an affair. I found out. That was that.'

'What, no second chance?'

'No.'

Stuart gave a bemused laugh. 'I almost feel sorry for him.'

'I suppose, being half-Italian, you think that kind of behaviour is acceptable.' She tried to tug her hand away from his, but he wouldn't let her.

'Not at all. It's just that ten years is a long time.'

'You're right, it is. Actually . . .' she paused. 'I suppose this would be a good time to tell you. Sean's coming here. He's due sometime tonight.'

Stuart dropped her hand. 'Was that your idea or his?'

'Neither. He's a photographer, and he's been commissioned to do the Amore shoot.'

He frowned. 'If I'd known this was going to

95

happen, I might not have suggested you use the palazzo for your shoot.'

'But then we wouldn't be together now.'

'That's true.'

'There's no need to worry, honestly.' She smiled up at him. 'Sean being here won't affect us. I'm not going to hide our relationship from him.'

'I hope you're not thinking of using me to make him jealous. I told you, Claire, I don't like being used.'

'Of course not!' She picked up his hand again and curled her fingers around his. 'I want to be with you. Sean and I are over and done with.'

'I hope so. The thing is . . .' Stuart hesitated, his eyes burning into hers. 'I think I could fall in love with you, Claire.'

Claire froze. His revelation was unexpected and, if she was honest, not particularly welcome. Even though he had given her a lot of pleasure, she had only just extricated herself from one serious relationship and wasn't ready to throw herself into another. She struggled to mask the horror she knew must be written on her face.

'I can see I've jumped the gun again,' Stuart laughed. 'I'm sorry. I don't intend to rush you to the altar or anything like that.'

She blushed. 'I didn't think you did.'

'I'm happy for now just to keep you company while you're in Venice. If that's OK?'

'Of course.'

He leant over the table and caught the back of her neck, bringing her face close to his. Then he kissed her, leisurely, expertly. He saw the desire that rose in her eyes and smiled.

'Oh, I'd almost forgotten. I have a present for you.' He reached into his pocket and brought out a box.

She took it uncertainly. It was wrapped in gold

tissue paper, and tied with gold satin ribbon. She put it on the table and unwrapped it. Nestling inside a black velvet box, on a lining of raspberry silk, lay a pair of bracelets. She looked at them, not knowing what to say.

'Here, I'll help you put them on.'

He took the heavy silver bracelets in turn and snapped them on to her wrists. Claire held them up to admire them against the tanned skin of her forearms. They had an exotic, almost barbaric beauty.

'What can I say?' She didn't try to hide the pleasure in her eyes. 'They're lovely, thank you.'

'As soon as I saw them, I thought of you.' He smiled wryly. 'Actually, I have to admit that my motives aren't entirely unselfish. There is something you can do for me in exchange.'

Disappointment flickered in Claire's eyes. She hated to hear his gift had strings attached. 'What's that?'

'Do you remember my friend Pietro? As well as doing murals, he sometimes paints portraits. I would like him to do one of you.'

Claire frowned at the eccentric request. What kind of portrait would it be, she wondered? She shook her head in confusion. 'I don't know . . .'

'You don't have to make your mind up tonight. Tomorrow will do. Just promise me you'll think about it.'

Sean Savage watched the other passengers' baggage chug its way around the carousel. There was still no sign of his gear. He hoped to Christ the airline hadn't lost it. It wouldn't be the first time. He raked his hand through his dark blonde hair. The Amore shoot hadn't even started yet, and it had already turned into a nightmare. First of all, he had had a wasted trip to Rome, then 24 hours at Heathrow, waiting for the agency's next instructions, not daring to go home in case he missed the plane he was supposed to catch. And now he had discovered that Claire was in Venice. He would never have accepted the Barker & Savage commission if he had known she was going to be involved. As managing director, she was usually above getting her hands dirty on shoots, but something had obviously happened to change that situation. Whatever it was, Sean cursed it. He was sorely tempted to book the first plane home again. The only thing that was stopping him was the fact that he'd already wasted three days, and needed the money.

He straightened as he spotted one of his metal cases emerge on to the carousel, and went to retrieve it. One down, two more to go. His mind snapped back to Claire. He hadn't seen her for three months, since the night she had confronted him about his affair. At the time, it had almost been a relief that she had found out about it; guilt had been gradually eating away at him, changing him into somebody he hardly recognised, and didn't particularly like. The irony of it was that he had just decided to call off his relationship with Caroline, when the whole thing had blown up in his face. As strange as it sounded, Sean honestly loved his wife, and hoped the confrontation would give them both the chance to clear the air, and start again with a clean slate. But her reaction had been a shower of cold water on his hopes. She hadn't shouted, she hadn't cried; he would have understood it if she had. Instead, she had just stared at him, her beautiful face as expressionless as a statue. Then she had turned on her heel, and brought a suitcase for him to pack. There were no recriminations, and so he didn't get the chance to explain anything, or even to suggest ways of repairing the damage.

At the time, he had been infuriated by her reaction. It was so like her. Even when he had first met her as a fresh-faced student, he had found it difficult to know what was going on in her head. As soon as she felt challenged in any way, emotionally or physically, the shutters would come down. The story was the same in bed. She favoured a no-nonsense approach, which was satisfying enough in its own way, but began to pale after a few years. Once or twice, however, he had succeeded in getting through her defences, and in coaxing her to let herself go. Whenever that had happened he had been astounded and delighted by the power of her response to him. But then, the day after, things had invariably reverted to normal again. The fact that she had given him glimpses of the potential in her made her usual reticence so much harder for him to bear. The result of that accumulated frustration was his affair with Caroline.

His initial anger at Claire's reaction had soon cooled, however. Not having had any choice in the matter, he had moved in with Caroline, who was in every way his wife's opposite: passionate, manipulative, melodramatic. The woman undoubtedly adored him, but drove him mad with her constant demands for attention. He couldn't even sneak a glance at a newspaper without her wriggling herself on to his lap. And she was jealous; Othello paled in comparison. Where had he been? Who'd he been with? He had started to think of her as a jailer, rather than a lover.

But of course, being with Caroline had it's compensations. Or one big one, to be precise: she would do anything – absolutely anything – for him in bed. At the beginning he'd been like a kid in a sweetshop – sex had taken an addictive hold on him that had made him reckless and blinded him to the damage he was doing to his marriage. It didn't take long, however, for his enthusiasm to wane, and for him to start longing for something gentler, less athletic. He shrugged.

It was over between him and Caroline now anyway. When he had left for this assignment he had moved his things into his brother's flat. That was another reason for not rushing back to London: he had nowhere to live. He felt like a gypsy.

None of these thoughts showed on Sean's face. To the two models and the stylist travelling with him he presented a relaxed, attractive figure. The women had not worked with him before, and were now watching him speculatively, noting the lean legs encased in jeans, the long green eyes above cheekbones like razor shells, and the way his hair curled on the collar of his denim jacket. The thing they found most interesting of all, however, was his lack of a wedding ring. Not that it would have made a lot of difference. On location, miles away from family life, most people regarded marriage as academic anyway. Tania, Lianne and Carol eyed each other critically, ready for battle. Which of them would be the lucky girl?

Sean bent to retrieve his duffle bag and the second steel case from the carousel, lifting them as if they weighed nothing. Slinging the straps over his shoulder, he strode past and tossed them a dangerous smile.

'Come on, you lot. Let's hope we're not too late to catch the boat.'

Chapter Seven

*T*he night air stirred the curtains, making them shiver like ghosts. Cherry could smell the tang of ozone from the sea, mingled with the faint scent of suntan lotion on her skin. She shifted in the bed, trying to get comfortable enough to sleep. But it was useless. As hard as she tried to close them, her eyes kept snapping open again, staring at the small cracks in the ceiling, while her mind danced with images of Quaid. Whenever she did manage to close her eyes for a few seconds, she would be back in the alleyway again with the American, overwhelmed by the touch of his hand on her thigh, his searching mouth on her breast. She groaned and kicked the sheet on to the floor. Why had she sent him packing? Whatever guilty impulse had made her do it, she was regretting it now. Her naked body was like a coiled spring, taut with frustrated desire. She ran her hands down it, smoothing her palms over the contours of her breasts, belly and hips. Then she cupped one breast in each hand, teasing the nipples with her fingers, before letting her arms fall on to the mattress again. She wished she had brought her vibrator with her.

But she hadn't dared to pack it: what if customs had insisted on searching her bags? She would have died of shame. She was too nervy and strung-out to satisfy herself with her finger.

Sighing, she got out of bed and went to the mirror. She stared at her reflection for a long time, at the full breasts, long legs, and at her slender shoulders and neck. And, finally, at her face. Her agent had told her that, perversely, it was her face that made her such a favourite with the readers of *Penthouse* and *Mayfair*. Unlike the other glamour models, who seemed to wear the same vacant, come-hither expression, Cherry's heart-shaped features were vibrant, full of life, her eyes simultaneously humorous and seductive, knowing and innocent. She lifted the weight of her hair off the back of her neck and arched her back, pushing her breasts into prominence like the professional she was. Then she smiled, as if she was looking into a camera, turning the corners of her lips up, making her eyes glow. It was like switching on a light. Just as abruptly, she switched it off again. What was she doing?

She wandered listlessly to the window and craned her head out so she could see the Riva degli Schiavoni at the end of the alley. There were still quite a few people coming and going on the promenade; not everyone had decided to have an early night. She cursed under her breath. Perhaps it hadn't been such a good idea. She marched back to the bed and threw herself on it, then lifted her head again to look at the clock on her bedside. It was still only half past eleven.

After another few minutes, she jumped up. She ran to the wardrobe and pulled out a dress at random, tugging it on over her head, then, without pausing to bother with underwear, she slipped on a pair of sandals, grabbed her room key, and left.

The Americans' hotel wasn't far from the Metropole: no more than ten minutes away, just off the Grand Canal. Cherry tried not to think while she was walking, but to concentrate simply on putting one foot in front of the other. But when she reached the hotel, she stopped. What if Quaid was out? What if – even more unthinkable – he didn't want to see her? She realised just how much she was gambling on this impulsive move. She hesitated, on the brink of changing her mind, when an athletic figure emerged from the swing doors of the hotel. Her heart thudded in her chest.

'Quaid?' she said, stepping into the light.

He hesitated a moment, then nodded, his eyes wary. 'Reckoned you might have been able to tell me and my brother apart by now.'

She shook her head, then by way of explanation for her being there, said, 'I couldn't sleep.'

'Me neither.'

She was suddenly conscious of her uncombed hair, and the breeze that was cutting through her sundress. She shivered. 'Listen, I'm really sorry about this afternoon. I know it wasn't your fault we were interrupted.'

He moved closer to her and looked searchingly into her face. Then, as if he had come to a decision, he put his finger on her lips. 'It doesn't matter. You're here now.' He ran his hands down her arms, and stopped when he felt the goosebumps on her skin. 'You're cold. Come inside.'

He took her hand and led her back through the swing door. She sensed him hesitate, before striding across the foyer towards the lift. He pressed the button. The lift was empty when it arrived. They got in, the door closed again, and they turned instinctively to each other. Quaid lifted her chin with one long brown finger, and kissed her experimentally, tenderly. His unexpected gentleness made her melt inside, she moaned and arched her fingers up through his hair. He caught his breath, deepened the kiss.

'Oh, Cherry,' he groaned against her mouth. 'I never . . .'

This time it was her turn to silence him with a finger on his lips. 'Shh.'

The lift opened and the American led the way silently to his room. They both slipped inside. He had left his bedside light on, and she saw that the room was luxurious. It had a deep-blue carpet, heavy velvet drapes at the window, and, most importantly of all, a huge king-sized bed. It seemed that cowboys were no different to the rest of their compatriots – they all liked to travel in comfort.

'Do you want a drink?' he asked, unsure of her again.

'No.' She shook her head, her eyes rivetted on his face. 'What I want . . . is to make love to you, Quaid.'

He stared at her, his usually sunny face clouded with some emotion. Then he shrugged and grinned. 'Who am I not to oblige a lady?'

His jesting expression melted, however, when she reached up to undo the zip at the back of her dress. Slowly, she shrugged it off her shoulders, then let it fall to the floor. She was naked underneath.

She heard his intake of breath. He stood as if nailed to the spot, staring at her narrow waist, her ripe breasts with their dark puckered areolas, and the curling nest of hair between her thighs. Cherry quailed under his scrutiny, and felt a blush spread from her cheeks down to her throat and collarbone. She was beginning to think that she would have to go to him, when he finally made his move. He approached her until he was standing so close that she could feel the warmth of him through his clothes. Then he grasped her shoulders, and dropped his mouth to hers. His hands moved down to clasp hers for a moment, before reaching up to her breasts. He stroked the globes lightly, without taking his mouth from hers, trailing his fingers across her nipples. She shuddered. Then his lips left her, and he scooped her off her feet, and carried her to the bed. He laid her there carefully, as if she was made of china, and, while her eyes devoured him, stripped off his jacket, then his blue checked shirt. She felt herself grow warm at the sight of his broad shoulders and the blonde hair that gleamed on his chest. He unbuckled his belt and kicked off his jeans, until he was only wearing nothing but his shorts and she could see his erection bulging against the cotton.

Then he surprised her. Instead of turning his attention to her more obvious charms, he began to caress her feet, taking first one and then the other in his hand and pressing a kiss to the instep of each. He rubbed them, feeling the delicate bones beneath the skin, easing her tension away little by little. When he had finished with her feet, he pulled them gently apart, knelt between her legs, and started to press light, nibbling kisses up her shins towards her knees. He teased her kneecaps with his teeth, making her squirm, and moved up, up her thighs, until she was moaning aloud.

Then, lightly, with infinite care, he spread the lips of her sex. She arched herself towards him, knowing he was feasting his eyes on the sensitive, swollen flesh. To her frustration he didn't do anything but look for a long, long time, until she thought she would burst with tension. She twisted her breasts in her hands, writhing as his hot breath branded her, until the moisture that pulsed into her sex could no longer be held there, and began to trickle down the cleft of her buttocks. Then, and only then, did he touch her. At first she thought she had imagined it, so lightly did he brush the outer lips of her vagina.

105

But the strokes of his tongue became swifter, surer, and she arched up to meet his mouth, pushing her glossy curls against him. He groaned and buried his face between her legs, fastening his lips unerringly on her clitoris. He spread her as wide as she would go with his fingers, and began to suck on the core of her pleasure, stoking a heat within her she had not felt before. She ached to have him inside her – his fingers, his cock, anything – but he confined his attentions to her clitoris, until all sensation was concentrated on that tiny, aching nub of flesh. She dug her fingers into his hair.

Then, suddenly, he left her. He straightened up and took off his shorts, reached in the bedside cabinet, and handed her a condom. She sat up eagerly, brushing her hair out of her eyes, and tore open the wrapper. Taking his cock in one hand, she slid the rubber over it, smoothing it down the shaft until he was groaning at her touch. He put his hands under her buttocks and pulled her towards him, so that she was resting on the edge of the bed. She moaned. She wanted to have his cock inside her, was mad for it, but again he spread her wide with his fingers, and pushed them into her, stretching her, exploring the lubricated channel.

'Please,' she gasped. 'Oh, Quaid. Please fuck me.'

He straightened up and jerked her hips towards him, ramming his cock into her. Cherry sighed and spread her thighs even wider, running her hands over the whipcord muscles of his back and shoulders. He lifted her buttocks higher to increase the depth of his penetration, so that he nudged the top of her womb itself, and began at last to move in her, and drive her towards her climax. She wrapped her legs around his waist, and he twisted slightly to vary the angle of penetration, determined to wring every drop of pleasure from her body. His grim expression spoke of

106

the effort it was costing him to hold back his own climax. With mischievous intent, Cherry clasped her legs around him more tightly, wanting to make him lose control as she had, but, even as she did so, her orgasm slammed into her. She would have screamed, but Quaid's hand fastened tightly on her mouth. He tipped her head back, kissed her chin, covered her throat with burning kisses, until she felt him grow momentarily even harder, and he pulsed his hot release into her. They collapsed back on to the bed together, slick with sweat, and lay there without speaking, until she felt him begin to shrink inside her. He pulled reluctantly out, holding the condom carefully in place with his fingers.

'I'm just going to the bathroom,' he muttered. 'Won't be a minute.'

Cherry lay back on the pillow, totally sated, her limbs heavy with pleasure. Idly, she listened to the water running in the basin, then turned her head to look around the room. The first thing she noticed, now that the veil of lust was no longer over her eyes, was a door that connected to the adjoining suite. Seeing the thin line of light shining under it, she realised why Quaid had covered her mouth: he hadn't wanted his brother to hear her. Thoughtfully, she climbed under the covers. The water turned off in the bathroom, and after a moment, the door opened again and her lover padded back to bed. He climbed in beside her, shivering a little in the air conditioning.

She smiled at him, but his grey eyes met hers uncertainly.

'Is there something the matter?' she asked, raising herself up on her elbow.

'I guess so. I got something to tell you.' He fidgeted with the sheet. 'Truth is, I'm not Quaid, I'm Harper.'

Chapter Eight

Cherry stared at the man in bed beside her for a long, long moment, then let herself fall back on the pillows.

'Bloody hell!' she gasped.

'I don't rightly know what made me do it. I guess I was jealous that you liked Quaid better than me. But I can't pretend I'm sorry about it now.' He peered down into her stricken face. 'Is it really so bad?'

'Oh, Harper,' she said wearily, 'you've just made a tart out of me.'

'Don't see it myself.' He stroked her hair on the pillow, capturing a strand to twist between his fingers. 'You're a stunning woman, Cherry.'

She snorted in exasperation. 'Why is it that men think that all they have to do is to pay a woman compliment, and they're automatically forgiven? You're like kids, the lot of you.'

Harper's fingers stilled in her hair. 'Didn't you enjoy being with me?

Cherry was about to give a sharp retort to his question when she looked at his face. Her answer mattered to him – a lot.

'Yes,' she sighed. 'Of course I did. It was wonderful. But – bloody hell, what am I going to say to Quaid?'

'Shh. Keep your voice down, unless you want to say it to him right now.'

Cherry frowned at the connecting door, then sighed and closed her eyes. 'I give up.'

Harper's hand reached out tentatively under the sheet to stroke her thigh, then paused before climbing once more to the damp curls between her legs. Cherry shivered, and, after a moment's hesitation, surrendered to the inevitable.

The scene in the palazzo ballroom was like something out of Dante's *Inferno*. Claire hardly recognised the room, once so airy, now teeming with lighting technicians, scene painters and various hangers-on. Everybody seemed to know what they were doing, however, which soothed her nerves a little. She searched the faces for one she knew, and finally spotted Ewan Jones, an art director from Barker and Savage, who was holding something up to the light by the windows. She picked her way through the trailing leads and lighting cases towards him.

'Ewan. How're thing's going?'

The young man turned and grinned at her through his thatch of dark curls. 'Not bad, considering. Here, what do you think of these?' He handed her a couple of Polaroids. It was hard to believe they'd been taken with all the equipment in the room: it looked almost as spacious as she remembered it, and twice as elegant, simply because of the camera angle and lighting.

'Pretty good,' she agreed. 'Where are the models?'

'We won't be needing them until tomorrow,' said Ewan.

'But they did get here safely?'

'Oh, yes. Last night. Sean told them to stay in the

109

hotel today to get some rest, but knowing them, they're probably at the lido.'

'I just hope they don't turn up with sunburn tomorrow.' At the mention of her husband's name, Claire's eyes slid around the room. There was no sign of him. 'Where is Sean?'

'He's gone to find Carol, the stylist. She went off to source some muslin for the curtains hours ago, and hasn't been seen since. He's in a rare bad mood.' He put the Polaroids in his pocket.

'I see the painter made it, though.' Claire nodded towards the far end of the room, where a team of artists were busy sketching out a fresco on to canvas that had been stretched over the wall. They had already finished one section, a Baccanalian scene of nymphs and satyrs. From a distance it matched the ceiling exactly in style and subject matter.

'I don't know where you found him, but the man's a godsend,' enthused Ewan. 'He works faster than Michelangelo on speed. Come and have a look.'

Claire followed him. Close up, the fresco was even better than she thought. No-one seeing it for the first time would have guessed that it had just been painted that morning: with its muted blues and pinks, it looked straight out of the *cinquecento*.'

'Wow,' Claire breathed, 'that's brilliant.'

'You like?'

Claire turned at the voice behind her to see an emaciated young man, with piercing, dark eyes and a goatee beard. He was staring critically up at the fresco, wiping his hands on his overalls.

'It is not as good as I would have liked, but I have had so little time. Another couple of days and I could have given it more depth, more feeling.'

'I wouldn't worry,' said Claire. 'It's very good. And through a camera it'll look marvellous.' She held out her hand. 'You must be Pietro Corolla.'

'I am.' He took her fingers and bowed over them. 'And you are Senora Savage. May I say that you are every bit as beautiful as my friend tells me.'

Claire threw an embarrassed glance at Ewan, who coughed and shuffled off. 'I'll be getting on then, shall I?' he said. 'I'll speak to you later.'

She waited until he was out of earshot. 'I don't know how to thank you for helping us out, Mr Corolla.'

'Please, call me Pietro.' He flashed a perfect set of teeth. 'I was glad to be able to. Any friend of Stuart MacIntosh is a friend of mine. He and I go back a long way. In fact, we were at college together.'

'At art college?' Somehow Claire had never pictured Stuart as an artist.

'Si, first in *Roma*, and then in *Firenze*.'

'Have you always specialised in murals?'

'Good heavens, no.' Pietro's eyes twinkled at her mischievously. 'I am, how do you say, a Jim of all trades. I do a bit of this, a bit of that: some scene painting; some photography; some portrait commissions. Anything, in fact, that will put food on my table.' He shrugged, watching her, noting with pleasure the way her cheekbones flushed dusky rose under her tan. 'It will be a privilege indeed to paint you, Signora Savage.'

Claire stiffened. 'I don't know what Stuart's said, but I haven't actually agreed . . .'

'But you must! You'll break my heart if you refuse.' He dropped his voice and leant towards her confidentially. 'Also, I need the money.'

'Oh.'

'Pietro! *Sa come si fa?*' One of the artist's boys was trying to translate a design into chalk on the canvas, and was having trouble with the lines of a drape.

'*Momento.*' Pietro took Claire's fingers again and kissed the tips. 'Excuse me, *signora*. It seems that I

111

employ monkeys! But I will see you soon, in my studio, no?'

Before she could answer, he stalked back to his fresco, shouting something unintelligible in Italian.

'Damn,' she hissed under her breath. Pietro's confession made it difficult for her to refuse to sit for him now. She wondered briefly whether Stuart might have put him up to it, but then shook her head. She was being paranoid.

'Hi.'

Claire had been so absorbed in her thoughts that she hadn't noticed Sean come into the room. Seeing her talking to the artist, he had hesitated at first, and then squared his shoulders to approach her.

'Oh, hello.' She bumped painfully back to the present, her stomach churning as if it was on a spin cycle. Sean was dressed as usual in jeans, with a plain white tee-shirt and black boots, but he looked browner and leaner than she remembered. Far better, in fact, than he had a right to. He was standing so close to her she had to tip her chin up to look at him.

'How are you?' he asked.

'Fine.' She smiled crisply. 'I'm glad to see you made it all right.'

'Eventually.'

'Do you have everything you need?'

'I think so, for now.' He raked his fingers through his hair. The familiarity of the gesture made Claire's mouth go dry.

'How long do you think the shoot will take?'

'Four days, maybe five. It's hard to tell. A lot depends on the natural light.'

'OK. But let me know if it's going to be any longer than that. I have to warn the client if we're going to go over budget.'

'Of course . . .' he paused. 'I never thought you would be here. If I had . . .' he let his voice tail off, and then smiled his lopsided smile. 'I didn't think you got your hands dirty with this kind of thing any more.'

Claire followed his gaze down to her fingers, to see that Pietro had managed to transfer a generous smear of cobalt paint on to them. She was too wound up to see the funny side of it.

'I don't usually,' she snapped. 'And I don't like the situation any more than you do!' She turned on her heel.

'Claire.' Her name, softly spoken, halted her in her tracks. 'We're going to have to talk to each other sometime, you know. Properly. There are things we need to discuss.'

'I know.' In spite of her efforts to keep her expression neutral, her mouth twisted. 'You must be anxious for me to sell the house. I'm going to put it on the market when I get back.'

'That wasn't what I meant, and you know it.' His emerald eyes bore into her,

She felt the prickle of tears in her throat, and disgusted with herself, she swallowed. 'OK, we'll talk. But not right now, we're both too busy.'

'Claire!' Ewan shouted to her from other side of the room. 'There's someone here for you.'

It was Stuart, who had turned up as promised to take her for lunch. He was standing by the door, relaxed and totally at ease, drawing interested glances from all the women in the room. His dark eyes, looking at them both, pulled her towards him like a magnet.

'I have to go.'

'I can see that.' Sean's eyes narrowed, cat-like, as they returned the other man's challenging stare. 'Why don't you give me a shout when you're less busy. You know where to find me.'

* * *

'Was that him?' asked Stuart, when they were safely out of the ballroom.

'Yes.' She didn't need to ask what he meant.

He was silent for a moment, before saying cryptically. 'As I said, ten years is a long time.'

Claire stopped. 'Believe me, I wouldn't talk to him if I didn't have to.' Then, without warning, the tears that had been threatening to spill over did so at last. She wiped them angrily away.

Stuart turned her to face him. 'Hey, I'm not going to give you a hard time about it. It seems to me that you're being tough enough on yourself.' He pulled her to him and stroked a tear from the corner of her eye. 'You have paint all over your face.'

'Have I?' She looked down in dismay at her fingers, that were still streaked with blue.

'Why don't you come and get cleaned up in my room?'

'Are you sure?'

'We can't go out for lunch with you looking like an extra in *Braveheart*, can we?'

Stuart led the way to a part of the palazzo Claire had never been in before. His room surprised her. It had a white tiled floor, white walls, and its only furniture was a wardrobe, chest of drawers and a single bed. Apart from an alarm clock there were no personal signs of occupation. Compared to the opulence of the rest of the Palazzo Giardino, it was almost monk-like in its simplicity.

'The bathroom's through there.' Stuart indicated a door in the corner. 'Help yourself to anything you need. Why not have a shower? It might make you feel better.' He sat down on the bed and reached for the phone. 'I can make some calls.'

In the bathroom, Claire stripped off her clothes and laid them carefully on a stool. The room was as plain as the bedroom, with a simple white suite and a tiled

114

shower cubicle. The only hint of luxury was the pile of fluffy towels that lay on a chair. She turned the shower on and went to the mirror over the sink. Her chin and cheek were smeared with blue, which, with her slanting eyes, gave her the look of a Red Indian squaw. She pulled her hair back off her face and grimaced. Seeing Sean had shaken her more than she liked to admit. How was she going to cope, working with him for the next five days? If it hadn't been for Stuart, she doubted that she'd be able to do it.

She had to confess that she'd enjoyed Sean's reaction to her new lover. She had seen by his eyes that he had guessed the nature of their relationship. Even as she stood beside Sean, she had felt the physical pull of Stuart across the room. It was as if he had her on an invisible leash. She knew what kind of leash it was: Stuart had woken her sensuality, and she wanted more of it. Had Sean sensed that, she wondered? Did he know her that well?

She stepped into the shower. The water was hot, and she let the jet sluice over her body, surrendering to its forceful caress on her skin. After a minute or so she reached for the shower gel that was hanging on a hook, and rubbed herself with it. It smelt of Stuart, so much so that she immediately felt a prickling warmth between her legs, making her heart beat more urgently. She carefully soaped her pubic hair, and let a finger slide up inside herself. She bit her lip, stifling a groan, then heard the bathroom door open.

She opened her eyes and blinked at Stuart through the water that jewelled her lashes. It was as if the scent of him had conjured him up, naked, smooth-skinned and leanly muscled like a dancer. He was already aroused. She took his hand and drew him into the shower with her. He looked down at the soap bubbles that were running down from her collarbone over her pointed breasts. He seized the slippery flesh in his hands, imprisoning it, making her moan with desire. Then, as the powerful spray gushed over them both, he released her and reached for the shower gel. She watched him as he soaped his hands, then closed her eyes as she felt them on her shoulders, her breasts, stomach and hips. He pulled her against him, and slid his hands over her buttocks. She began to run her hands over him, revelling in the musculature of his chest, stomach and thighs. There was not a trace of fat on him. She reached up to rake her hands through his hair, sleek with water, and felt the curls spring under her fingers. She took in every detail of his face, watching how the rivulets ran over the heavy brows, and beaded his lashes with sparkling drops. She smoothed his eyebrows and ran a wondering finger over the tip of his lashes, then down to his beautifully moulded mouth. Of all the parts of Stuart's body it was his lips – full and sensuous – that always took her breath away. He growled low in his throat and bit her finger, nipping it between his teeth. She leant weakly against him.

She could feel him trembling with the force of his desire, and the knowledge that he wanted her so badly sent a white hot surge of lust through her own body, making her arch against him, pushing her breasts against his chest. He took her face between his hands and kissed her, deeply, savagely, as if he were going to devour her whole. She could hardly breathe through the water and his lips on hers, his tongue plundering her mouth. He dropped his hands to dig his fingers into her buttocks, making her groan aloud with both discomfort and desire. Hoisting her up against the wall, he spread her thighs, and she felt his cock nudge the swollen lips of her sex. But even on this wave of intense arousal, she still felt the stirring of common sense.

'We can't,' she gasped. 'Not without a condom.'

116

He stopped and stared unseeingly down at her, almost as if he had lost consciousness of who and where they were. She thought for a moment that he was going to ignore her, to push himself inside her regardless, but then relaxed as she saw awareness return to his face. He shook the water out of his eyes.

'I don't have one here.'

Disappointment surged through her, but was swiftly replaced by another emotion. All was not lost. She pushed him away from her, and dropped to her knees. Guessing her intention, Stuart moaned and thrust his groin towards her. When she enclosed his penis with her lips, he closed his eyes and leant back against the wall. Water lashed down at her as she cupped his balls, and felt them tighten at her touch, and his cock jerked spasmodically inside her mouth. She took him in deeper. He clutched the side of her head, so that she couldn't pull away from him, and began to move his hips, drawing himself in and out of her throat with long, unhurried strokes. Claire stiffened, and tried to back off a little, but he just gripped her more tightly. She squeezed her eyes shut and concentrated on the sensation of having him in her mouth, feeling the tickle of wet curls on her chin, the nudge of the tip of his glans at the back of her throat, savouring the male scent of him even through the teeming water. He was moving more urgently now, blind to everything but his own satisfaction. Using her. She experienced the same sensation that she did whenever he tied her up, the same perverse thrill of power, a wave of pure animal desire. In and out he thrust, his body stiffening as he approached his release. Claire reached up to dig her nails into his buttocks, and he began to sob, slamming into her again and again. Then, with a bitter cry, he exploded in her mouth. She let him pulse into her throat, then slump against her, still clutching her head. When his breathing had steadied again, he pulled her up to stand beside him. His eyes were dark, fathomless, as he reached round to turn off the water. The silence was deafening.

He put his hands either side of her head and kissed her, more considerately this time. Claire returned the kiss impatiently, her own unfulfilled desire making her less gentle. She didn't want his consideration, but something wilder, darker. She caught hold of his lower lip with her teeth and nipped, not hard enough to draw blood, but enough to make him flinch and draw back. He laughed. She saw the speculation and pleasure in his eyes.

'So you want to play?' As he spoke he began to caress her left nipple, teasing it with fingers that were slightly abrasive, wrinkled from their time in the water. Then, without warning, he pinched it hard. She gave a squeak of surprise. 'Have you ever thought of having your nipples pierced?' His fingers tightened again as he rolled the tight button of flesh between them. She groaned and leant her head back against the wall. 'No? Perhaps you'd prefer a stud somewhere else?' He let his hand fall, between her legs to capture one of her labia between his finger and thumb. 'Here perhaps?' He nipped the fleshy lip, making her shiver even as she melted inside. 'On second thoughts a ring might be better than a stud, then I could chain you to my bed.' He rubbed his face against hers. 'If only I could.' The thought of being bound in such an intimate way raised goosebumps all over her. He released the lip of her labia, and slipped his fingers inside her vagina, rubbing the tips over the tender frilled flesh. He found her clitoris. After rubbing it a moment, he caught it between his thumb and forefinger. 'But I think I would prefer to chain you to me by this.' Blood surged into the delicate nub, and he increased the pressure on it until

118

it throbbed beneath his fingers like a tiny panting tongue.

'I think you already have,' she murmured. She could feel her moisture trickle on to his hand, hot and sweet. Sweat broke out on her upper lip, and she licked it away distractedly. With a cry he bent to savage her mouth with his own, and nip her chin with his teeth, still maintaining his exquisitely debilitating hold on her clitoris. He dropped his other hand to caress the globes of her buttocks.

'Has anyone ever told you that you have the most delicious arse?'

She shook her head, half laughing, half gasping.

Stuart ran his fingers, still slick with shower gel, up the cleft of her buttocks, lightly at first and then more deeply, until they were teasing the puckered entrance itself. Claire shuddered, but was too far gone with pleasure to make any protest. Slowly, he pushed a finger up into the tight channel. Delicious shivers ran through her, turning her body and her mind to jelly. At that moment she would have done anything he asked of her: she was completely in his power. She sobbed as he released her clitoris, and thought at first that it had gone numb, until he brushed it again with his thumb. The effect was electric. She bucked against him.

'Please, Stuart, please.'

He obliged, sliding first one, then two and three fingers into her sex, so that she was impaled both front and rear. Then his thumb began to work on her clitoris, battering the tortured nub of flesh. Her legs started to shake and she was forced to lean against him to remain upright, only barely conscious of his cock, rigid again, pressing against her thigh. Stuart watched her avidly, his face dark, intensely aware of the friction of her skin against his cock, both hands buried in her scalding heat, forcing satisfaction on her like a punishment. She had no chance of holding anything back against that relentless onslaught, and came at last, hot and shuddering, soaking his fingers with her juice. When it was over, she went limp and her head fell forward on to Stuart's shoulder. Moments later his own face twisted as he ejaculated over her thigh and belly.

They stood like that for a long time, just holding each other. Stuart was the first to move: he stroked her face, then turned the water on again. He soaped them both, rinsed them off, and helped her out of the shower. She shivered as he wrapped a towel around her, too drained to do anything but acquiesce. He led her to the other room and laid her on the bed. Lying naked next to her, he pushed her wet hair out of her eyes.

'I've never . . .' she began.

'Shhh.' He raised her chin and kissed her. Even through the bulk of the towel she could feel that he was still hard.

The phone rang.

'Damn!' Stuart twisted round to pick it up. Claire watched his face sleepily as he listened to the voice on the other end. 'What, right now?' he said, frowning. Then, resigned, 'OK.' He slammed the receiver down. 'Damn!'

'Who was it?' She propped herself up on her elbow.

'Vittorio. He wants to meet you.' Stuart's gaze swept around the room suspiciously. 'I swear the man has eyes in the back of his head.'

'What do you mean?'

'Nothing. Let's get dressed. He's waiting in the garden.'

After the air conditioning in Stuart's room, the heat outside was like plunging into a pool of warm water.

'So tell me, Signora Savage,' said Giacomo Vittorio,

120

after they had shaken hands. 'What do you think of this city of ours?'

'It's beautiful,' she smiled. 'I'm sorry, that seems inadequate, doesn't it?'

'Si, it is much better in Italian. *Bellissima*.' Vittorio rolled the word around his tongue. 'It is easy to see why Italian is the language of love, no? Please, let us sit.' He waved towards a table that had been laid in the dappled shade of a plane tree. 'I thought you might like some lunch. It is getting late.'

Claire looked at her watch, and saw with surprise that it was almost three o'clock. 'I should really be getting back to the shoot,' she said.

'Nonsense. You cannot work on an empty stomach.'

Her eyes slid to Stuart, to see that he had already taken a seat at the table. His hair was still wet from their shower, and was slicked back off his face so that his features was shown at their perfect best, achingly beautiful, but expressionless. She shrugged. She was hungry. 'Thank you. That's very generous.'

'*Non importa*. It is a pleasure.'

Vittorio rang a handbell, and three women appeared immediately, weighed down with trays of food. There were lobster, oysters, smoked tuna, and huge *gamberoni*, or prawns, still in the shell, their delicate pink antenae bristling. As the women placed the trays on the table, Claire saw that the nearest woman was staring at her. The liquid eyes held hers for a moment, gentle, almost pitying, before sliding away again.

'Please, help yourself,' urged Vittorio.

She saw that Stuart had already begun to fill his plate, and watched the other man under her lashes as she did the same. It was impossible to tell how old her lover's client was. With his steel-coloured hair swept back from a face that was curiously wrinkle-free, he could have been anything between forty and sixty. There was an aura of vigour about him, that was emphasised by his powerful features; he had eyes the colour of stone-washed denim, high cheek-bones, and a nose that jutted like a blade over full lips. His mouth had the same kind of sensuality as Stuart's, but more exaggerated, caricatured even, to the extent that it was almost off-putting.

'Do you like seafood, Signora Savage?' he asked.

She nodded.

'In Venice it is very expensive, in spite of the fact that we're on the coast. But I think it's worth paying for. The good things in life always are, don't you agree?'

Claire stared as he deftly cracked open a lobster claw and prised out the tender meat. Seeing her interest, he held it out to her.

'Would you like it? It is the best part.'

Claire stared at the pink, exposed flesh in his manicured fingers and shook her head. 'Sorry, I'm not keen on lobster.' It was a lie, but he wasn't to know that. Somehow she couldn't bring herself to accept it from his hand, like a pet.

'Then at least let me pour you some wine.' Before she could stop him, Vittorio filled her glass. 'It is Sicilian. Like everything from Sicily, it is a little rough, but with a big heart.'

'Are you Sicilian?' she asked, more out of politeness than any real interest. She bit into one of the prawns she had peeled and found it was delicious.

'*Si*, Palermo. As a boy I thought that noisy, godless city was the only one in the universe that would satisfy me.' Vittorio shrugged. 'But I quickly discovered it was not so. I can find what I crave anywhere.' He turned to Stuart and patted his knee. 'Signora Savage must come and see us in when we are in London, eh?'

122

'I imagine that she is a busy woman,' said Stuart, breaking his silence at last.

'Ah, you young people, you'll never learn. You work too hard. It would be a pity if such a beautiful lady as the Signora could not find time to play once in a while.'

Claire blushed. She knew she didn't look her best: the shower had robbed her of her make-up, and her hair was frizzing because of the hasty way she had dried it.

Stuart smiled at her, but the smile was stiff and didn't reach his eyes. 'Yes, it would be a pity,' he agreed.

She smoothed her skirt self-consciously under the table, and as she did so she saw that Vittorio's fleshy hand was still resting on Stuart's knee. A jolt of shock ran through her. She flashed her eyes up to her lover's face again, to find him staring at her, with some intense emotion that she couldn't fathom.

'Tell me,' continued Vittorio. 'How is your business coming along in my ballroom? Do you think you will be here long?'

She recovered herself quickly. 'About a week I should think.' Both of Vittorio's hands were employed once more in devouring his lobster. She pushed the rest of her food aside; she wasn't hungry any more.

'A pity. It pleases me to see the palazzo filled with young people again. A place like this, it needs life, no?' He looked at her, one eyebrow raised questioningly. Then he smiled, showing white, slightly uneven teeth. 'But it is good that you will be here for my birthday party on Saturday. You and your colleagues are all invited, of course. My guests are selected very carefully, but even so, I flatter myself that it is the event of the season here in Venice.' Vittorio licked his fingers, then looked at his watch.

'It is a pleasure to meet you in the flesh at last.' He stood up and kissed her hand. 'But I'm afraid I must go. Please, feel free to finish your lunch. There is no hurry for you to leave.' He turned to Stuart, and said something to him in Italian but spoke too quickly for Claire to catch it. Then he bent and kissed the younger man on the lips. '*Ciao, amico mio.*'

When Vittorio had gone, Claire just sat there, staring at the ruins of the prawns of her plate. Then, because she had nothing better to do, she took a large draught of wine. It was rough and stung the back of her throat. She gagged and wiped her mouth with her hand.

Stuart folded his serviette, his eyes boring into her face. 'I imagine you'll be wanting to get back to the shoot?'

'Yes,' she said, dully. 'I should check how Pietro's getting on with the frescoes.'

He paused, before asking: 'Have you thought about what I asked you yesterday, about the portrait? You're not here long.'

She stood up and tossed her serviette on to her plate, covering the prawns. When she looked into his eyes at last, her own were glittering like emerald chips. 'Don't push me, Stuart,' she snapped. 'I'm not in the mood.'

Chapter Nine

'The dome immediately above you, the Pentecost Dome, was the first in the Basilica to be decorated, with mosaics representing the nations whose languages were given to the apostles on Pentecost Sunday. On the wall of the right aisle, over there, you'll see another mosaic masterpiece, also 12th century, The Agony in the Garden . . .'

Cherry, eavesdropping shamelessly, craned her neck to see the scene the tour guide was talking about. The interior of St Marks was too much to take in on one visit; it dazzled the senses with its lofty arches and domes covered with shimmering mosaics. Even though the day was dull, and there was no sunlight slanting in through the high windows, it still hurt her eyes to look at them. The guide and his group moved on into the baptistry, leaving Cherry sitting in her pew. She was far from alone, however. The air rang with the exclamations of tourists, and the sound of their feet tramping over the boards that had been laid to protect the floors. Her neck ached with looking up for so long, so she dropped her eyes to the exposed sections of floor, decorated with richly

125

coloured marble, porphyry and glass in swirling geometric mosaics. At last, sighing, she stood up and stretched like a cat. She had been sitting there for almost three quarters of an hour, her mind blissfully blank, but now it was time to go back to the real world.

Outside, the weather was overcast and there was a raw breeze blowing over the lagoon into the Piazza San Marco. Cherry shivered, glad of the long sleeves and skirt she had had to wear in order to be admitted into the basilica. She paused in the doorway, wondering whether to go straight back to the hotel, or find somewhere where she could sit indoors and have a coffee. The pavement tables in the square looked wind-blown and inhospitable, and there were only a few hardy souls sitting at them. Before she had time to make up her mind, however, her elbow was taken in a firm grip.

'There you are.' One of the Albright twins turned her to face him. 'Your friend Claire said I might find you here. You and me need to talk.'

Cherry frowned. Was it Harper or Quaid? By the no-nonsense tone of his voice, she guessed that it was the older twin. His mouth was set in a grim line, grey eyes flinty. Yes, it must be Quaid. Harper had no reason to be angry with her – just the opposite, in fact. She quailed inside. Had Quaid found out about her and his brother? He steered her across the square towards the quay, where they could talk without drawing attention to themselves, then released her arm.

'I've been thinking about yesterday. And, the more I do think about it, the more it seems to me that you have some explaining to do. It was a cruel trick to run out on me like that.'

Cherry sagged with relief. He obviously didn't know about Harper. But he was still angry, and hurt.

126

She turned to stare across the choppy water of the lagoon, reluctant to look him in the eye.

'I'm sorry,' she said. 'I don't know what came over me. You caught me by surprise in the alley. One minute I was in the mood, and the next minute, I wasn't. I'm sorry.'

Quaid scowled. 'There's a word for women like that. Two words, in fact. Neither of them very nice.' He caught her elbow again and turned her round to face him. 'Listen, I'm not some greenhorn you can lead on and then drop again when the fancy takes you. The way I see it, you either want me, or you don't. So tell me right now, which is it? Yes or no?'

Cherry stared at him in consternation. What could she say? She had enjoyed sleeping with Harper, but Quaid was the twin she had been immediately attracted to. His straightforwardness excited her. Even now, right in the middle of the quayside, the memory of his big hands on her breasts, between her legs, stirred her blood and made her breath quicken. He was watching her, frowning, his arms crossed over his chest.

'Well . . .?' In spite of his aggressive body language, the tone of his voice betrayed his anxiety. 'Yes or no?'

She slumped. It was no use fighting it. 'Yes,' she whispered.

They didn't make it as far as the hotel. Once again, the alleyway proved too much of a temptation for Quaid.

'What if someone comes past, like they did yesterday?' whispered Cherry nervously.

'I don't care.' He took her hand in his and pressed her palm urgently to his groin. 'I have a powerful ache, darling.'

Cherry explored the bulge in his jeans, tracing the length of it with her fingers. As she touched the tip of his erection through the denim, he gave a bass groan, like a bow being drawn across a cello. The sound sent a thrill through her. Trembling, she pulled his face down to hers and kissed him, snaking her tongue against his.

After a minute, she pulled away again, her heart thudding in her chest. She didn't want to risk someone stumbling on them having full sex, and wouldn't be able to relax enough to enjoy it, anyway. A solution occurred to her. She dropped to her knees. In the shadow of doorway, hidden behind Quaid, anyone passing might not see her.

'Jesus, darling, you don't have to do that . . .' Quaid's voice was gruff with anxiety and hope.

'Shh. Someone might hear us.' Being careful not to split her nails, she undid the button at the top of his fly and released his prick. It leapt at her between the teeth of the zip, just as long as his brothers, with the same golden hair curling at the base, but a little thicker. He sucked in his breath. She cupped him in both hands and pressed her lips to the throbbing tip. Now he groaned in earnest. Cherry dipped the tip of her tongue into the tiny slit, like a cat lapping cream, and tasted the moisture that had pearled there. Just for a moment, she bared her teeth and let the American feel them on the most sensitive part of him, before covering them with her lips again and taking him into her mouth properly. She swallowed him centimetre by centimetre, opening her mouth wider to accommodate him, until she had taken the whole length as far as it could go. She could feel the tip of his cock pressing against the bottom of her throat and the tickle of pubic hair on her chin. Then she withdrew slightly and reached for his balls. They were pressed uncomfortably by the zip of his jeans and Cherry freed them, feeling the skin wrinkle and ripple at her touch. She stroked them lovingly, testing their weight and rolling their hairy resilience between her fingers. Quaid arched himself up, and Cherry felt his cock nudge against the base of her throat once more. She drew back a little and then began to work him properly, smoothing and creasing the delicate skin on the iron shaft, rubbing her lips up and down it, sucking the end like a luscious lollipop and savouring the seashell scent of him before taking him into her throat again, stroking his balls all the while. The American's stomach muscles tightened and relaxed, then tightened once more. Cherry wished that she could see his face, wanting to relish her triumph as he submitted to his pleasure, but her victory was sweet even without it. She felt the shaft stiffen in her mouth, going absolutely rigid for a second before his stomach muscles rippled once more and he arched to meet her, filling her mouth with his salty release. She withdrew and smiled up into Quaid's dazzled face before swallowing.

He leant back in the doorway, breathing heavily as he recovered his composure. Then he pulled her up to stand beside him and buried his face in her hair. She put her arms around him.

'Do you still want that coffee?' she whispered, grinning.

He shook his head. 'I have a better idea.'

He took her hand and pulled her into the alley – not towards the quayside, but in the other direction, away from it.

'Where are we going?'

'You'll see.'

The alley went straight on for two or three hundred yards and then split into two – one lane leading to the left over a bridge towards the centre of the city, and the other to the right. They took the right turn, which narrowed as it passed between two rows of houses, their brickwork faded with sunlight and mottled with damp. Then, on one side the houses gave way to ornate railings with vegetation pushing through. Two of the railings were missing. Quaid squeezed his rangy body through the hole with some difficulty, and Cherry slipped through after him.

'Where on earth . . .?'

'Sh.' He pulled her through the tangle of bushes into a clearing.

'Oh!'

They were standing in a churchyard. It was overgrown and neglected, the stones almost smothered by weeds and grass. In one corner there was a tiny church, the door boarded up, its stonework crumbling, its windows blank and broken.

'What a shame,' murmured Cherry. 'How did you find it?'

'I came upon it by accident yesterday morning. I've never been able to resist a gap in a fence!' He smiled, showing his teeth in his tanned face. 'As soon as I saw it, I thought of you.'

'Why?'

He lifted an eyebrow.

Cherry looked around her again. The clearing was so quiet it was hard to believe that they were in the middle of the city. The only sound was the cheeping of swallows nesting in the tower of the church, that were looping to and fro across the uninterrupted expanse of sky. There were no houses overlooking them. Sunlight dappled down on to the slabs that were scattered around the clearing like dominoes. The largest stone was set a little apart from the others, away from the clutch of the bushes and weeds. It was square and low, like a coffee table. Or a bed.

She went over to it, and traced her fingers over the mossy inscription.

'Maria Battisti,' she read. '1740 to 1821.' She

frowned, calculating. 'It must have been unusual to live to that sort of age in those days.'

'That's not the best of it,' chuckled Quaid. He brushed away the dirt from the rest of the inscription. 'It says here that she was married four times.' He pointed to a plaque on the wall, in the shadow of a yew tree. 'It mentions her fourth husband over there.'

She went to investigate, and her eyes widened. 'But he was only twenty-one when he died in 1822. That means . . .'

'He was her toyboy!' Quaid had selected a short stalk of bristling grass from the clump around the tomb and was chewing on it thoughtfully as he watched her.

'I didn't think there was such a thing in those days.' She rejoined him and stroked her fingers over the stone. 'She must have been seventy, at least. The randy old thing.'

'It just goes to show, I guess, that there's nothing new in this world.' He lifted her up to sit on the slab. The stone was warm on her buttocks through her skirt.

'Do you think we should, here?' she whispered, staring into the eyes so close to hers.

'Don't worry. I reckon these are memorial stones, not graves. The bodies are probably in a catacomb somewhere.' He moved even closer, took the stalk from between his lips and stroked the bristled end over her cheek, then trailed it slowly down the line of her throat to the v where her breasts were shadowed at the neck of her blouse. She shivered and felt her nipples stiffen. Quaid saw the reaction and stared at the small bumps pressing against her cotton shirt. He circled them with the stalk of grass, tickling them into even greater prominence.

'Why don't you take off your shirt, darling?'

She hesitated.

'Please.' His plea was no more than a whisper.

She obliged, slipping the pearl buttons out of their buttonholes, shrugging off her blouse to fall on the stone behind her. She was wearing a front-fastening bra with push-up cups, that gleamed white against her dusky skin. Quaid's face darkened and he slipped the stalk of grass under the material. She moaned as it pricked the tender tip of her nipple, and let her head fall back. He withdrew to tease the other nipple, watching the colour flush over her collarbone, throat and cheeks. Then, with one hand, he unclipped her bra to let her breasts spring free. He applied the tip of the stalk directly to one nipple and watched the areola tighten, until it was pointing at him accusingly. Cherry leant back on her elbows, breathing heavily, staring up at him through half-closed lids.

After returning her stare for a moment, the American gave a roguish grin and dropped the stalk of grass to brush her kneecaps. She shuddered and parted her legs instinctively at the 'open sesame'. Then she closed her eyes, her whole body tightening with anticipation. The stalk stroked higher under her skirt, skimming over her thighs as light as a feather, leaving a tingling trail wherever it passed. She pulled up her skirt until it was bunched in her fists. Quaid searched out the softest skin on the inside of her thighs and prickled it. She trembled at the sensation, which was one of irritation rather than pain, but too gentle to be either. Less than an inch away from that tormenting stalk of grass, her sex tingled. She was so hypnotised by it that she hardly felt Quaid reach up and pull down her pants, but she did hear him breathe in sharply at the sight of her. She arched herself up, aching to feel the stalk on the very centre of her. But Quaid merely stroked it up the vertical mouth of her vulva. It pouted imperceptibly at first

132

and then puffed out a little fuller, revealing the blushing inner lips and the moisture oozing there.

He slipped the stalk between them and she cried out as it pricked her clitoris, provoking a little explosion of moisture from deep inside her. She was overwhelmed by pleasure. The stabs of the bristle grew faster, darting round her clitoris like tiny daggers, while Quaid's fingers slipped into the channel of her vagina, to revel in the feeling of her contracting and blossoming open again under the torture he was inflicting.

Cherry cried out and tossed her head from side to side. Every time she thought she was coming, the pricks of pain pushed her to a new level of pleasure, until she felt she was teetering on the edge of a precipice.

'Let it go, darling,' Quaid renewed his attack with the grass, deepening the probing of his fingers to match its rhythm. But still she clung on. Her pleasure rippled out, catching her in the cross-currents until she finally tumbled over the edge.

Her elbows gave way under her, and she fell back, her body heaving with spasms of delight, her clitoris throbbing and raw. Quaid spread her thighs and replaced the stalk with his tongue, soothing the tormented, over-excited flesh until she became aware of a more slow-moving pleasure beginning to build inside her. He climbed up on to the gravestone and hauled her along it by her armpits, scraping her buttocks against the stone until he was able to lie full-length on top of her. She submitted to the manhandling, enjoying the feel of his hands on her, and of his weight as he pressed himself on top of her. She was aching with the need to have him take her properly. He kissed her and she reached up to clasp him around the neck. His hands moved over her, touching her everywhere, demanding, prying, until she felt herself

133

open to him. He slid into her, his mouth soldered to hers, and began to move in and out, each thrust sending currents sparking through her body.

'Harder,' she begged, digging her fingers into his shoulders.

She gasped as he slammed into her, bruising her against the stone until she began to tremble again with voluptuous pleasure. Instinctively, she raised her knees higher until they were almost touching her chin. They both climaxed together, crying out with the force of their satisfaction.

Afterwards, as they lay together on the tomb, Cherry opened her eyes and stared up at the sky. Then she smiled. For a moment she had imagined Maria Battisti grinning toothlessly down at them, clapping her horny old hands in approval.

Then Quaid accompanied Cherry back to her hotel and left her with a kiss and a promise to meet her later that night. She had only just put her key in the lock of her door when she heard the phone ringing inside, and had to scramble to answer it.

'Hello?'

'Hi. I've been trying to get you all day.' She didn't need to ask who it was: 'You're not avoiding me, are you?

'No, Harper, it's just . . .'

'I'm glad. I've been thinking and dreaming about you ever since last night. What are you doing now?'

'I was going to have a shower.'

'Can I come over and join you?'

'Well, I don't know.'

'Please.'

As sated as her body was, Cherry tingled at the need in his voice. 'OK,' she sighed. 'But don't take too long.'

Chapter Ten

'*I* think it's just as well we're having a night on our own tonight,' commented Claire. 'You look worn out.'

'You're not kidding. I'm knackered, and that's the truth.' Cherry slumped on her bar stool. 'I'm glad of the chance for a chat, too. There's a problem I need your advice on. Well, two problems, actually.'

'Oh?' Claire swirled her olive around in her martini with her finger. 'I take it they have American accents, these problems of yours.' She looked at her friend. 'Listen, I'm really sorry if I dropped you in it by telling one of them you were at St Marks yesterday. I didn't know whether you wanted to be found or not.'

Cherry smiled, but her face was tense. 'Don't worry about it. I dropped myself in it well before then. The thing is . . .' she sipped her drink, choosing her words. 'I've been spending time with both of them. They're so different. Harper's a bit on the shy side, and artistic, while Quaid –' she grinned. 'He just marches in, with both guns blazing.'

In spite of her mood, Claire also smiled at the

image. 'When you say you've spent time with both of them, you mean . . .?'

Cherry rolled her eyes.

Claire raised her eyebrows.

'Yes,' spluttered Cherry, finally. 'If you must know!'

'What happened to your resolution?' Seeing her friend's look of chagrin, however, she decided not to press the point. 'So you've slept with them both and still can't choose?'

'They're both so different. They look the same, but it's weird. I suppose you could say that they complement each other.' She grinned. 'I always did like sweet and sour.'

'Hmmm.' Claire sucked at the olive. 'I admit that it would have been a lot easier for you if one of them had been a real stud between the sheets.'

Cherry grinned. 'Actually, they both were, in their own way. That's the problem. It would also help if I thought that either of them was serious about me. I want to settle down.'

'You haven't known them very long, remember. It's impossible to tell what a man wants after less than a week.' Claire wrinkled her brow, thinking suddenly of Sean. 'God knows, it's difficult enough after ten years. Do they know that you're sleeping with them both?'

'I'm not sure. They're awfully close.'

'Well, then, that's your answer. They don't want to get too involved with you, in case they tread on each other's toes. Or some other – more painful – part of their anatomy.'

'Claire!'

Claire ignored her friend's gasp of mock outrage and signalled to the barman for another martini. 'Do you want one?' she asked Cherry.

'No, ta. I still have most of this one.' She frowned at Claire's empty glass. 'Are you OK?'

'Yes. I'm fine. Dandy. Ticketty-boo.' Then she sighed. 'No, I'm not.'

Cherry looked at her, her dark eyes full of commiseration. 'It must be hard for you, seeing Sean every day.'

'It is. In fact,' said Claire with false brightness, 'I think I'm going to go round the bend. Wherever I go, he seems to be there – in and out of the palazzo. I even bumped into him in the foyer here at lunchtime. He said he was picking something up.'

'And what about Stuart?'

Claire grew sombre again. 'Let's just say that things have got complicated in that particular direction.'

'You are still seeing him though?'

She shook her head. 'I don't know.'

The barman brought the martini to the table, letting his eyes linger on both of the women. 'There is a package for you in reception, Signora Savage,' he said. 'You want that I should bring it to you?'

'A package!' squeaked Cherry. 'What do you think it is?'

'I wouldn't get too excited, it's probably something for the shoot.' Claire nodded at the barman. '*Si grazie*, bring it in here.'

But as soon as she saw the note taped to the parcel, she knew it wasn't from the agency. She tore it off, and pushed it into her pocket.

'Aren't you going to read it?' asked Cherry.

'Later.'

Cherry eyed the parcel jealously.

'Go on then,' laughed Claire, 'open it for me.'

Cherry tore into the package with eager nails, ripping the brown paper to reveal a velvet box. She looked enquiringly at Claire, who nodded for her to open it.

137

'Oh, it's lovely,' breathed Cherry. 'It matches your bracelets.' She threw her friend a sudden look of horror. 'You're not going to send it back, are you?'

Claire lifted the heavy silver collar from its nest of velvet. 'No. I suppose it will give me something to wear at the party. If I go.'

'What party?'

'Vittorio's birthday party, at the Palazzo Giardino, on Saturday night. I have some invitations upstairs for you too. It's a masked ball, apparently. I dare say you can bring both of your problems with you, if you haven't solved them by then.'

'But I'm supposed to be going home on Saturday morning,' Cherry's face drooped with disappointment.

'Oh God, I'd forgotten that. I can't believe the time has gone so fast. Listen, why don't you stay on here with me until after the shoot's finished?'

'I'd love too, but I can't afford it.'

'I can lend you some cash, if you like.'

Cherry shook her head. 'Thanks for the offer, but I couldn't.' Then she added: 'Actually, there might be another way.'

'What's that?'

'I've had a job offer. Here in Venice.'

'What kind of job?'

'The most important kind – cash in hand. I was going to turn it down, but now . . .' Her voice tailed off.

Intrigued by her friend's unusual reticence, Claire tried her best to discover what the secret commission was. But no matter how much she cajoled her, Cherry would say no more.

Later, in her room, Claire took the collar from its box and put it on in front of the mirror. The silver band encircled the column of her throat snugly and was so heavy that it looked more like a means of restraint than a piece of jewellery, in spite of its intricate engraving. With a dry mouth that wasn't entirely caused by too much martini, she took Stuart's note from her pocket and tore open the envelope. The writing was bold, masculine, and flowed across the expensive paper. As Claire began to read, however, she realised that his confident handwriting was at odds with the way he was feeling.

Claire,
   You've been avoiding me, and I can guess what you must be thinking. But please, judge me with your heart and head, not your eyes. Talk to me. Meet me at Pietro's studio tomorrow morning at eleven, 41a Calle San Francesco, behind the Campo di Confraternita. It will do us both good to get away from the Palazzo Giardino for a little while. Please come.
   Yours, Stuart.
   Ps. I hope you like the necklace.

When she had finished reading, Claire looked up and stared into the eyes of her reflection. They glittered with an unusual, feverish light. Seeing that look, she knew she had no choice but to keep the appointment.

The next morning, Claire went to the palazzo early. But as eleven o'clock crept closer, it seemed that everything was conspiring to make her late for her meeting with Stuart. First of all there was a problem with the sample bottles of Amore provided by the client, which were empty rather than full, as requested. Claire and the stylist, Carol, had to resort to filling them with weak tea to make them look convincing on film. Then one of the models – Lianne – went missing.

Claire found the girl huddled on a bench in the garden. Her head was bowed, her painstakingly ringletted hair falling forward to hide her features. When she heard Claire approaching over the grass, however, she lifted her face and Claire saw that it was streaked with tears.

'Mrs Savage.' She made a hasty attempt to blot her eyes.

'Lianne. Everyone's looking for you.'

'Are they?' The girl spurted fresh tears.

Claire sat on the bench beside her. 'What's the matter? Whatever it is I'm sure we can help you sort it out.'

But the girl just shook her head.

'Is it your costume, your make-up?' Claire hid her irritation. Lianne's crisis was costing them precious time, but she knew that it needed careful handling. In spite of their stunning looks, the models' egos were as fragile as egg shells. A sharp word, an impatient gesture might send the girl rushing for the airport, and then the agency would be in serious trouble. 'Has someone upset you?'

The model sobbed.

Inspiration struck Claire. 'Is it a man?'

'I don't know what I'm going to do, Mrs Savage.' Her beautiful face twisted as she wrung her tissue in her hands. 'He must be laughing his head off at me. I can't concentrate on the shoot, I can't.'

Claire gave her a fresh handkerchief. 'Listen, every woman has made a fool of herself over a man at some time or other. The thing is not to make things any worse by letting him see you're upset about it. I take it he's in the crew?'

Lianne threw Claire a sideways look and nodded.

'Well, what do you think he's going to think when

he sees you in this state? If he is laughing at you, he's not worth worrying about. Personally, I wouldn't give him the satisfaction.'

Gradually, Lianne's tears subsided. Claire waited, hiding her impatience, breathing in the earthy scent of the garden. Finally, the model straightened up.

'I think I'm OK now.' But then she stared in consternation at the mascara on her tissue. 'My make-up. It's in ruins. I can't go back in like this.'

Anticipating more tears, Claire was quick to come to the rescue. 'Don't worry. I'll send Susan out to you.'

Inside, Claire found the make-up artist chatting to Ewan Jones. 'Lianne's in the garden,' she said. 'Would you mind going out to her?'

'Sure, no problem.' The girl gathered her brushes into her case.

Sean strode up to them. 'Have you found her?'

'Yes. Susan's just going to do a quick repair job, then she's all yours again.'

'Thank God.'

Her mercy mission accomplished, Claire headed for the door, but Sean stopped her.

'You promised me you'd find time to talk.' He let his gaze wander over her, noting the flushed cheekbones and air of distraction.

'I know.' Her eyes slid away from his. 'But we've both been so busy.'

'Look, in spite of everything I'm already ahead of schedule today, and should finish early. Why not have coffee with me this afternoon?'

'I don't know.' Claire's eyes met his briefly, green on green.

'Please. We might not get another chance.'

She looked at her watch, oblivious to the words he had loaded with meaning. It was already quarter to

141

eleven: she was going to be late. 'OK. But I can only spare an hour or so.'

'I'll see you in the Metropole lounge at five, then.'

She was already gone.

Sean resisted the urge to smash his fist into the door frame, only barely managing to master his frustration. The last couple of days had been nothing short of disasterous. First of all, the situation with Lianne had quickly become impossible. Right from the beginning, the model had made it clear she was attracted to him. Then, the night before, she had been waiting in his bed with a bottle of champagne. There is no easy way for a man to tell a naked woman that he isn't interested in her. It had made working with her difficult, to say the least.

But Lianne was only a minor problem, compared to Claire. Since he had arrived at the palazzo, Sean had reacquainted himself with all his wife's once-familiar gestures: the way she brushed the hair back from her face, the graceful way she moved, the habit she had of raising one eyebrow when she was listening to someone. He was always aware of her when she was around, even if he couldn't see her. The sound of her laugh, low and throaty from another part of the room, had the power to wipe his mind blank. He couldn't concentrate.

Seeing her with the Scotsman was even worse. They were clearly lovers: whenever the other man was near, Claire seemed to give off a subtle, incandescent glow. Sean had never thought of himself as a jealous man, but whenever he imagined his wife in bed with MacIntosh – which was too often – a fist clenched around his chest, and squeezed, hard. Now he knew how she must have felt when she found out about Caroline. He shrugged: he supposed it served him right, but it still didn't make it any easier to bear. He had to talk to her, to tell her he had made a mistake. She might not want him back, but at least he could say he had tried.

He reached up absent-mindedly to adjust a light. Right at that moment, five o'clock felt like a lifetime away.

Claire found the address behind the Campo di Confraternita surprisingly easily. She looked up at the building, and jumped as she saw a cat glaring down at her from the stone window ledge above. Ignoring its baleful gaze, she pressed the buzzer in the panel beside the peeling doorway.

'Come up.' She recognised Stuart's voice, despite the distortion through the intercom. She climbed the stairs slowly, wrinkling her nose against the odour of boiled cabbage and garlic. The stairwell was badly lit, and she paused at each of the doors. They were all shut, however, until she reached the top landing, where one stood ajar, waiting for her.

She knocked and stepped into the room.

'Claire!' Stuart was silhouetted against a huge window that ran from floor to ceiling. She couldn't see his features against the light, but heard the relief in his voice. 'I didn't think you were coming.'

She shrugged. 'I was held up.' Scanning the room she saw that it was practically bare, except for a few canvasses, an easel, and an old velvet chaise longue against the wall. 'Is Pietro here?' she asked.

'He's coming later. I wanted the chance to talk to you first.' He moved so that she could see his face. There were dark smudges under his eyes. 'Why didn't you call me?'

'You said in your letter that you know why.'

'I do. But I want to hear it from you.'

She shook her head. 'I can't . . .'

'OK. I'll say it then. You think that Vittorio and I are lovers.'

She tried to keep her voice as disinterested as she could. 'Aren't you?'

'I'm not going to lie to you. We used to be.'

'So . . .' she paused, the words refusing to form themselves in her mouth. 'Are you . . .?' But she had to stop again.

A wry smile curled the edges of his lips. 'Am I what? Am I gay?' He shook his head. 'I discovered a long time ago that I'm more interested in women than men. I thought you, of all people, would have realised that.'

'But, Vittorio?' Her words hung in the air between them.

'He was philosophical about it. His taste is not exclusively reserved to men, either. He has many lovers, of both sexes. One more, or less, means little to him. I'm merely useful for business.'

'So you – you don't sleep with him any more?' She was surprised at her shattering feeling of relief.

'Not for years. But sometimes Vittorio likes to give that impression. He enjoys teasing people.' Stuart closed the distance between them. He took her hand, and crushed it to his lips. 'I thought he'd gone too far, and scared you off.'

'He almost did.' She gave a rueful laugh.

He pulled her possessively to him and kissed her. His lips tasted slightly salty. Claire could feel his arousal through their clothes. She reached up to trace one curving cheekbone and the delicate whorl of his ear.

'Did you like the necklace?' he asked against her hair.

'It's beautiful. Thank you.'

'You're not wearing it.'

'It's hardly the kind of thing that goes with a skirt and blouse.' She pointed to the bag she had dropped

144

on to the floor when he had taken her in his arms.
'It's in there, with the bracelets.'

'Will you put them on for me?'

'What, now?'

He nodded. 'Please.'

'OK.' She took the jewellery from her bag and was
about to put it on, when he stopped her.

'Not like that.'

Claire raised an eyebrow. Stuart began to unbutton
her blouse, then her skirt. Stunned, she made no
move to stop him. He quickly and efficiently stripped
her of her clothes, then took the bracelets from her
fingers and snapped them on to her wrists. When he
had also fastened the collar he stood back to look at
her. She was utterly naked, her only adornment the
barbaric jewellery that gleamed like moonlight on her
skin. The effect on him was electric. He reached for
her roughly, all tenderness vanished, replaced by a
dark driving need that drew his body taut and made
his movements harsh and jerky. Trembling with the
force of his desire, he lifted her off her feet. Because
of the rough floor boards, the only possible place for
them to lie was the chaise longue, but instead of
placing her on it as she expected, he turned her over,
and pressed her, face down, over the high arm. With
no preamble whatsoever, his fingers probed
impatiently into her, not with the aim of giving her
pleasure, but merely to see if she was ready for him.
She was. The act of being stripped by him had fired
her blood to such an extent that she had practically
melted inside. His hands left her for a moment and
she heard the zip of his fly and then crackle of a
condom wrapper. She lay perfectly still, waiting. He
delved once more into her vagina, making her writhe
beneath him. He coated his fingers with her juice, and
withdrew them to lubricate the cleft of her buttocks,
anointing the tight, virgin entrance to her backside.

Then with no hesitation, and without asking permission, he buried himself to the hilt inside her. Claire gasped and squirmed beneath him, trying to escape from that punishing rod of flesh. But she was pinned as surely as a butterfly. Her discomfort lasted no more than a moment, however, for as he began to move in her, he reached round to pull her labia wide with his thumbs, and began to work in the oily cleft between them. Her whole body flooded with ambiguous sensations. Driven half mad with pleasure and pain, she was suddenly aware that he had taken her as he would take another man. Her mind flashed with the unbidden image of Stuart and Vittorio together: the younger man's lean body bent beneath Vittorio's powerful one, being pierced, crushed by it. She was seized with a tremor so powerful, so violent, that it communicated itself to Stuart's cock. He sobbed aloud and increased the speed of his thrusts. Claire's legs, belly, sex and breasts were aflame, and as she bent beneath his onslaught she was forced to draw breath in great shuddering gasps as if she was drowning. Still Stuart's fingers worked ruthlessly between her legs, and his hips grinded against her buttocks, making them quiver with each thrust. Then, suddenly, his fingers abandoned her clitoris. He grasped her hip with one hand, and buried his other fist in her hair, arching her backwards towards him. He gave a hoarse shout of pleasure, then collapsed over her.

When he withdrew, a minute or so later, she could feel every centimetre of him pull out of her. She heard him discard the condom. Then he turned her around to face him. He covered her eyes, her cheeks, her chin with grateful, scalding kisses, then caught her breasts in his hands. Her nipples were hard and almost painfully swollen, so that she flinched at the contact. He soothed them with his tongue, spiralling it round and round until Claire was moaning aloud. Gently,

146

he pushed her back on the chaise longue, and arranged her legs to his satisfaction, placing one leg so that her foot remained on the floor, and hooking her other knee over the back, so that she was pulled wide enough to expose the button of her clitoris, pulsing in the delicate folds. He groaned and, using all his fingers, stretched her wider still. She shuddered at the flush of cool air on the burning core of her, then arched with ecstasy as he bent his head and took her clitoris between his lips. She buried her fingers in his hair, tugging at it. Invisible flames licked over her skin, tightening her nipples and surging towards her belly and thighs. He pushed a finger deep into her vagina and began to spiral around her clitoris with his tongue, biting, sucking, teasing her until her thoughts were reduced to an incoherent jumble. She lifted her arms over her head in abandon and clutched at the velvet, lifting and lowering her buttocks to accommodate his tongue, oblivious to everything except the pleasure that was surging through her. He groaned into her, prompting her to look down at him through lashes that were spiked with moisture. His dark head was moving on her like a machine, framed by the pale gold of her thighs. She felt herself begin to contract. He gripped her buttocks, digging his fingers into her, increasing the urgent strokes of his tongue. Claire's tremors increased, shaking her more and more until they finally lifted her up and flung her back down again on to the chaise, wringing a cry from her that echoed loud in the empty room.

Drenched with pleasure, she lay without moving, Stuart's head resting on her belly. He began to trace idle circles on her thigh with his fingers. She sighed.

'Are you happy?' he asked.

'Of course.'

'I'm sorry I was rough with you, at first. I was so

147

tense, imagining that you weren't coming. Then, suddenly, you were here. All I could think of was being inside you.'

She squeezed his shoulder.

There was a stealthy step on the boards behind his shoulder. '*Mi scusi*,' whispered Pietro, 'I do not wish to disturb.'

Claire tensed, her whole body poised for flight, but Stuart continued to stroke her thigh slowly, soothingly, never breaking the mesmeric rhythm. Her body was still so sensitised after her orgasm that she shuddered under him and closed her eyes.

'Please,' he murmured, 'don't move. You can't imagine what you look like right now.'

Claire tried. What she saw in her mind's eye was enough to make her moan with mingled shame and excitement: she saw herself languid with satisfied lust, her legs spread, the juice still glistening between them. Silver gleamed at her throat and at her wrists that were lifted above her head, thrusting her round and rosy breasts into prominence. She felt the artist's dark eyes sweep over her, and felt a renewed ache between her legs. She squeezed her eyes even more tightly closed, and so didn't see the subtle nod Stuart gave to his friend. She knew that she should feel nothing but shame, exposed as she was, and yet she was clothed in sexual satisfaction as surely as if she was wearing a cloak. Stuart moved silently back, while the artist set up his easel as quickly and as quietly as he could.

'*Che bella*. Ah God, she is perfect. Don't let her move, Stuart. Talk to her.'

Stuart, still fully clothed, sat on the floor. Claire opened her eyes and her gaze, still glazed with lust, met his.

'Forget Pietro,' he whispered, his eyes hot and dark. 'Let him work, while you listen to me. You're so

148

lovely. Let me tell you all the things I want to do to you, when we have the time and know each other better . . .' As Stuart spoke his rich Scottish tones took on more of a Mediterranean lilt. His words washed over her like waves on a tropical beach, arousing her, telling tales of tongues, and fingers, and lips, of things she had hardly imagined possible between two people. Her head shimmered with dark images of delicious pain, and slow-moving ones of pleasure, scouring her body with tingles of anticipation and dread. Her second orgasm took her by surprise. She arched herself up as it leapt up from her toes to quiver over her thighs and shiver between her legs. Seeing her abandonment, Stuart moved closer.

'But that's nothing, Claire,' he groaned, 'compared to what I want you to do to me. Listen . . .' He went on, painting explicit pictures with his tongue, his eyes never leaving Claire's face. She moaned again, unable to satisfy the tingle between her legs.

Meanwhile the artist blocked his ears and ignored the bulge in his trousers. Professional pride took over from lust, and his brush flew over the canvas, desperate to capture the moment before it was lost. This would be his masterpiece, or his name was not Pietro Corolla!

Sean slumped deeper into one of the Metropole's armchairs, trying not to look conspicuous. It wasn't easy. He was the only person in the lounge, and had been for almost an hour.

'Another expresso, while you are waiting, *signore*?'

'No, *grazie*.' Sean scowled at the waiter's smug expression. It was becoming obvious, even to himself, that he had been stood up. Vivaldi's 'Four Seasons', playing on a repetitive loop over the hotel sound system, was grating on his nerves. He looked at his watch again. Claire wasn't coming.

In spite of his claim that he was ahead of schedule, he'd had to rush to make his appointment with her, and in the end had been forced to leave Ewan to wrap things up. He didn't like to think about the mess the young Welshman was probably making of it. And he didn't like to think what had kept Claire. He drained his coffee cup and set it down with a bang on the glass table. Enough was enough. If she wanted to get her own back for him messing her around with Caroline, he could understand it. But there was only so much he could take. From now on, as far as his wife was concerned, the kid gloves were coming off!

Chapter Eleven

*A*s Claire was walking through the hotel foyer towards the lift, her passage was blocked by a waiter carrying a tray of coffee. She smiled at him as he stepped around her, but then her smile wavered into a frown. She slowed her steps and finally stopped altogether just outside the lift. Oh God! Sean! She retraced her steps and peered into the lounge, but there was only an elderly couple there, being served by the waiter. If Sean had ever been there to meet her, he was long gone. Claire felt like banging her head against the wall. How could she have forgotten? She headed wearily for the lift again and almost collided with her friend, who was coming out of it.

'Hi there,' breezed Cherry.

'Hello. I don't suppose you've seen Sean at all this afternoon?'

Cherry shook her head. 'No. Should I have?'

'I was supposed to meet him here two hours ago.'

'Oh dear. He's not going to be a happy man, is he? What happened?'

She grimaced. 'I was, um, detained.'

'Really?' Cherry's eyes were mischievous. 'Sounds interesting.'

'It was.'

'Care to fill me in on the details?'

'No way.' Claire smiled. 'Where are you off to?'

Cherry's eyes lost their sparkle. 'Work. Remember that commission I mentioned? I accepted it.'

'But that's great! That means you'll be able to stay for the party.'

'I didn't want to miss it. And besides, I have another two good reasons for wanting to stay, remember?'

Claire eyed the vanity case her friend was carrying. 'Isn't it a bit late to be going on a shoot?'

Cherry shrugged.

'Who did you say the commission was for?'

'I didn't.' Cherry gave a brittle smile. 'Nice try, though. You have your little secrets, and I have mine. See you in the morning.'

She stared as Cherry marched towards the door, then called after her. 'Call for me at eight o'clock. I've made an appointment at the mask makers. You can come too.'

'OK, I'll be there.'

Claire stepped out of her bath and wrapped herself in the fluffy bathrobe provided by the hotel. For the first time since coming to Venice she had the luxury of a whole evening to herself. Even if Stuart hadn't been working, she didn't have the energy to see him again so soon after their session at the studio. It had been late when Pietro had finally allowed her to get up from the chaise longue, by which time her lust had cooled to the point where she felt faintly ridiculous. But Stuart had hugged her, and kissed her worries away, before escorting her back to the hotel. He had been so successful in soothing her anxiety that she had even promised Pietro one final sitting, the following afternoon.

She tried not to think about her afternoon as she waxed her legs, plucked her eyebrows, and gave herself a manicure. By the time her nail varnish had dried, it was still only nine o'clock. She dropped into an armchair and switched on the TV. After a while flicking through the channels, she gave a sigh of disgust: every programme was a cheesy gameshow, hosted by men who looked like used-car salesmen and women with improbably filled bikinis. She threw down the remote control. In spite of her initial pleasure in having some time to herself, she was bored. And she wanted a drink. Room service was expensive, and she didn't want any of the supercilious hotel staff to think she was the kind of woman who would drink alone in her room – even if she was.

After another half an hour of bikinis and inane grinning, however, she had had enough. She switched off the TV, swapped her bathrobe for a pair of jeans and a sweater, grabbed her room key and went out.

It was only two minute's walk to the convenience store just off the Campo di San Zaccaria. She deliberated over the range of wine on offer, before choosing two bottles of Spumante. Then, hugging her purchases to her chest, she hurried back to the hotel.

In the foyer, she was dismayed to see a tall figure leaning over the reception desk, speaking to the porter. It was one of Cherry's Americans. He straightened up when he saw her coming.

'Hi. I was looking for Cherry.'

As if she hadn't guessed. 'She's gone out.'

'So Guiseppe here tells me. Do you know where she's gone?'

Claire shrugged. 'Sorry, I've no idea.' She felt conspicuous standing in the foyer with her bottles of wine. Even though they were wrapped in paper, it was obvious what they were. It was also irritating to be quizzed on her friend's whereabouts – if Cherry had wanted the man to know where she was, she would have told him herself. She was about to excuse herself and make a dash for the lift, when she heard the door behind her swing open, and saw the American's face change.

'Harper,' he growled. 'What the devil are you doing here?'

She turned to look at the other twin. She really couldn't tell them apart: they had the same build, the same colouring, and the same hostile look in their grey eyes.

'I might ask you the same thing. You told me you were too tired to go out tonight.'

'I was. But I perked up, and figured I'd come pay Cherry a visit.'

'I guess that makes two of us, doesn't it?'

Claire looked from one brother to the other and back again. The air crackled with tension. 'Look,' she said wearily. 'Cherry's not here. I don't know where she is. If you'll excuse me, I have to go.' And so she left them there, scowling at each other like gunslingers in a stand-off.

Back in her room, she changed into her bathrobe again and poured a generous measure of Spumante into one of the glasses in the bathroom. It was lukewarm, but pleasant enough. Then she settled down to watch the TV again – somehow it didn't seem quite so bad with a glass in her hand. As the room grew darker around her she didn't bother switching on the light, but let the images on the screen fill the room with blue flickering shadows.

At twenty past twelve she was about to turn in for the night, when there was a knock on her door.

'Who is it?'

154

'Me.'

'It's not locked.'

Cherry poked her head in. 'I heard the telly. Do you mind if I keep you company for a bit?'

'Of course not.' Claire nodded towards the bottles on the dressing table. 'Help yourself to some wine, there's still some left. There's a spare glass in the bathroom.'

Cherry disappeared into the en suite. 'What have you been doing with yourself tonight?' she asked in a disembodied voice.

'Nothing much. A bit of grooming. Getting drunk. Watching TV. And fighting off your admirers.'

Cherry emerged, glass in hand. 'What do you mean?'

'The Albright brothers were here, looking for you.'

'What both of them?'

'Yes. At the same time.'

Cherry rolled her eyes. 'Bugger!' She poured herself some wine and threw herself on the bed at Claire's feet.

'I think they were a bit surprised to see each other,' said Claire.

'I bet they were. Still, I suppose it had to happen sometime. Do you think they know yet that I'm sleeping with them both?'

'I'd be amazed if they didn't at least suspect it.'

'Bugger,' said Cherry again, more mildly this time. 'What do you think I should do now?'

Claire shrugged. 'How should I know? I suppose you're going to have to make up your mind which one you want.'

Cherry took a large gulp of wine. 'I don't think I can.'

'In that case, you'll have to say goodbye to both of them. You would have to soon enough, anyway.'

'I don't think I can do that either. Not yet.'

'You're an impossible woman,' said Claire with a smile in her eyes.

'Tell me about it.' Cherry smiled too, and turned her attention to the TV. 'What are you watching?'

'I'm not sure, really. Some third-rate soap. But the male lead looks like Billy Zane.'

'Mmm. It can't be all that bad, then.'

'I wish that was true. Actually, it's dreadful.'

Cherry picked up the remote control and started to flip through the channels. She stopped abruptly when the screen was filled with writhing flesh. 'Aha. This is more like it.'

Both of the women watched the scene that was unfolding on the TV. Although the participants seemed to be Hungarian, or some other central European nationality, no translation was needed. Two men had a woman tied naked to a bed, and were taking it in turns to torment her with a dildo, while the other one toyed with her nipples. The woman was obviously enjoying the attention: she was making more noise than a stadium full of football supporters.

Cherry turned the sound down a bit, and wriggled up the bed to prop herself against the pillows beside Claire, who refilled their glasses with Spumante.

The two men brought their captive to a climax, then left her to shudder out her orgasm alone, with the dildo still thrust inside her. After a moment another woman appeared, gently removed the dildo and began to kiss the captive. In contrast to the voluptuous woman on the bed, she had a boyish figure and cropped hair, and wore leather pants and braces. Her breasts were bare, however, and her rouged nipples danced as she thrust her tongue into the other woman's mouth. She reminded Claire of Charlotte Rampling in *The Night Porter*. Heat began to tingle through her limbs – she didn't know whether it was because of the drink or the film.

'Claire?' said Cherry, taking a gulp of her wine, her eyes never leaving the screen.

'Mmm?'

'Have you ever – you know, with another woman?'

Claire eyed the actresses, who were now rubbing their breasts vigorously against each other. 'Good God, no!'

Cherry giggled. 'Me neither.'

They watched, enthralled, as the thin woman mouthed her way down the other woman's body, tugging at her nipples, snaking her tongue into her belly button, and nuzzling at last against the glossy curls that lay between her legs. Through the alcohol that was misting Claire's brain, the scene seemed both incredibly funny, and arousing. She could feel that her own sex had begun to ache and moisten. She shifted uncomfortably. The thin woman stroked her partner's sex, as she might a kitten, then gently insinuated one finger between the reddened lips. She began to frig her enthusiastically, making the other woman groan and squirm in delight, not stopping until she was on the very verge of her climax. Then she gave a wicked, sensual smile. The camera zoomed in artistically, as she pulled the other woman's labia wide apart with carmine-tipped fingers.

'Bloody hell,' spluttered Cherry. 'Do we all look like that?'

The captive's vagina was revealed in all its glory: pink, swollen, glistening, its sensitive membranes pulsing with desire.

'I don't know. I've never really looked.'

'Me neither.'

The thin woman dipped her head and began to lap at the delicate flesh, with slow, appreciative strokes of her tongue.

Cherry squirmed and giggled. Claire smiled, but it was an effort. The sensation between her legs was becoming harder and harder to ignore. The buxom woman was groaning even louder now, arching up and smearing her own lipstick against her hands, then rubbing it over her throat and breasts. Every groan heightened Claire's arousal, until she felt she would burst with it. The thin woman increased the thrusts of her tongue, darting it in and out of the other woman, pressing her face into the glistening curls, while her captive spread her knees to open herself as wide as possible, fingers tugging at the cropped hair. She was practically howling now.

Cherry dissolved into giggles, picked up a pillow and hid her face.

'It's no good,' she gasped. 'I can't watch any more. I'll have to go to my room and sort myself out.'

'You can do it here, if you like.'

Cherry slowly lowered the pillow and looked into Claire's eyes. 'Are you serious?'

Claire nodded, her mouth dry. 'As long as I can do it too.'

Cherry giggled again. 'What, to me?'

'No, you idiot. To myself. We can watch each other.'

Cherry hesitated, before giving a devil-may-care grin. 'Why not? I'll try anything once.' Before Claire could stop her, she had pulled her dress off over her head. She lay down on the bed, facing her. She was wearing white bra and pants, that gleamed against her dusky skin. 'God,' she said. 'I'm so turned on.'

'Me too,' said Claire. She was naked under her bathrobe, and would have done anything to cast the cumbersome thing aside, but she hesitated. Cherry read her mind.

'Why don't you take that off?' she said. 'You'll be more comfortable. I'll take these off too.' She unfastened her bra and wriggled out of her pants, letting her ripe breasts swing free, exposing the luxuriant v of hair between her thighs. Claire blushed and shrugged off her robe, then lay down facing her friend on the bed. By the groans and sighs coming from the TV behind them, they could tell that the voluptuous captive still hadn't reached her second climax. Claire tried not to stare at her friend's body, illuminated by the flickering light from the screen. She had seen her naked before, of course, in the pages of *Penthouse* and *Forum*, but it wasn't the same. She was genuinely aroused now. Her large dark nipples were puckered and swollen, and there was a deep flush over her breasts, neck and face. Cherry closed her eyes and began to explore her own nipples with the tips of her fingers, making the goosebumps harden and stand to attention even more. She stroked her hands over the skin of her stomach and hips, then found the junction between her thighs. Sighing, she slid one finger deep inside herself.

Claire gasped and closed her eyes. She was intensely, feverishly aroused, so much so that she could feel her heart pounding in her right breast, making it pulse against the coverlet. Gingerly, she reached up to feel her nipples, and gasped as her fingers found the button-hard nubs of flesh. She rolled them between her fingers, feeling the skin tighten and her loins flash with fire. Unable to resist any longer, she dropped her hands to her sex. Even through the curls, she could feel her labia were puffed up and sensitive, only barely managing to contain the juice that had gathered there. She sighed and slowly slipped her thumb between them. She moaned. It was like plunging it into a ripe plum. Her clitoris was plumped up and slippery. Soothingly, she ran her thumb over it, and cried out with the force of the delicious sensation. She opened her eyes and found herself staring into Cherry's melting brown ones, her pupils huge and bottomless.

'I could do you, if you like,' murmured Cherry. 'While you do me.'

Overwhelmed by lust, she merely nodded. Cherry wriggled closer, until her chocolate nipples were almost brushing Claire's coral ones. Claire closed her eyes again. This was too absurd. But it was incredibly beautiful too. She had no intention of chickening out. She sighed as she felt a touch, as light as a butterfly's wing, on her right nipple. Cherry's hand closed gently around it, holding it between her thumb and forefinger, then Claire felt her friend's other hand skim over her belly, and delve unerringly between the lips of her sex. She moaned and opened herself wider to the questing fingers.

'You're so wet,' whispered Cherry.

Claire just murmured in response. She opened her eyes and saw that her friend had her own squeezed shut in concentration as she explored. Her gaze dropped to Cherry's breasts, that were resting heavily against each other. She fought off the urge to take one of the nipples between her fingers, or in her mouth, and dropped her own hand to the junction between her friend's thighs. Her wrist bumped against Cherry's as she manoeuvred herself into a better position, then prised the succulent lips apart with her newly-varnished fingers. Cherry groaned and shuddered.

Claire insinuated her fingers into Cherry's vagina. It was a peach to her plum. She was plumper, looser than Claire, more generous, the hot welcoming flesh cleaving to her finger, and refusing to let her withdraw. Cherry increased pressure on Claire's clitoris, scalding her with pleasure and making her bolder. Claire pushed her index finger deeper into the enticing cleft, wriggled it, then withdrew to find the hidden fleshy pad just inside the neck of the channel – the G-spot. She tickled it, and the effect was instantaneous. Cherry swooned against her, gasping.

Yet, even though she was half dazed with pleasure, she mirrored Claire's action, finding the same sensitive spot within Claire's vagina with her own fingertips. Heat shimmered through Claire's veins, causing a rush of moisture to flood between her legs on to her friend's hand. Yet she kept her own finger agitating, teasing, spiralling, in time with her own spasms. The two women arched against each other, their bodies taut as bow strings, breasts crushed together, groin pressing hand against hand, against groin. Claire's pleasure swirled around her like a whirlpool, before concentrating in one spot, and threatening to suck and gurgle her down into it.

They came almost together, Claire only slightly before Cherry. They both cried out into the room, their cries competing with the screams of the voluptuous woman on the screen, whose lover had at last succeeded in coaxing another orgasm out of her. Then they lapsed into a dazed silence.

'Wow,' said Cherry, at last. 'That beats the hell out of DIY.'

Claire murmured her agreement, too sated and tired to speak properly. Cherry scrambled off the bed to retrieve the remote control, which had fallen on to the floor. She switched the TV off, then climbed back beside Claire in the darkness, wrapping her arms around her. Claire fell asleep immediately, comforted by the fragrance of Cherry's hair against her cheek.

Chapter Twelve

*T*he rays of the early-morning sun failed to penetrate the mist that lay over the lagoon, but gilded
the droplets of moisture instead, so that they hung
suspended like thousands of glow worms or fairy
lights. Sean pressed the shutter release, hoping that
he'd chosen the right kind of film for the conditions,
then walked on, deeper into the heart of the city. It
was only six o'clock, and Venice was still sleeping,
veiled in mist and her own mysteries like an Arabian
houri.

He was still smarting about Claire's failure to turn
up at the Metropole. In fact, he had hardly slept that
night, but had tossed and turned in his bed, imagining Claire with MacIntosh, until the sheets had tangled themselves around his legs, and his skin was
sheened with sweat. When he had pushed the curtains aside and seen the mist, he had thrown some
clothes on, loaded his Ricoh with film, and slipped
out of the hotel.

Taking photographs always soothed him, no matter
how restless or agitated he was. When he looked
through the lens of a camera he forgot himself,

becoming nothing more than an eye on the hunt for the perfect composition. Venice had everything to satisfy him. Wandering around the sleeping canal sides he found plenty of subjects: an abandoned mannequin in a gondola; a line of washing, pearled with dew; a prowling cat that appeared through the mist like some mythical beast; solemn statues on a church facade, their profiles etched in pink by the rising sun. He took shot after shot, only pausing to reload his camera, his thoughts of Claire gradually replaced by awe at the city's beauty and his compulsion to capture it on film.

'I hope you don't mind me waking you so early. But you and me need to talk.'

'I know. I wasn't sleeping anyway.'

'You want to go for a walk?'

'Uh-huh. Just give me a minute to put some clothes on.'

A little while later, the Albright twins stepped out of the door of their hotel. The mist was beginning to clear, allowing the occasional patch of sunlight to gleam briefly before disappearing again. The two men walked without speaking for several minutes, their boot heels ringing on the pavement, before Quaid broke the silence.

'It appears to me that we've gotten ourselves riled up over the same woman.' His tone was carefully neutral. 'I take it she's been sleeping with you, too?'

His brother's face had a shuttered, stubborn expression.

'Damn it, Harper, answer me. I won't get mad, I promise. Just tell me the truth.'

Harper glanced at him, and relented. 'She went to bed with me before she did with you.'

Quaid bit back a curse and turned away so his brother couldn't see his face.

'To be honest, she thought I was you.'

'You let her think that?'

Harper didn't answer, but looked down shame-facedly at his boots.

'How could you do that to her? To me?'

'It was only that first time, I swear. After that she knew what she was doing.' Harper's expression became even more obstinate. 'I'm not going to give her up, Quaid. Not for you, not for anybody.'

Quaid stared at him, then sighed. 'Hell, I don't blame you.' They walked in silence for another minute or so before he spoke again. 'If she'd wanted to choose between us she'd have done it by now. It seems to me that she's happy stringing us both along.'

'I don't think so.'

'Oh?'

'She's not a schemer, Quaid. Just confused.'

'She's not the only one. What about us? We've always shared everything – our home, our work, our friends. This could easily spoil what we have. I'd be real sorry if that happened.'

Harper frowned. 'Me too. But what are we going to do?'

His brother looked thoughtful. 'How about doing nothing?'

'What do you mean?'

'You know, just let things tick along the way they're going. We'll be leaving Venice in a couple of days anyway. Why spoil the time we have left with jealousy?'

Even though they had found a solution, a depression descended on them both.

'I can't imagine not seeing her again,' muttered Harper.

'Me neither.'

'So what are we going to *do*?'

* * *

Sean straightened up from where he had been kneeling to capture a view between some railings, and sighed. He would have to be getting back to the hotel to shower and change for work. By coincidence, he found he was standing on a bridge over the canal that ran alongside the Palazzo Giardino. He leant on the balustrade and took a deep breath. He wasn't looking forward to the day ahead, knowing he would have to confront Claire about their missed appointment.

He was about to move on, when his eye was caught by a movement on the canal, at the palazzo's jetty. There was a motorboat tied alongside it, with a chauffeur waiting at the helm. The man flicked his cigarette into the canal as the door leading on to the jetty opened, and two burly men emerged, followed by a woman. She was dressed in black, like the men, but to much more stunning effect. Her long evening gown set off the pearly skin of her shoulders and neck, and the silver hair that was swept off her face. She was astonishingly beautiful, in a pure, old-fashioned way, like a twenties' film star – an impression that was heightened when she pulled her scarf up around her face, framing her fragile features to perfection.

It was too good an opportunity for Sean to miss. He screwed his zoom lens deftly on to his camera, framed the shot and pressed the shutter release, capturing her face forever. As he did so, she looked straight at him, right into the lens, and stiffened. Alerted by her expression, the two men spotted him too.

To Sean's surprise they began to run along the wooden boardwalk towards him, shouting and making furious gestures. Acting purely on instinct, he sprinted over the bridge away from them.

He led them on a complicated dance through the winding streets and canal side paths, not wanting to lead them back to his hotel. As he ran, Sean laughed. He was enjoying himself, knowing that he was fitter than either of his pursuers, whose laboured breathing he could hear behind him. He would have outpaced them easily, losing them in the maze of streets, if he hadn't made a fatal mistake. He dodged down an alleyway he was not familiar with, only to find that it ended in a cul-de-sac after only a few yards. He didn't have time to retrace his steps: the two men were too close on his heels. They stopped, gasping, at the mouth of the alley, then straightened up when they saw they had him trapped. They took their time to recover their breath, and began at last to walk towards him. When the larger of the men grinned, Sean saw he had several teeth missing.

'Hey, what's the problem, boys?' he joked. 'I wasn't breaking the law or anything. Why don't we talk about this . . .' He barely had time to clench his stomach before the first meaty fist slammed into it.

Quaid and Harper heard the fight before they saw it. They followed the unmistakable sound of knuckles on flesh through the deserted streets until they were standing at the mouth of the alley. Quaid looked at Harper.

'Seems to me that two against one's unfair.'

Harper nodded in agreement. 'Seems that way to me, too.'

Quaid grinned. 'Why don't we even things up a bit? Hey, *amigos*!'

At his shout, the two Italians turned to face them, and Sean took the opportunity to smash his fist into the jaw of the larger one. The brothers waded in. With the fight more than equalled up, it only lasted a few minutes. The Americans handled themselves well, landing several expert blows on Sean's assailants. Realising they were outclassed as well as outnumbered, the Italians ran off up the alley, clutching their injuries.

Quaid helped Sean to his feet, grinning. 'You all right?'

Sean nodded, too winded to say anything.

Sucking the knuckles of his right hand, Harper retrieved what was left of Sean's camera from where it lay on the cobbles. 'Guess you might need a new one of these.'

Sean took it and grimaced

'You a journalist?' asked Quaid.

Sean felt his gums gingerly with his tongue and spat blood on to the pavement. 'No,' he gasped. Photographer.' He straightened up and put out his hand. 'You've no idea how pleased I am to meet you. Although I thought for a moment those bastards had given me double vision.'

The brothers grinned.

'I'm Quaid Albright. This is my brother, Harper.' Quaid's grin faded into a frown when he took a closer look at his new friend's face. 'I hope you don't mind me saying so, mister, but you look as if you could do with a trip to the emergency room.'

The first thing Claire saw when she woke was Cherry, watching her. Their eyes locked and held for a moment before they both burst out laughing.

'My God,' spluttered Cherry. 'I don't believe what we did last night.'

Claire rolled over and looked at the ceiling. 'Me neither. It must have been the wine.'

'Or just being here, in Venice.'

'I know what you mean.' Claire swung her legs out of bed. 'This city has a strange effect on people.'

'Weird, isn't it? I tell you what, though, it's a good job we both like men so much.'

'Or we might make a habit of it?' Claire pushed her

hair out of her eyes and looked at Cherry. 'Seriously though, I wouldn't want to risk our friendship.'

'Me neither.'

'OK. Let's make a deal to stick to men.' They shook hands jokingly, then Claire pulled Cherry out of bed. 'Come on, we have shopping to do.'

Cherry went to her own room to shower and change, and met up with Claire three quarters of an hour later in the foyer of the hotel. They were both dressed for some serious shopping in sundresses and comfortable sandals.

'What shall we do first?' asked Cherry eagerly. 'Frocks, shoes, or masks?'

'We have an appointment at Signore Moretti's at eight-thirty.'

'Do you know where it is?'

'Stuart drew me a map.' Claire consulted the scrap of paper in her hand. Stuart had assured them that Moretti was the best mask-maker in the city, and that if they mentioned his name, he would help them find something for Vittorio's party. 'It's in the *mercerie*. Not far.' She looked at her watch. 'Which is just as well, because it's twenty past already.'

The Piazza San Marco was still fairly empty. Half a dozen hawkers were setting up their stalls, watched by a handful of early rising tourists and the ever hopeful posse of pigeons. The mist had cleared completely, leaving the air fresh and sweet smelling. The clock tower struck half past as the two women hurried through the archway under it, into the twisting lanes of the *mercerie*.

After a few minutes, Claire stopped and looked at her map again. 'I think it's here somewhere,' she said, pointing down a dark, shop-lined alley.

'It doesn't look very promising. Are you sure he'll be open?'

'He did say to come at half eight.'

'Hey, Cherry!' They were were brought up short by a shout, and turned to see the Albright twins hurrying down the street towards them, accompanied by a third man.

'My God,' breathed Claire. 'Is that Sean? What on earth's happened to his face?'

They stood, stunned, until the men caught up with them.

'What are you doing up so early?' asked Quaid.

'I could ask you the same thing,' countered Cherry. 'What's going on?'

'We're just taking our friend here to the hospital. He got mixed up with some bad company.'

'I thought your fighting days were over, Sean,' said Claire

'You guys know each other?' Harper's eyebrows rose.

Claire and Sean threw each other a wry look.

Cherry snorted. 'Know each other? They're only married, for heaven's sake!'

'Separated,' corrected Claire.

The twins stared.

'Well, I'll be darned,' said Quaid. 'How about that?'

'Here, let me take a look at you.' Claire stood on tiptoe to scrutinise Sean's battered features. 'It's difficult to see what damage there is, for all the blood, but I don't think it's too serious. Does it hurt much?'

Sean shook his head. 'I feel more numb than anything else. My skull took the worst of it, and as you know, it's pretty thick.'

'Mmm,' said Claire sceptically. 'Why don't you come back to the hotel with me, and I'll clean you up a bit. Then at least we'll be able to see if you need to bother with the hospital.'

'Sounds like an offer I can't refuse,' said Sean.

* * *

169

'So what happened?'

Sean winced as Claire dabbed away the blood from his eyebrow. 'There isn't much to tell. I took a photograph of a woman coming out of the Palazzo Giardino, and her two gorillas took exception to it. They must have thought I was paparazzi. Next thing I know, they're wading in to me with their fists.'

Claire frowned. 'You're sure it was the Palazzo Giardino?'

'Of course I am. I haven't had *all* the brains knocked out of me.'

She straightened up. 'I think you could do with some stitches in that. It looks nasty.' She moved on to the cut above his other eye.

Sean looked thoughtful. 'Do you think Vittorio could be mafioso?'

'What? Just because one of his friends didn't like you taking her photograph?' Claire laughed. 'Don't be silly.'

'He's certainly rich enough. What does he do for a living?'

'No idea. All I know is that he's a businessman, and he comes from Palermo.'

'Aha!'

'Don't be ridiculous. Not everyone who comes from Sicily is the Godfather, you know. I've met Vittorio, and I think he's perfectly charming.' That wasn't strictly true, but she wasn't about to explain to Sean why she didn't like the man.

'Well, I still think there's something dodgy going on.' His eyes narrowed, watching her. 'Of course, if Vittorio is running some kind of racket, it would mean your friend MacIntosh is mixed up in it too. Ouch! That hurt!'

'Don't be such a baby.' Claire bit her lip as she continued cleaning up Sean's face. Right at that moment, Stuart was the last person she wanted to think about – particularly in connection with Vittorio. She moved on to Sean's mouth.

'How are your teeth?' she asked. 'None loose, missing?'

Sean grinned to show her they were all present and correct. 'No. Just a split lip.'

'Pity.'

He hesitated. 'I suppose you think I had it coming?'

'I must admit there was a time, not so long ago, when I felt like doing this to you myself.'

'And now?'

She shrugged and dropped the cloth into the bowl. 'Now I'm over it.'

'Is that why you stood me up yesterday?'

Her hands paused as they wrung out the cloth. She'd wondered when he would bring that up. 'I'm sorry about that. I forgot the time'

'Can I ask what you were doing to make you forget?'

She stiffened.

Sean sighed before she could answer. 'Sorry,' he said. 'I'm not trying to pick a fight. I've had enough for one day.' His eyes grew speculative as they rested on her face. 'But I do think you should make it up to me.'

She raised an eyebrow. 'Oh, how?'

'By letting me take you to dinner tomorrow night.'

She stood back to look at him. One of his cheekbones was bruised, his bottom lip was split, and he had a deep cut over his right eye, which was already beginning to blacken like a banana. But he was still powerfully attractive, and knew it. His green eyes held hers, pleading. 'Please,' he said. 'We wrap up the shoot tomorrow, and I'd like to celebrate with you.'

'OK,' she said finally. 'But only if you promise to have that eyebrow seen to. If I'm going to have to look at you over my food, I don't want you to be any more gruesome than you need to be.'

Later that afternoon, Claire was early for her appointment at Pietro's studio. The downstairs door was propped open, so she walked straight up and knocked on the studio door. There was no answer. She knocked again. Still no answer. She sat on the top stair to wait for Stuart and the artist, and as she waited, the cat she had seen on her first visit wandered up the stairs and began to wind itself around her legs.

'Hello there. What's your name?'

Ignoring her, it stalked over to the coir mat outside the studio door and began to sharpen its claws on it. A thought occurred to Claire. She felt under the mat, and smiled as her fingers closed on something cold and metallic.

'Thanks, puss. I'm sure Pietro won't mind if I wait inside.'

She let herself in with the key. The studio was as she remembered it, almost empty except for the chaise longue, a few wooden chairs and Pietro's easel and materials. A cloth hung over the easel, Claire realised that the canvas underneath it was probably her portrait. Trying to ignore it, she went to the windows. The view over the roof tops of the city was stunning: she could just make out the temple-like roof of the church that stood in the Campo di Confraternita, standing ghostly above the patchwork of sun-faded tiles, and beyond that, the glitter of the sea. She turned back into the room, and looked at the easel. It was too much of a temptation. Tiptoeing over to it, she lifted the cloth. And caught her breath.

She hardly recognised the woman on the canvas. Under Pietro's hands (or had it been Stuart's?) she had undergone a voluptuous transformation. With the silver collar at her neck and the bracelets at her wrists, she had the look of a biblical seductress – Salome or Delilah. In spite of the provocative, almost pornographic pose, Pietro had captured her with delicacy and feeling. But it was the look in her eyes that shocked her the most: they stared out of the painting, challenging the viewer, veiled and fiercely sensual. Shaken, she let the cloth drop again and went to sit on the chaise longue.

The sunlight was warm through her clothes. She dropped her bag on to the floor, leant back against the velvet and closed her eyes, savouring the heat on her skin. She hadn't realised she was so tired.

When he arrived some time later, Pietro was surprised to discover that the door to his studio was unlocked. He pushed it open.

'*Ciao,*' he called. 'Signora Savage?'

But there was no answer. He soon saw why. Claire Savage was lying on the chaise longue, turned towards him, one hand tucked under her cheek and the other thrown up and over her head, her breasts slowly rising and falling in her sleep. He drew up one of the rickety wooden chairs and sat on it, staring at her. He watched the way the strands of her hair that had fallen over her face blew softly against her cheek as she breathed, and the way the buttons of her blouse strained to contain the swell of her breasts and her sleeping breath.

As he sat motionless, staring at her from his chair, she stirred and raised one of her legs, throwing it over the arm of the sofa with a luxurious, abandoned movement. Pietro almost groaned out loud. Her movement had caused her skirt to ride higher, exposing a length of tanned flesh.

His eyes travelled up her leg, from the top of her sandal, up the beautifully moulded shin to her knee, then higher, to rest at last on the hem of her skirt. The garment was so crumpled and had ridden so high, that the artist could see the peep of white cotton in the shadowed v between her legs. Holding his breath, he slipped off his chair and shuffled closer until he was kneeling right next to the chaise longue. His gaze devoured her sleeping face, moving from the sweep of her lashes, over the curving cheek to her mouth, which was open slightly to reveal the gleam of teeth. The last time he had seen this woman she had been in the most vulnerable of positions, open and glistening with the effects of lust. He had sternly held his own desire in check, eager to capture her on canvas and aware also of his friend's presence in the studio. He could hardly have been unaware of it – Stuart's murmured words to the woman had seeped into Pietro's ears and brain like a drug, tormenting him with visions of tangled limbs and panting mouths. The hours he had spent working on Claire Savage's portrait had been some of the most disturbing and frustrating of his life. After the sitting he had been so aroused that he had hurried home. His girlfriend had been baking *ciabatta* in the kitchen, and he had surprised her by lifting her off her feet and on to the table, where he had made love to her like a man possessed, covering them both in flour.

Now as Pietro watched Claire, he was aware of Stuart's absence. He also knew that his friend wouldn't be joining them, as planned, for the sitting. *Dio mio!* Did Stuart think he was a saint? It was too much to expect of him, to be so close to such a lovely woman and not to touch. He wanted to brush her lips with his own, to explore that wet space with his tongue, or better still, his cock. He swallowed and let his eyes slide down the curve of her throat to the neckline of her blouse. The white cotton was straining, the top button only barely fastened. He lifted his hand, and then dropped it again, his eyes anxiously scanning the sleeping woman's face. Then his own face took on a determined expression as he reached slowly for that tempting button. It slipped surprisingly easily out of the button hole, and the blouse fell open a little to reveal the swell of her breast. The gleaming flesh rose and fell under Pietro's riveted gaze. He moved lower and undid the rest of the buttons very slowly, one by one. Finally the blouse fell open completely. *Ah, che bella!* His cock stirred in his trousers and he shifted uncomfortably. How far could he go, he wondered, before she would wake? He knew he should stop now, fasten her buttons, wake the *signora* and give her the message that Stuart wasn't able to come. Then they could resume her portrait. But somehow his body refused to obey the sensible commands of his brain. He couldn't move, but stayed kneeling on the floor in front of the woman, like a pilgrim praying to the shrine of lust.

He stared at the beautiful flesh exposed before him. Then he raised a finger and delicately traced the curve of her breast, as light as gossamer on the skin until it met the frothy top of her bra. He increased the pressure a little and eased the lace down gradually, exposing the top of the areola, and then, finally, the nipple itself. The bud popped out over the bunched up lace, and Pietro touched it lightly with his finger. Claire moaned, but didn't wake. He looked at the coral nub where it was pushed up by the bra, and flicked it two or three times, until it was standing to attention like his cock, which was now straining against his flies. He dropped his mouth to the nipple and licked it with the tip of his tongue, feeling the rubbery resistance of it. Then he gave in and took the whole of it into his mouth, sucking it and rolling it on his tongue. After a few moments of greedy sucking, he reached down to put his hand on Claire's ankle, then stroked it up her shin to her knee, pausing for a moment to caress it, before travelling higher. It slid over the skin, until it stopped at the rim of her pants.

Pietro paused and checked the woman's face for any sign of distress. But there was none. He pushed her skirt higher, until he could see her pants properly. Because she had one leg raised, and the other curled under her, there was an inch and a half of intriguing cotton space where they joined. He had a violent urge to press his face into it, but resisted. Instead, he ran his finger over the soft skin at the top of her thigh and insinuated the tip under the rim of her pants, running it down beneath the elastic towards the space between her legs. When he felt Claire's pubic hair springing against his knuckle, he knew he had gone too far to stop. He eased his body into a better position, resting on his elbow above the sleeping woman, and pushed the elasticated material to one side, wriggling his finger further into the curling hair and snaking it towards the cleft of her sex. He almost sobbed as she shifted a little, giving better access to his questing finger. The lips were pouting slightly now, and damp. Pietro held his breath and watched Claire's flushed face as he slid his first knuckle between them. She stirred and he closed his eyes. When he had recovered himself he looked back down at her face and pushed his finger deeper into her. She was deliciously tight. He withdrew his finger and sought the tiny nub of her clitoris. Then slowly, he began to stroke it.

Claire frowned in her sleep, and bit her lip. Pietro would not be evaded, however, and continued to tease the tingling bud, rolling it this way and that, bringing more fingers into play. She moaned, low in her throat. Pietro's shifted his weight slightly, and then captured her nipple with his warm lips once more, his goatee tickling the tender flesh. Her eyes squeezed tighter, then she began to shake. He made soft shushing noises and reached up to stroke her face with one hand, the fingers of his other hand still moving determinedly inside her.

When she came, she arched her body and drew her knees together, crying out into the dusty air of the studio.

Pietro leant back and watched Claire's face, his fingers still buried in the drenched heat of her sex. Slowly, her eyes flickered open and looked into his. He almost reeled at the force of the invitation he saw there. He withdrew his hand, but she caught it in her own and forced it back down to the warmth.

'No. Don't go.'

Pietro felt himself blush. Had she been awake all the time? By her enigmatic expression he couldn't tell. He searched it for a clue to what she wanted him to do next. Claire smiled and his prick throbbed.

'Fuck me, Pietro. Please.' She reached down and pressed her hand to the swell of his groin. '*Per favore.*'

He didn't need telling twice. He slipped off the chaise longue and on to his knees, pulling her round to face him so that her knees were either side of his. He bent down and catching the white cotton of her knickers, pulled them off and over her feet. She kissed him, teasing his lips, her small hand fumbling for his flies. He closed his eyes as she tugged the zip down and released his cock. Her hands cradled him, and he thought he was going to come there and then. She watched a single salty drop of liquid squeeze from the tip of it, then bent and lapped it off with her tongue.

'*Dio!*' Pietro's voice was hoarse, his face flushed as he pushed her back on the sofa. He pulled her skirt up and spread her knees. She leant back and closed her eyes as he gently opened her labia with his fingers. The soft folds glistened, and she moaned as

Pietro slid a finger inside her again. He pushed her back down and pulled her blouse out of the waist-band. One nipple was still peeping at him cheekily from the top of her bra and he sucked it while he fumbled to free the other breast from its lacy prison.

'Un momento.' Claire struggled to sit up again and wriggled her blouse off. Then she unhooked her bra to free her breasts completely. He stared at them, then grasped her hair with one hand and pulled her face towards his, grabbing for her breasts with the other, kneading them in his fingers. He kissed her wetly, sucking at her lips and tongue, before looking back down at her sex. He could see his burning prick pressing against the edge of the sofa, only inches away from her inviting warmth. He grabbed her by the hips and pulled her towards him, until the tip of his cock was resting against the soft folds of flesh and he could feel the teasing prickle of pubic hair. Claire clutched at his shoulders as he dug his fingers into her buttocks and lowered her on to the shaft of his prick. She cried out and grasped him harder, while he groaned at the exquisite sensation of her engulfing him. Her eyes opened and met his. A single tear squeezed out of the corner of her eye, and he licked it away before beginning to move inside her. Claire wriggled herself impatiently further on to his prick.

His face twisted as she continued to move experi-mentally up and down, up and down, held in position by the stiff rod of flesh. He could feel his own pleasure gathering speed. But still he watched the woman's face, so close to his own. She was gasping now, her breath coming in shudders.

'Sono ... pronto. I'm ready' At her hoarse words, he was bowled over suddenly by a heat that shook him to the marrow of his bones and carried him to the edge of consciousness. It flashed through him. A moment later, the woman also reached the point of

no return, shouting her pleasure to the ceiling, then fell gasping and spent on Pietro's shoulder

Afterwards, he courteously helped her resume her position for the portrait, fastening the silver collar and bracelets with gentle hands.

He looked into her eyes. 'I hope there is no need to tell Stuart of this?'

'Of course not,' she said, horrified at the thought.

'*Grazie*. If I lost the goodwill of my friend, I would starve. He puts much business my way. You understand?'

Claire nodded. She understood.

Chapter Thirteen

'*I* don't understand.' Stuart glowered at her, then swung away, out of the bed. He reached for the bathrobe on the floor. 'Why did you agree to have dinner with him?'

'We need to talk. There are things to sort out, the flat, the mortgage . . .'

'You don't have to do it over dinner.' He looked at her accusingly. 'You still find him attractive, don't you?'

'My marriage is over, Stuart.' Claire didn't answer his question.

He fell silent, staring out of the window at the people coming and going on the Riva Degli Schiavoni.

'You're acting as if you own me,' she said quietly. 'We've known each other less than a week.'

His shoulders slumped as he came back to the bed and sat down beside her. 'I know. I'm sorry. It feels like longer.' He reached out to stroke her shoulder, and brush the hair from her eyes. His expression was tender. 'I just don't want you to get hurt, that's all.'

'There's no chance of that.'

'Really?' The intelligent eyes bored into hers.

'Really.'

'I'm glad.' He dipped his head and kissed her, exploring her lips, while she slipped her hand beneath the bathrobe to feel the smooth skin beneath.

'Come back to bed,' she whispered.

He shrugged off the robe and joined her under the sheet. She shivered to feel the heat of his body along the length of hers, cupped his buttocks and pulled him hard against her, so that she could feel his burgeoning cock brand her thigh. She trailed her lips across his chest, that smelled faintly of lemons, and captured one nipple between her lips. He moaned and rolled her on top of him, kissing her chin, her mouth, her throat. Pushing him away, she sat up to straddle him, and reached for a condom on the bedside cabinet.

He groaned and closed his eyes as she smoothed the sheath over the eager rod of his cock. Her face and chest flushed with passion, she looked down at him. He really was beautiful, with his long black lashes, straight nose and stubborn chin: just looking at him almost brought her to orgasm. She raised herself on her knees and slowly lowered herself on to his cock, taking him in little by little, until she had completely engulfed him. She arched backwards, pressing him deeper, forcing a guttural sigh from him. This time she had him in *her* power, and it was up to her to dictate what would happen next.

His eyes opened, flashing with lust, and he reached out to imprison her breasts with his hands. But she grabbed his wrists and pulled them away from her, then, with a throaty laugh, pinned them down on to the pillow. Their faces were only an inch or two apart and she could feel his breath fan her cheek, stirring the curtain of her hair that had fallen over her forehead. His cock leapt inside her as he read the wanton expression in her eyes. She began to move on him, lazily, lasciviously, raising herself so that his cock was almost completely exposed before swallowing him again and squeezing him with her most intimate muscles. She repeated the movement again and again, tortuously slowly, until he was writhing under her, arching his hips up to hers whenever she withdrew. But she refused to end his exquisite torment, taking her pleasure in watching his face. His eyes were squeezed shut, his face was flushed, and his breath was coming in gasps. As she raised herself up, he gave a frustrated heave of his hips to bury himself again, but she evaded him. She paused a moment, before sliding down on him, then up again, laughing as his cock tried to cleave to her moist, burning flesh. He struggled to pull his hands out of her grasp, to clutch her to him, but she tightened her grip. Luckily, he was too distracted to put up much of a fight. He began to twist his head from side to side as his pleasure increased. Satisfied that he was past the point of resistance, Claire grasped both of his wrists in one hand and reached behind her to tease his scrotum with her fingers. He sobbed aloud. He was very close to orgasm now. His balls were tight and swollen, tucked up high on the the base of his cock, slick with her own moisture. She continued to move on him, slowing her pace still further, her muscles aching with the effort, until she felt him grow even more rigid inside her. Then she raised herself up on her knees as high as she could, until only the very tip of his cock was held, trembling, between the lips of her sex. She stroked her fingertip over the sensitive flesh of his balls. They tightened spasmodically, his whole body stiffening under her, face twisted as if in pain. She felt his cock twitch once, twice, before plunging herself down on to it, hard. He arched up, his cock pulsing again and again, until he was completely spent.

* * *

182

Afterwards they lay together peacefully, until the room grew dark, and Stuart reached over to switch on the lamp.

'I forgot to mention that Pietro phoned me to say his portrait of you is finished,' he said, lighting a cigarette. 'He says it's the best he's ever done.'

'Oh?' Claire squinted against the light and tried to keep the tone of her voice neutral. 'When can I see it?'

'You can't. It's for my eyes only.'

'But that's not fair!'

He kissed her splutter of indignation into silence. 'That's the way it goes, I'm afraid.' Then he flicked his cigarette into the ashtray. 'Listen, I'm working tomorrow, so if I'm not seeing you tomorrow night, the next time will be at Vittorio's party.'

'Oh.'

'Did you manage to find Moretti's shop from the map I gave you?'

'In the end.' Claire frowned, remembering the diversion, but then grinned again at the thought of the purchase she had eventually made.

'You look pleased with yourself.'

'I am. I bought the most gorgeous mask.'

'You'll have to give me a clue what it's like, or I won't be able to recognise you.'

She laughed. 'Surely you know my body well enough by now?'

'But you'll be wearing clothes, I hope!' Stuart pulled her against him. 'Actually, perhaps I'd better warn you. Vittorio's parties can be a little unconventional.'

'Really? In what way?'

'How can I put this? Let's just say some of his guests are exhibitionists, and can get a wee bit carried away.' He kissed her, and then his eyes grew serious.

'I wish we didn't have to go, though. It will be our last night together.'

It was true. Claire had booked flights for herself and Cherry, leaving at lunchtime on Sunday. Although she had been quick to point out to Stuart that she had only known him for a little while, he had managed to get through her defences disturbingly easily. It was difficult to imagine not seeing him again.

'Why don't we give the party a miss?' she asked.

'We can't. Vittorio's invitations aren't so much invitations as orders, and he's expressly said he wants to see you – us – there.'

She bit her lip, and said nothing.

'You don't like him much, do you?'

'Not a lot.'

'Forget about him.' His fingers stroked up the inside of her thigh, trailing in the juice that glistened there. 'Let's enjoy the time we have left.'

As he rolled on top of her, Claire marvelled at his powers of recuperation: he was already hard again. Sighing in anticipation, she opened herself for him.

Later, as she was walking down the hotel corridor towards her room, Claire paused outside her friend's door. There was no light showing under it, so she started to walk on. Then she stopped: there was a muffled noise coming from inside. If it had sounded like lovemaking she would have ignored it. But it didn't. It was softer, more subdued. She tapped on the door.

'Cherry? Are you all right?'

There was no answer, but she heard the shuffle of feet on carpet, and the door swung open.

'What are you sitting in the dark for?' Claire switched on the bedside lamp and looked at her friend. 'Oh.'

Cherry's lovely face was stained with tears, her eyelids swollen and blinking in the light.

'What on earth's happened?'

'Oh Claire, I feel awful. Everything's gone wrong.' She sniffed into her paper hankie and climbed back into bed. 'I've finished things with Quaid and Harper.'

'Both of them?'

She nodded. 'I couldn't go on like that. Two-timing them. And so I thought that if I couldn't have them both, I'd be better off with neither.'

'That was brave.'

'Was it? Right now it feels like the stupidest thing I've ever done.'

'How did they take it?'

'It was hard to tell. I did it on the phone. Quaid wanted to know why, while – while Harper just went quiet.' She sobbed fresh tears into her hankie. 'I never thought I could feel this miserable.'

'What did you tell Quaid?'

'I gave him some old guff about not wanting to settle down and get serious with anyone. It's the biggest lie I've ever told.' Her face crumpled again.

Claire took Cherry in her arms and held her. 'Shh. You've done the right thing. You would have had to say goodbye on Sunday anyway. Imagine what it would have been like if they both turned up at the airport to see you off?'

'It's better than nobody being there.'

'There's just tomorrow and Saturday to get through. You'll be all right.'

'But what about the party? They're both going. I gave them their invitations yesterday.'

'I wouldn't worry about it, honestly. With a bit of luck there'll be lots of people there. And they might not even recognise you in your mask.' Claire held

185

Cherry away from her and searched her face. 'Unless you'd rather not go?'

'Are you kidding? I took that commission specially so I could stay for it. And I've spent a fortune on my dress. Wild horses wouldn't keep me away.'

Claire brushed a streak of mascara from under Cherry's eyes with her thumb. 'That's my girl.'

'What about you?' sniffed Cherry. 'How did Stuart take the news that you're seeing Sean tomorrow night?'

'Pretty badly at first. But I told him there was no chance of me and Sean getting back together, so he's OK about it now.'

'He believed you then?'

'Of course he did, why shouldn't he?' Claire avoided Cherry's eyes. 'After what Sean did to me, I'd sooner wrestle with an alligator than tangle with him again.'

Chapter Fourteen

*S*ean smiled, his teeth gleaming in the candlelight. 'As you can see, I only had to have one stitch in the end.' He waggled his eyebrow up and down, making Claire laugh.

She sat back in her chair and sighed happily. She couldn't remember the last time she'd eaten so well. They had had an Italian antipasto to start; roasted aubergines, red peppers, artichokes and smoked tuna, washed down with a ruby Corvo wine. Seafood linguini had followed, and then an obscenely large portion of cassata ice cream. The restaurant was small but bustling, with unpretentious red and white checked tablecloths and Swiss-style furniture. The waiter, an old man that reminded Claire of Pinocchio's father, winked at her as he squeezed past with a bottle of wine for another table.

'You look like the cat that's got the cream,' said Sean.

She patted her stomach. 'I'm stuffed.'

'Do you fancy a liqueur?'

'I'd better not. I think I've had enough to drink.'

'Nonsense.' He tipped the last of the wine into her glass.

'If I didn't know better, I'd say you were trying to get me tipsy.'

'What if I was? It wouldn't be the first time.' His eyes were warm on her face.

She looked at him seriously. 'I hope you're not trying to have your evil way with me.'

'It wouldn't be the first time for that, either.'

His eyes held hers for a long moment, then she laughed. 'You're so sure of yourself, aren't you?'

He looked affronted. 'Not at all. I don't know what you mean.' But the amusement that shone in his eyes contradicted his words.

'I think you'd better take me back to the hotel.'

He grimaced, but signalled for the bill. 'Your wish is my command.'

When the waiter returned Sean's card, he leant confidentially towards him. 'It might be a good idea not to go outside just yet, *signore*. The rain is very heavy.'

Claire looked out of the window and saw that it was true: the rain was bouncing down on to the cobbles, and pitting the surface of the canal. 'I don't have a coat with me,' she groaned.

'Me neither,' grinned Sean. 'It looks as if fate's against us. We'll just have to stay here until it eases off.'

She frowned. She knew that if she spent much more time in Sean's company, she was in danger of doing something she would regret.

'You want a ride, *signora*?'

Claire turned to discover who had spoken and saw a man leaning on the bar behind them. He was wearing the traditional white shirt and black *pantaloni* of a gondolier. He saw her hesitate. 'My gondola has a cabin.'

That clinched it. 'Yes, please.'

Sean groaned. 'You're mad! Come on then, let's get soaked, if that's what you want.'

They watched from the doorway of the restaurant until the gondolier had brought his boat alongside, then ran through the rain to reach it. They climbed in, laughing and gasping at the violence of the shower, struggling to keep their balance as it rocked under them. The tiny cabin was furnished with cushions, and was damp but comfortable.

Sean smoothed the water from his hair, laughing. 'A typical Venetian downpour! Do you remember the firework display on our honeymoon? We nearly drowned.' The gondola backed out from the quay, throwing the man and woman together in the intimate interior. He put his arm around her shoulders. 'Have you enjoyed yourself?'

'Yes, I have. Thank you.' Claire refused to look at him, and ran her fingers through her own hair. 'I must look a mess.'

He shook his head, serious suddenly. 'You're beautiful. Come here.'

She resisted slightly as he pulled her on to his knee, and stared into her eyes. She was half reluctant, half desperate for his touch. He brushed her damp hair off her face, and then bent to kiss her. His kiss was slow and measured. He let the tip of his tongue explore the edge of her teeth and then the inside of her mouth. When he pulled away again, she saw him wince.

'Is your mouth too sore?' she asked.

'No way.' To prove it, he kissed her chin, her eyebrows and her jaw, his hand cupping her face and tilting it to bring each part to his lips. It made her feel as if she was a glass of vintage champagne, and he was sipping her slowly. She closed her eyes to savour the feeling and he kissed her eyelids in turn. Then his mouth dropped lower to the pulse of her throat and he buried his face in the black curtain of her hair, inhaling deeply.

'You smell marvellous.'

Claire just sighed, although she could have said the same thing; Sean's aftershave was subtle, yet she could smell it evaporating in waves off his hot skin through his shirt. She closed her eyes again as his hand explored the curve of her shoulder. He touched her as if she were made of porcelain, running his finger over the bones beneath the skin, tracing the level line of her collarbone to where it ended in the dip at the base of her throat. He pressed his lips to the spot and she stirred against him.

'The gondolier – '

'Forget him,' Sean whispered. 'He's watching the canal, not us.'

She relaxed into his arms. He kissed her again and then trailed his fingertips down to the swell of her breasts above her flowery cotton dress. He took the thin skin between his fingers and pinched it lightly here and there, like a curious child, leaving a row of blushes across the flesh. She looked at his face through her lashes and thought she had never seen a man so striking. With his blonde, almost Slavic looks, he couldn't have been more different to Stuart. She was distracted from the comparison, however, as Sean unfastened the top buttons of her dress and pulled it lower to reveal the areolas of her nipples. She wasn't wearing a bra. He bent down and licked the swelling half-moons, and Claire felt him harden under her buttocks. She moaned as he cupped a breast and lifted it, squeezing one of the tight nipples through the cotton. He undid some more buttons and pushed the material lower still, to expose her breasts completely, and she shivered as the cool air caressed her skin and made her nipples pucker.

'I've missed you so much.' Sean took a breast in his

190

hand and felt its weight. She opened her eyes and turned slightly to see that the gondolier was watching them. Sean followed her gaze.

'*Guardare diritto,*' he growled.

'*Si, signore.*'

Claire wanted to reach up and touch Sean's bruised, fallen-angel face, but her arms were restricted by her dress. He reached down and brought one of her breasts to his mouth, sucking on it gently at first, flicking the nipple with his tongue and then nipping it in his teeth. She felt the sweet ache of wanting him spread from her breasts, down to her stomach, slipping between her thighs and turning her legs to water. He released her breast from its slippery prison and pushed her gently down on to the cushions, so she was lying flat on her back across him, her legs bent coyly and her feet still on the bottom of the boat. He pressed the material of her skirt to mould against her thighs, throwing the smooth curve of her sex into relief. Because her bottom was on his knees, the mound was pushed up and silhouetted prominently against the dark interior of the cabin. Sean stroked it, and she pressed herself up against his finger. The slap of water against the hull of the gondola was running along the whole of her body, making it vibrate like a tuning fork. She was aware that they had slowed down as they approached a junction with a smaller canal, and wondered whether the pedestrians crossing the bridges above them were able to see her semi-naked, provocative position. She hoped not, but didn't want to stop to close the curtains properly: Sean had opened the floodgates. She arched her sex up, begging for his touch. He lifted her skirt a little and looked up it.

She felt his hand skim her knees and then travel up the smooth skin to brush her skirt higher, and push one leg of her French knickers to one side. She knew he would be able to see the honey of her arousal, even though her legs were pressed together. She arched up towards him slightly, relaxing her buttocks so that her legs parted and her sex pouted at him.

'Please.'

In reply, he slipped his hand beneath the silk and stroked the begging lips. They swelled and opened wider at his touch, moisture glinting between the curls. She arched up again, so that his finger dipped into her, just a little. He pushed her legs gently further apart with his other hand. Then, using all his fingers, he opened her wide to look at her properly. He took in every detail; the lush hair that curled damply on the outer lips, and the pink folds of the inner lips, half hiding her clitoris like an oyster hides a pearl. He opened her wider still and pushed a finger into the supple tunnel of her vagina. She gasped and ran her hands over herself, kneading and pinching her breasts and nipples – she felt as if she were a piano, and Sean was playing her chord by subtle chord. He insinuated two more fingers into her and began to rub her clitoris, circling the stiff pearl with the fingers of his other hand. For a while, both hands were busy in the heat of her sex. Feeling herself begin to contract, she moved her buttocks with little gasps to help his fingers accomplish their task. He withdrew one of his hands to tease her nipples, leaving moisture glistening on her breasts as he moved from one painfully taut island to the other, and then back again. Meanwhile, his other fingers never stopped their slow, tantalising work inside her. Her contractions increased, gripping her tighter and tighter still, until they rippled through her, lifting her up and shaking her again and again until the boat beneath them rocked in the water.

As soon as her orgasm had passed, Claire pushed herself up on the seat and looked at Sean. She could tell by his flushed face and the bulge in his trousers that he had been very aroused by her abandoned release.

'Will you come back to my hotel with me?' he asked.

She hesitated, but only for a moment. She wanted him. 'OK.'

He turned to give the new address to the gondolier, ignoring the smirk on the other man's face. When they arrived at the hotel it was no longer raining. Claire got out and waited while Sean paid the gondolier, then hurried with him through the doors, only remembering at the last minute that the hotel was full of Barker and Savage staff. But she needn't have worried. It was past midnight, and the foyer was empty.

In the intimacy of Sean's room, Claire felt suddenly awkward.

'Do you mind if I tidy myself up?' she asked.

'The bathroom's through there.'

She splashed cold water on her face, and as she straightened up, her eyes met those of her reflection in the mirror above the sink. They were sensuous, challenging: they were the eyes of the woman in Pietro's portrait.

'Are you OK?' Sean had come into the bathroom behind her and was watching her with his own slanting green gaze. The bruises on his face looked yellow in the flourescent light.

Claire pushed her hair off her forehead. She wasn't OK, and knew that he could see it. He bent down to kiss the pulse throbbing behind her ear, letting his lips trail down her neck to the silky skin at the top of her shoulder. She shivered, and he wrapped his arms around her.

'We don't have to do anything if you don't want

to,' he said. His eyes still held hers in the mirror, dark with desire.

'I know. I want to. It's just . . .'

'You think too much. Why don't you just relax and go with it.'

Relax and go with it. That was more or less what Stuart had said to her the first time they had made love in the palazzo. She closed her eyes at the bitter sweet memory and let herself slump into Sean's arms. He felt her surrender and pulled her harder against him, so that she could feel the dampness of his clothes and his erection against her buttocks.

'You're so beautiful, Claire.' His fingers trembled slightly as he undid the buttons of her dress, and pushed the material off her shoulders to fall in a pool around her feet, leaving her dressed in nothing but her French knickers. He reached round to cradle her breasts in his hands, pulling her to him and burying his face in her neck. She opened her eyes to see herself clasped intimately against him and watched as he twisted her nipples in his fingers, teasing them to rigidity. His hands were dark against her own lightly tanned skin, that looked almost pale in the harsh light. Sean's hands roved lower, over her hips, to capture her buttocks through the silk. After a moment, he slid his palms up and under the legs of her knickers to find the bare flesh beneath, stroking and kneading, before reaching round to the tops of her thighs to the junction between them. She sighed and spread herself wider as his fingers dipped into her, and he began to rub his fingertips up and down in the juicy cleft. Watching Sean's hands move rhythmically under the oyster silk, Claire leant back and raised her arms to clasp her hands behind his neck. She tugged at the rain-darkened curls of his hair, and ran her hands over his stubbled chin. He caught her ear between his teeth, making her stiffen against him,

194

and pushed his thumb deep inside her, lifting her off her feet. She cried out with pleasure, and felt his confined cock pressing against her buttocks. His thumb buried inside her, he continued to tease her with the fingers of his other hand, until she reached her orgasm, trembling, her body arching against him, and the tunnel of her sex clenching spasmodically.

He lowered her to the floor, and she turned to face him. Desperate to see him naked, she began to tear at the buttons of his shirt, ripping the damp material in her haste. Her hands were shaking so much he had to help her with his belt. He shrugged off his trousers and boxer shorts and stood naked in front of her. Bruises bloomed beneath his tan, one on the pectoral muscle close to his left nipple, and another, larger one on his stomach, above the hair that curled at the junction of his stomach and groin. His penis was heavy with blood. She reached for it, curling her fingers possessively around the shaft. He groaned, and pressed her backwards into the sink. Bending his head to hers he began to kiss her feverishly, with no heed for his hurt lip. A thought struck her. She hesitated and pushed him away.

'What's the matter?' His eyes were hazy with lust.

'What about Caroline?' she whispered.

'Caroline?' His gaze cleared a little as he stared at her. 'That's over. I've moved out. The whole thing was a mistake. It's you I want, Claire – I knew that the minute I laid eyes on you again.' He seized her lips with his own once more, bruising them against her teeth, and thrust his cock against her hands. 'Can't you tell how much I want you?' Her hands closed around him again and she returned his kisses hotly. He reached down and practically tore her knickers off her, then lifted her up so she was sitting on the edge of the vanity unit. He bent to suckle one nipple in his mouth, then he stood back and pushed her knees apart.

'Let me look at you.'

Claire closed her eyes with the force of the lust that swept through her. She leant back and clutched at the taps behind her for support.

'Wider,' he whispered, pushing her knees as far apart as they would go. 'That's it, love.' He dropped his head so that his face was level with her sex, and looked into her. She groaned, feeling as if her very soul was exposed to his gaze. He gently spread her labia with his fingers and then slipped his tongue between them, flicking it into the coppery channel. He opened her wider still with his thumbs, and then began to lap and nibble at her clitoris. She groaned and ran her hands through his hair, digging her fingers into his scalp. Invisible flames were licking through her veins, threatening to burn her up. He probed her with his thumbs and increased the pressure of his tongue on her aching clitoris. Still sensitive from the orgasm he had given her just a few minutes before, she came immediately.

'Now it's my turn.' He picked her up, the spasms of pleasure still thrilling through her, and carried her into the other room, where he lay her on the bed. She heard him open a drawer, close it again, then felt the tip of his rubber-clad penis nudge against her sex. He hesitated there a moment, before he squeezed his eyes shut and pushed fiercely into her. She groaned loudly and clutched at the coverlet, bracing herself as he began to plunge in and out of her with long, hard strokes. Their bodies clung together, slick with sweat. He bit her chin, while she dug her nails into his back to drive him on, wanting to feel him deeper inside her. She wrapped her legs around his hips, and dropped her hands to his buttocks, running a finger up the sensitive cleft between them until a tremor rippled through him. As she pushed the tip of her finger into the tight channel of his anus, his cock stiffened and he ejaculated into her with incoherent, passionate words of love.

She watched Sean as he slept, resisting the compulsion to kiss the bruises on his eyebrow, cheek and chin, in case she woke him up again. She knew she had surprised him by the directness of her love-making. They had both changed while they were apart. There had been no mistaking the emotion in his eyes as he had thrust into her, and she guessed that his regret was genuine. Could they have a future together, she wondered? On the strength of the hours they had just spent, it seemed possible. Her thoughts were interrupted by the phone. She snatched it up.

'Hello?' she whispered.

'Who's that?' It was a woman's voice, heavy with suspicion.

Claire pushed her hair out of her eyes and sat up. 'Do you want to speak to Sean? I'd rather not wake him.'

'No. I've changed my mind.' The voice sounded familiar. 'Who *is* this?'

Resentment rippled through Claire. 'His wife,' she snapped, 'if it's any of your business, which I doubt!'

The line went dead, and Claire suddenly remembered where she had heard the voice before. She replaced the receiver.

Sean stirred beside her, and put his arm around her waist. 'Who was that?' he asked sleepily.

'Lianne.' She wriggled out of his embrace.

He opened his eyes.

'Are you fucking her, Sean? I thought you said you had decided you wanted me back?' Jealousy made her angry and irrational.

He sat up. 'I did. And it was the truth. I'm not sleeping with her.'

Claire slid out of the bed, retrieved her dress and knickers from the bathroom and put them on with shaking hands. She was dangerously close to tears. 'She told me someone had treated her badly, but I never guessed it was you. I suppose I might have known. Some things never change, do they?'

'You're being ridiculous. How many times do I have to tell you that I am not sleeping with her. And even if I was, you could hardly complain. You've been glued like a limpet to that bloody Scotsman ever since I got here.'

'That's different.' She picked up her sandals and rammed them on. 'It was you that cheated on me, remember. Not the other way around.'

'How can I have cheated on you with Lianne when we weren't even seeing each other? I wouldn't dream of seeing anybody else now that we're back together.'

Claire's cheeks drained slowly of colour. She turned to face him, eyes glittering. 'Back together? That's one hell of an assumption, isn't it?' She lifted her chin. 'One fuck does not mend a broken marriage.'

'A *fuck*?' Sean raked his hands through his hair. 'Jesus! I can't believe you said that. What the hell's got into you?'

'I've come to my senses, that's what.'

He jumped out of bed as she rushed for the door, but wasn't quick enough to get there before her. 'For God's sake, Claire, be reasonable.'

She drew herself up. 'Tomorrow's the last day of the shoot. After Vittorio's party, we can communicate through our solicitors. We won't have to see each other again, which I'm sure will be a relief to us both. Goodnight.' And with that, she flung herself out of the door and slammed it shut behind her.

Chapter Fifteen

Claire applied her third coat of mascara and stood back to admire the effect. She was wearing more make-up than usual: her eyes, subtly outlined with kohl and fringed by mascara-slick lashes, were huge in her face. She pushed her hair behind her ears to attach her earrings, fake diamond pendants that made her throat look long and fragile. She had considered wearing the collar and bracelets Stuart had given her, but had decided against it: they didn't go with her new dress, and besides, when she fastened them on they felt like manacles – a symbol of subjugation or even slavery. As much as Stuart excited her in bed, she had no intention of becoming a slave to him, or to her senses.

She slipped her bathrobe off and let it fall to the floor. Underneath she was naked, her only adornment the ruby varnish on her toes and fingers. She looked at her reflection briefly before reaching for the underwear she had bought. The tissue paper rustled under her fingers as she pulled out the ruby satin and velvet basque, and held it against her cheek for a moment. It was wonderfully soft, the velvet pile complementing the slippery satin trimming around the cups and on the panel down the front. How she loved the ritual of dressing up! She adored the glamour and sensuality of it, that made her delight in the fact that she was a woman. Today she was determined to savour it even more than usual: it helped to take her mind off her argument with Sean. She sighed as she began to lace herself into the basque. She should have known better than to fall for his careless charm again. Hadn't she already discovered, the hard way, just how little she could trust him? And yet, the memory of his hands parting her legs, stroking her, made her shiver.

She thrust the thought away and examined herself in the mirror again. The basque was old fashioned, pushing her breasts up high so that they were almost spilling out of the cups, and nipping her waist to improbable slenderness. The rich ruby velvet suited her colouring, making her look mysterious and exotic. She reached for her stockings, rolling the first one over her foot, pulling the gossamer silk slowly over her calf, knee and thigh before snapping the satin-covered suspender clips of the basque securely on to the stocking top. Then she repeated the process with her other leg, letting her hands linger on the smooth band of flesh between stocking and groin. With a flush of surprise, she realised that she was aroused. It might have been because of the sensual process of dressing herself, or the thought of Sean, or Stuart, or both. She didn't know, but her whole body was tingling with anticipation. Her fingers rustled through tissue again as she pulled out her new shoes from their box. They too were red velvet, high heeled and trimmed at the front with scarlet feathers. They were terribly impractical, but she hadn't been able to resist their flirtatious appeal. She put them on and admired them in the mirror, noting how they accentuated the length of her legs. Her gaze continued on, up past the dark triangle of her sex, up the velvet-clad torso to the areolas of her breasts that were peeping over the top of the basque like rising moons. She resisted the urge to slip a finger inside herself, and reached instead for the panties that matched the basque. She was about to wriggle into them, when she changed her mind. Tonight was going to be her last night with Stuart. She could imagine his delight when he discovered that her sex was unfettered above the intriguing boundary of her stocking tops.

Her dress was hanging on the back of the bathroom door. She took it down carefully, and stepped into it. It was a red velvet sheath, long and snugly fitting, the neckline running straight across her collarbone, leaving her shoulders naked and only barely covering the top of her nipples. She surveyed the effect with satisfaction: she looked as good as she ever had: her hair was glossy, and her skin radiant with good health. It must have been all the sex she was getting. She smiled at the thought and then reached for the last part of her outfit. The mask was fashioned from scarlet feathers, totally obscuring the top part of her face, except for her eyes, that glittered through the eye holes like emeralds. Her reflection in the mirror had been transformed into a bird of paradise, an enigma. But it still needed the finishing touch: she carefully applied her ruby lipstick, stretching and pouting her lips below the tiny jewelled beak.

There was a knock at the door. Claire went to answer it, as quickly as her tight-fitting dress and high heels would allow. But when she opened it, she saw a stranger standing in front of her. The woman was clad in a Victorian style dress, dark and glossy as a starling's wing, tight at the waist, low at the neck, gathered into ruches at the hips to emphasise the voluptuous figure beneath. She wore long black lace gloves, and her features were hidden by a black leather mask, except for the mouth, which was a deep, dark plum. But the most startling thing about her was the mane of dark hair, that had been teased into a jumble of curls and fell over her shoulders, almost to her waist.

'Bloody hell!' exclaimed Cherry. 'You look brilliant!'

'You too. Wherever did you get that dress?'

'It's antique, I think. I found it in a shop in the Stazione Marittima.' She twirled round. 'Do you think it suits me?'

'It's lovely.' Claire pulled her friend over to the mirror so they could inspect their reflections together.

'Don't you think it's a bit spooky?' said Cherry. 'We don't look like ourselves at all.'

She was right: the two women stared back at them with strangers' eyes. They looked like exotic creatures who could – and would – do anything.

Claire shivered, breaking the spell. 'Are you OK?' she asked. 'You haven't seen Harper or Quaid have you?'

'No.' Cherry's eyes darkened behind her mask, and Claire kicked herself for asking. She considered telling Cherry about her scene with Sean, but then thought better of it. She didn't want to put even more of a dampener on things.

'Are you ready?' asked Cherry.

'I think so.' She grabbed her shoulder bag.

'Come on then, we don't want to miss anything.'

The windows of the Palazzo Giardino shimmered with the light of hundreds of candles as the water taxi powered its way over the water towards it, jostling with other boats to deposit their passengers on the jetty. The water caught the reflections from the windows and weaved them with the reflected flames of the sconces on the wall near the door. Cherry squeezed Claire's arm as their boat bumped alongside another one at the jetty.

'Look! Isn't that Conrad Karlsson?' she hissed.

Claire turned to look in the direction Cherry was pointing. The passenger in the boat that had drawn up alongside was masked, but unmistakeable. The actor's muscled body, only barely restrained by his tuxedo, was one that both of the friends had lusted over at some time or other, although they were used to seeing more of it. Famous for his macho all-action roles, Karlsson was usually stripped to the waist.

'He hasn't made much of an effort to disguise himself, has he? That little scrap of a mask's not going to fool anyone,' whispered Cherry in disgust.

'I suppose if you were famous you'd probably want people to know who you were.'

They were helped out of the boat by one of the burly doormen, who examined their invitations and then pointed them in the direction the other guests were taking. Claire was surprised at the change Vittorio's decorators had wrought since the shoot had finished the day before. In that short space of time they had hung the corridors with violet muslin, and lined them with extravagant displays of lilies whose waxy petals gleamed in the candlelight, filling her nostrils with their scent. The party-goers were carried along from one pool of light to another, following the sound of music and chatter that drifted down from the floor above, until they were ushered at last through the carved double doors of the ballroom.

Claire and Cherry blinked at the two huge chandeliers that hung from the ceiling. They were also filled with candles, whose flickering light bounced around the room from one mirror to another, reflecting off the polished parquet floor. As they looked at the other guests, the same thought occurred to the two women: thank heavens they had made an effort with their appearance. It was simply the most glamorous gathering either of them had ever been in. Some of the guests were dressed in evening dress, and some in costume, but all had entered into the spirit of the party. Their masks were astonishing. There were boars, demons, satyrs and other mythical creatures, rubbing shoulders with birds of paradise and peacocks. Everywhere the women looked, jewels glittered on fingers, throats and ears.

'Bloody hell,' breathed Cherry. 'Pinch me, I think I'm dreaming.'

'Champagne?' A waiter bent towards them with a tray of glasses. He was stripped to the waist, his face and torso painted dark blue and white, his black hair encircled with a wreath of vine leaves. Cherry's eyes dropped to the lower part of his body, and she gasped to see that he was wearing nothing but a pair of tight leather briefs. They each took a glass of champagne.

'What kind of party is this?' giggled Cherry when he'd disappeared into the crowd.

'Who cares? Let's enjoy ourselves.'

'*Benvenuta, signorinas*. Welcome to my party.'

A tall man had approached them. He was wearing a *bautta*, the traditional white long-nosed mask of Venice, that was moulded into a malevolent expression and covered the whole of his face to his lips. Faded denim eyes stared out at them from the glowering eye holes as he took Cherry's hand in his.

'I hope you will have an entertaining evening.' He kissed her fingers, and then took Claire's hand. She realised he had spoken in English, and so had guessed their identities. Vittorio's eyes flickered over her breasts, before sweeping around the ballroom. 'It is a little crowded at the moment, *naturalmente*, but as the evening wears on it will become more . . . select. I do hope you can stay until then.' While he was talking his thumb had been rubbing her palm intimately. He pressed a lingering kiss into it. Then he was gone.

'Yuk.' Cherry wiped her fingers on her dress. 'That man gives me the willies.'

'I know what you mean.' In spite of Vittorio's intrusion, however, Claire's enthusiasm had not been dampened. She began to tap her feet to the beat of the salsa that the band was playing, and watched the people who were swaying on the dancefloor.

Another half-naked waiter passed with a tray. Cherry reached eagerly for one of the things on it, then squealed.

'Look!' It was not a vol au vent, as she had hoped, but a discreetly-wrapped packet of condoms. 'They're handing them round like sweets!'

Claire emptied her champagne glass quickly. Stuart had said that Vittorio's parties were unconventional, and she was beginning to see that he hadn't been exaggerating. She didn't care: after her fraught scene with Sean she was in the mood to have some fun.

'Do you want to dance?'

Cherry looked at the bodies undulating on the dance floor and grinned. 'Why not?'

Sean watched Claire as she danced. He hadn't recognised her in her mask and red velvet dress at first, and probably wouldn't have done if she hadn't been with Cherry. Together, however, the two women were unmistakeable. He had to admit, they both looked fabulous. But it was Claire who drew his attention. He cursed under his breath. Would he ever understand her? She had given herself so freely to him the night before, and he had responded instinctively, overflowing with his love for her. And then she had called it a fuck. A fuck! He swore again, more loudly this time, making people nearby turn to look at him.

He continued to watch the two women, knowing that he wasn't the only man in the room who was doing the same. They both danced well, moving their bodies sensuously in time to the Latin beat. As he watched, a slender man dressed in the black and scarlet costume of a matador approached Claire, while his friend bowed to Cherry. The women smiled and began to dance with them.

Sean grabbed another glass off a waiter and swallowed the contents quickly. He had been lucky to get into the party at all. Only his mask had saved him from being recognised by a doorman, who was one of the thugs that had trapped him in the alley. Luckily the black velvet concealed his features and his bruised eye. He looked around for another waiter, and beckoned him over: now that he had succeeded in getting in, he had every intention of getting as drunk as possible, as quickly as possible.

Cherry laughed as her partner swept her to a halt, and joined in the applause for the band. She saw that Claire was clasped firmly in her matador's embrace, and turned to the man beside her. The party was in full swing now, she had to shout for him to hear her over the laughter and chatter.

'I have to take a break.' She pulled a face. 'I have to go to the ladies' room.'

'*Signorina*, I am desolate. I will wait for your return.' He bowed and grinned below his mask.

Flushed from the exertion of the dance, Cherry threaded her way through the crowds towards the ladies' room. As the crush thinned out, she began to notice that there were quite a few amorous couples barely hidden in doorways and curtained window alcoves. She tactfully averted her eyes from the entwined limbs and grinned. In the perfumed sanctuary of the bath-room, she freshened her face with water, retouched her make-up and replaced her mask.

She was just coming out again, when she looked up and felt her heart clench in her chest. Two men were strolling down the corridor towards her, both dressed in tuxedos and wearing identical black masks. They were the same height, had the same blonde hair, and an identical loose-hipped way of walking. They hesitated when they saw her, and then quickened their pace.

She fought the urge to run away, lifted her chin and kept on going, intending to walk past them.

'Cherry!'

'We have to talk to you.'

Their voices were low and urgent as they stopped, one on either side of her.

'Oh?' She tried to keep her own voice light, glad of the mask that hid her flaming cheeks.

'Not here.'

'Somewhere private.'

'Well, I don't know if I . . .' she stammered.

But they had no intention of letting her argue with them. One of them pushed open a nearby door, peered around it and then pulled her inside. The room was dimly lit. When Cherry's eyes had grown accustomed to it, she saw that it was quite small, and lined in red velvet. She was distracted from the strangeness of the room, however, by the question that was hurled at her.

'Why did you run out on us?' The tone was heavy, hurt. The other brother was silent, watching them. Noting that he had said 'us', her shoulders slumped.

'You know why.'

He sighed. 'Yeah, I guess so. But all the same, it was a mean thing to do.'

Cherry's eyes behind her mask grew round. 'Are

207

you saying you'd rather I carried on sleeping with you both?

The American shrugged. 'Me and Quaid had already talked things over and agreed there was no point being jealous.'

The elder twin, who had been unusually silent, stepped forward. 'The thing is, we're so close, it's a bit like being jealous of yourself.'

'That's easy for you to say.' Cherry was sceptical. 'But you were squabbling over me like kids with a toy.'

'We've sorted that out now. No more rivalry.' His tone lowered seductively. 'You even can put it to the test, if you like.'

'H – how?'

Quaid's answer was to cup her chin and lower his mouth to hers. He kissed her thoroughly and deeply, and then, while she was still dazed and still had her eyes closed, she felt his lips leave hers to be replaced by another, cooler pair, more gentle but just as effective. Her heart hammered in her chest, and she opened her eyes to see Harper grinning down at her.

'Darling,' he whispered. 'Neither of us wants to give you up.'

'Oh.' She leant back against the door and gave a hopeless shake of her head. 'You're both confusing me. I don't know what to think.'

'Then don't think,' murmured Quaid. 'Feel.' He slipped behind her, swept the hair from the side of her neck and pressed his lips to her tawny skin. She melted against him and closed her eyes. Harper moved silently to stand in front of her, and kissed her on the mouth, stroking his fingers over her cheeks, her throat, and then down to the neck of her dress. Quaid pulled her hips against his erection while Harper's long fingers eased under her dress to find her nipples, which sprung pebble hard beneath them.

208

Gently, he teased them out of her dress. She sighed and pressed herself further back into Quaid's embrace, and he groaned and reached round to cup her breasts. He weighed them in his palms, before moving on to the nipples, rolling them between his fingers. She caught her breath as his fingers tugged the sensitive tips, pulling them to rigidity. Harper kissed her throat and collarbone, his mouth becoming more and more greedy, until Quaid fed one of her nipples into his mouth. He fastened on it, licking and sucking, as Quaid continued to tease her other nipple from behind.

'Wait,' Quaid whispered hoarsely. Hands and mouth quit her breasts as he turned to lock the door behind them, and then stooped to unfasten her dress. The men stood back and watched as the dark material rustled to her feet, leaving her standing in nothing but a pair of black panties, her long gloves, shoes and mask, curls cascading over her shoulders and breasts. She shuddered at the caress of cool air on her skin, and then at the heat of Quaid's hands as he cupped her buttocks through the lace.

Hardly daring to take their eyes from the woman in front of them, the brothers hurried to strip off the dinner suits, shirts, underwear, and finally their masks. Cherry looked at them through lust-heavy lids. In the dimly lit room they looked like matching erotic statues, with their lean golden bodies, and identical, trembling erections. Misunderstanding her hesitation, Quaid took her by the hand and led her to the divan where he sat down and pulled her on to his knee.

'You're the most beautiful thing we've ever seen. We'll be real gentle with you, we promise.' He reached to cradle her breasts once more, stroking his thumbs over the nipples, while Harper knelt on the floor in front of them, his expression rapt. She moaned and pressed her buttocks against Quaid's erection. Harper eased her panties off, sliding them down over her thighs and over her shoes. Quaid arranged her so that her knees were on either side of his, and slowly spread her thighs apart. Harper drew in his breath as the dewy outer folds of her sex were exposed to him. Cherry, teased to a sweet delirium by Quaid's fingers at her nipples, arched her body up, begging. Quaid's hands left her breasts and dropped to her sex. Then slowly, very slowly, he drew the lips apart, until she was completely exposed to the avid scrutiny of his brother. Heat scalded through her as Harper ran his fingertip around the curls, spiralling it around her throbbing clitoris and slipped it into her heat. They all groaned in unison, and she felt Quaid's cock twitch against her buttocks. It leapt again when his brother dipped his head and flicked his tongue across the burning nub of her clitoris, and she bucked, making the man beneath her moan. Quaid lifted her slightly, so that she could feel his cock press against the entrance to her vagina.

'Can I darling?'

Cherry nodded, too drenched with desire to speak.

They all paused a moment, and then Quaid lifted her even higher, bringing her down slowly on his long, hot cock until she was stuffed full of it and could feel it right at the very neck of her womb.

Harper spread her as wide as he could and began to lap at her more vigorously, pausing every now and again to suck on the tight button at the centre of her and to nibble the lips that usually enclosed it. Quaid's fingers gripped her thighs to keep them apart, and she squirmed involuntarily, twisting on his cock so that he had to squeeze his eyes shut with the effort of not coming. Harper's tongue flickered lower, to taste Cherry at the very point where his brother's cock pierced her. Her muscles clenched in response. It was

210

too much for Quaid. With a hoarse cry, he clasped her to him, and pumped his release into her, then lay back, exhausted on the divan. Cherry was still on the brink of her own orgasm. She desperately wriggled free of Quaid's softening cock and pulled his brother up so that he was standing in front of her, his carbon-copy member thrusting only inches from her face. She kissed it, seeking out the very tip with her tongue, making him tremble.

'I don't have another rubber,' he groaned, stricken.

'There's one in my bag.'

Harper quickly found the condom Cherry had taken from the waiter, and fitted it over his cock. She watched him as he did it, lying back luxuriously on his brother, her legs spread in open invitation. Then she guided him into her. She was so slick he slid easily inside, and made tiny sucking noises as he began to move in and out. Cherry's orgasm was close, but elusive. She wriggled and panted, thrusting her hips up to grind them against the base of Harper's cock. Quaid stirred underneath her, took her ear in his teeth, then slid both hands between her stomach and his brother's to find the honeyed heat of her sex. His fingers moved up from the pumping root of Harper's cock to find her clitoris, and began to rub it, hard and fast.

Vittorio sighed with satisfaction and a tight, mounting pleasure. He had come into the viewing room to check that his video equipment was ready for later in the evening, and had been surprised and delighted to see the impromptu scene that was unfolding through the two-way mirror. The sight of the half-caste English woman and her tall Americans was an unexpected bonus. It had prompted him to grab his companion, a curly-haired, melting-eyed Sicilian, still young and inexperienced, but with a promising propensity for pleasure.

He stroked the raised buttocks of the boy kneeling under him, and pumped his cock in and out of the dark channel between them. He caressed the silky skin of his back, grasping the narrow hips as he thrust in and out, eyes glazed and staring at the scene on the other side of the mirror. He came at the same time as the brunette, biting the neck and shoulders of the boy to stifle his cries. When he felt himself start to soften he pulled out, carefully keeping the condom in place with his fingers, and flipped the boy over on to his back. The scene behind the mirror had aroused him too. He was breathing heavily as he stared up at Vittorio with a mixture of defiance and lust, his cock sticking up between his legs like an accusing finger. With a groan, Vittorio groped for the nubile, angry-looking flesh and fed it into his mouth.

Chapter Sixteen

Cherry lay sandwiched on the divan, sweat cooling on her skin.

'I think we should be getting back to the party,' she whispered.

'In a minute,' soothed Quaid, kissing her neck, smoothing away the curls that were sticking to it.

Harper grinned at her. 'Now do you believe us when we say we're not jealous of each other?'

She smiled. 'I might do.' She shifted, savouring the unique sensation of having two cocks pressed against her. 'But I really should be getting back. Claire will be wondering where I've got to.'

'Can you see Cherry anywhere?'

Stuart craned his neck to scan the crowd as he led Claire off the dance floor, then shook his head, 'She must have decided to sit this one out.'

'That sounds like a good idea,' laughed Claire. 'I'm exhausted!'

He put his hands around her waist and kissed her. 'Not too exhausted, I hope. This is our last night, remember.'

She kissed him back, raking her fingers through his hair. 'How could I forget?' She pressed herself closer, revelling in the heat of him through his matador trousers, aware of the champagne that was bubbling through her veins. 'You look great in that costume. Very sexy.'

He grunted and bit her ear. 'I could say the same about you. That dress is such a turn-on.' He took her hand and pressed her palm to his groin. He was hard.

She whisked her hand away playfully, but he caught it again in his own.

'Come on,' he said, pulling her towards the door.

'Where are we going?'

'You'll see.'

He led her away from the ballroom to a part of the palazzo where the passageways were darker, and there were only a few party-goers drifting in and out of the shadows. Halfway along a curtain-lined corridor, he pushed one of the curtains aside and pulled her into the alcove behind it.

'What's this?' she asked.

'One of Vittorio's surprises for his guests.'

She pulled him to her by his lapels and smiled up at him saucily. 'A nookie room? That's very thoughtful of him.'

He grinned. 'Not exactly, but close. Look.' He pulled her over to the far wall, where there was a raised step, and another shallower curtain above it. He helped Claire on to the step and pulled the curtain to one side. She had to bend slightly to look through the peephole that was revealed there.

The room beyond was a bedroom similar to Stuart's, only more lavishly furnished, with a brass bed, fur rugs and pictures on the walls. It was empty, and she was about to draw away from the peephole to say as much to Stuart, when the door opened, and three people burst in. There was a man and two

214

women, laughing and obviously half drunk. They closed the door behind them and fell back against it, giggling. The man had an arm around each of his companions. One was dressed in white with long silver hair and a slender figure, while the other was a more voluptuous redhead, whose breasts strained against the taffeta of her dress. All three were wearing masks. The man turned his head to kiss each woman in turn, pressing his body towards them. They pushed him back against the door and started to undress him, their fingers tearing at the bow tie first, before peeling off his shirt, trousers and socks.

'Do they know we're here?' whispered Claire.

'Shh. He'll hear us.' Stuart's breath was warm against her ear. 'The women know there's probably someone watching, but he doesn't.'

Claire knew she should look away, but somehow she just couldn't tear herself from the peephole. She was held there by a hot voyeuristic urge. The man was naked now, apart from his boxer shorts. He was neither tall nor heavily muscled. In spite of the drink he'd consumed, there was an imperious bulge under the material of his shorts. The redhead raked her nails down his chest, then delved into his shorts. He shuddered and grinned as she wrapped her fingers around him. Claire shivered too, feeling herself grow warm. Stuart began to stroke her, running his hands over the velvet of her back and hips.

The man made a grab for the silver-haired women, but she laughingly evaded him and, turning her back to him, shrugged herself out of her dress. As she straightened up in her white silk slip, she looked straight into Claire's eyes and winked at her. Claire was embarrassed and amused, and then her amusement turned to something hotter as the woman slid one hand under the bodice of the slip and teased her nipple, her eyes behind her mask never breaking contact with Claire's. After a moment, she turned back to the man. He, meanwhile, had succeeded in freeing the redhead's breasts from her dress. They hung huge and heavy in his hands, while he slathered the nipples with his tongue, tormenting them to rigidity. Claire's sex began to ache and moisten with anticipation. Behind her, Stuart's hands stroked lower, to explore the tight moons of her buttocks under the velvet.

The women pulled the man away from the door, towards the bed, where they pushed him down on to the cover and efficiently removed his shorts. His cock was surprisingly chunky, the head lilac and shiny. He grinned as the two women each took a wrist and fastened it to the brass bedstead. The redhead sat on the bed and took out a black rubber dildo from the bedside cabinet. The man's grin vanished momentarily when he saw it, but returned again as she began to run her tongue lasciviously from its base to the tip of the knob, never taking her eyes from his. She eased the bulbous head of the dildo between her lips, then slowly took it into her mouth, stretching her lips wide to accommodate its girth. She drew it in and out of her mouth, sucking the tip luxuriously whenever she pulled it out. Then she reached for the other woman, grabbing her buttocks through the silk, and pulling her towards her. The silver-haired woman groaned and ran her hands over her body, pinching her hard little nipples through the silk, bunching the slippery material in her hands, until her lower body was exposed to the man and the woman. Her sex was shaved, startling in its nudity. A flash of heat ran through Claire at the sight. The redhead pulled her companion closer and bent to cover her inner thighs with biting little kisses, then began to tickle the bald sex with her tongue, flicking it up and down the enticing slit. The other woman pushed herself on to

216

the redhead's face, then brought both of her hands down to spread the lips of her sex apart, making herself even more accessible. Claire and the man on the bed stared into her, while Stuart's hands caressed Claire's legs, pushing up between her stockings and her skirt.

The redhead lapped at the juicy folds of flesh exposed to her, then slowly eased the black dildo up between the lips, pushing it into the other woman right to the hilt. The silver-haired woman moaned, the man on the bed muttered an oath, and Claire had to bite her own lip to stop herself from crying out, particularly as Stuart had now pushed her skirt up completely over her hips, and his hands had found the bands of flesh above her stocking tops. He began to tickle the dampening patch of hair between her legs, and she pushed her bottom up to allow his fingers better access. Meanwhile, the redhead was teasing her friend with the dildo, drawing it in and out of her vagina with one hand, pressing her other thumb to the clitoris. Then, with a wicked smile, she pulled the dildo out of her friend's sex and turned to the man on the bed. She pressed the glistening head to his lips. At first he kept his mouth shut, but then the silver haired woman slid her hand down his cock to grasp it firmly at the base, and he groaned. The redhead took the opportunity to thrust the dildo, sticky with the other woman's juice, between his lips. He took it deep into his throat, while the other woman pumped her hand up and down on his cock. The dildo was driven in and out of his mouth, until it had been sucked clean and the man was arching his hips up, on the very brink of orgasm. Suddenly the two women stopped their ministrations. The man gave a sob of frustration, and the women swapped places so that the silver-haired one was at his head, and the redhead at his groin. The silver-haired woman climbed on to the bed, and ripped his mask off. Claire gasped. The features of young Ewan Jones and his mop of black curls were plainly visible, but only for a second, because the woman straddled his face with her knees, and spread herself wide. Claire caught a glimpse of gaping wet flesh before the woman lowered herself down and began to smear herself on Ewan's face, trapping his head between her thighs.

Claire groaned, and Stuart's fingers slid inside her. She was very aroused, and bucked as his fingers found the hot, hard button of her clitoris. The redhead climbed on to the bed too, facing away from Ewan, and lowered herself on to his cock. Claire watched, gasping, as the turgid flesh was swallowed a centimetre at a time by the woman's sex. When it was buried inside, the redhead arched backwards and thrust her fat breasts towards Claire, and began to clutch and squeeze them as she thrust herself down again and again on to it. Stuart was rubbing Claire's clitoris urgently now, his fingers almost brutal, and she could feel his cock pressing into her thigh. She closed her eyes, and braced herself with her hands against the wall, preparing for the violent release she knew was coming. She opened her eyes again just as Ewan, entirely at the mercy of the two women who were riding him, shouted his pleasure into one slick sex while his cock spurted into the other. Claire came, drenching Stuart's fingers.

Sean lit a cigarette. He drew the smoke into his lungs and then breathed it out again, letting it snake into the shadows. On a jealous impulse he had followed his wife and her lover from the ballroom, but had lost them when they had slipped into the curtained passageway. Not knowing which of the alcoves they had gone into, he had settled down to wait. He wasn't sure what he was waiting for, but had already seen and heard enough from his hiding place to make his hair curl. One half-naked couple had stumbled into him, too far gone in their mutual lust to care if anyone saw them. He didn't like the idea of Claire being mixed up in some kind of orgy, even if she was with MacIntosh.

As if the thought of Claire had conjured her up, she emerged suddenly from one of the curtained alcoves with her lover, and then disappeared again into another one further down the passage. Grimly, Sean ground his cigarette beneath his heel and moved closer. It was none of his business, and yet he was driven by the need to know what was going on.

The scene through the peephole in the second alcove was already well under way. The room was larger, and this time no attempt had been made to hide the numerous peepholes that ringed the room. The occupants were dressed in shiny black rubber, their costumes designed to be as titillating as possible. One woman, whose jouncing breasts were framed by leather straps fastened on to a collar, was riding another woman around the room, kicking her with high heels. Her mount was naked, with rouged nipples that hung down towards the floor. As Claire watched, the woman on top reached round to stroke the other woman's bare rump, then pushed her gloved fingers deep into her sex. The woman beneath her gasped and sank down on to her elbows, which brought a sharp rebuke from her rider, and a slash from a riding crop. She lifted herself up and began crawling again, round and round the room, red-faced and gasping, driven by the crop and the ruthless fingers that were working away inside her.

Claire was both repulsed and fascinated. Her own sex throbbed rawly.

'Don't worry,' whispered Stuart. 'They're professionals. Nobody's getting hurt.'

Claire's gaze swept around the rest of the room, and locked on to a man who was spread-eagled facing the wall, his feet kept forcibly apart by what looked to be an iron bar between them. He was manacled and naked, slick with oil, the bunched muscles of his back rippling as the black tongue of a whip flicked over him. The whip was wielded by a woman clad from head to foot in leather. Maintaining a bored expression, she let the lashes fall lower, until they were curling around the man's buttocks, only just missing the delicate sac dangling between his legs. The man grunted and ground his groin into the wall, and as he did so, he turned his head slightly. Claire recognised Conrad Karlsson, the film star. She had no time to absorb this scene, however, because a younger man – no older than eighteen – stepped up to him and gestured for the woman to stop. The youth dipped his fingers into a jar, and spread the oily contents over the actor, smoothing it over the muscular shoulders and back, letting it trickle down into the cleft of his buttocks where it clung in droplets to the curling hair beneath. He kneaded the buttocks luxuriously for a few moments before slipping his thumbs between them and prising them wide to reveal the pucker of the other man's anus. Karlsson tensed, but was unable to close his legs because of the iron bar between them. Claire clenched her own buttocks together instinctively. The boy ran his fingers around the orifice, until the actor was shivering and sweating, then took the whip off the woman, smeared the handle with the contents of the jar, and applied the tip of it to the sensitive cleft. The older man bucked, and, with a vicious twist of his features, the boy thrust the handle of the whip all the way in. Karllson groaned out loud, his anus stretched to capacity by the unforgiving leather. Smiling, the boy ran his hand over the muscled back again, fingers dipping to caress the balls that were tightening below the leather-stuffed buttocks. Then he reached round to grasp the other man's cock, pressing his own erection against his buttocks. Claire moaned softly, wondering what the actor's fans would think if they could see their macho hero in such a submissive position. Stuart took her ear between his teeth.

'Are you turned on?' he whispered. 'Do you want to fuck me?'

Claire nodded, but didn't look at him. Her attention was still on the men in the room beyond. The boy continued to work his hands up and down the shaft of his prisoner's cock, his hips grinding against the spread buttocks. Although hands and cock were hidden, pressed against the wall, it was clear the boy was teasing Karlsson cruelly, stopping whenever he was on the brink of his climax. Claire wanted to burst into the room and ram the poor man's cock inside her, to put him out of his torment. A sheen of sweat had formed on her upper lip. She licked it away and turned her head to watch the third and final scenario that was being played out.

There were two more women, one white, one black. The black one was a real beauty. He hair was spread out on the floor beneath her, contrasting with her red stockinged legs, that were wrapped around the other woman's waist. The white woman was suckling her breasts, raising and lowering herself carefully so that the spectators could see the strap-on dildo between her legs, moving in and out. As Claire watched, the dominatrix who had been whipping Karllson knelt down behind the couple, took the globes of the top woman's buttocks in her hands, then slipped her fingers beneath the strap of the dildo to penetrate her, so that with every thrust the woman made with her artificial penis, she was invaded herself by grasping fingers. The room was filled with gasps, groans, sighs, and sucking noises. The woman who was being ridden finally collapsed, shuddering on to the floor, the gloved fingers of her passenger still buried in her vagina. Claire twisted round to face Stuart.

'Why are you showing me this?'

'Why do you think?' He kissed her deeply. 'I want you to know every pleasure.'

She gasped as his palm found the mound of her pubic bone, and ground against it through the velvet.

They both stiffened as the curtain was pushed aside.

'So here you are, Stuart. I hope I am not disturbing anything.' Vittorio stepped into the alcove. The blue eyes beneath his mask fastened on Claire's flushed face. 'I was wondering, Signora Savage, how you are enjoying my entertainment?'

Claire was momentarily speechless. Stuart's hand remained on her sex, cupping it possessively, as he scowled at Vittorio. The older man drew closer, staring down at Claire's breasts where they were heaving above the neck of her dress, and licked his fleshy lips. She pressed herself further back into the wall

'It's very interesting,' she whispered.

'You think so?' He smiled at Stuart. 'Did I not say the signora had good taste? I was wondering if you would both care to join me in my private apartments? There are only a few of us there, but you might find it . . . even more interesting.'

Stuart's hand tightened fractionally on Claire as his eyes met Vittorio's. 'I don't think so. We are quite happy here – alone.' The last word was said with emphasis.

Vittorio's gaze fell to Stuart's hand, and he smiled slightly. 'So I see. It is a pity. Ah well, if you change your mind, you know where to find me.' He turned and disappeared through the curtain.

Stuart dropped his hand. 'I'm sorry,' he said.

Claire shrugged. 'Is he always this possessive of you?'

'Of me?' he laughed. 'You're the one he's desperate to get into bed.'

Claire's eyes widened.

'I thought you might have guessed.' He looked as if he was going to say more on the subject, but then changed his mind. By the sounds that were seeping through the partition wall, they could tell that the stage-managed scenarios were reaching their finale. He leant against the wall and locked his gaze on to hers.

'I wish you weren't leaving tomorrow,' he said.

'Me too.'

'Perhaps I should come with you?'

She raised an eyebrow.

'Seriously. I've been away from London for too long.'

'What about Vittorio?'

'He would have to manage without me for a while. I'm due for a holiday.'

Claire smiled, unsure how else to respond to Stuart's proposition.

Sean pressed himself back into the shadows as Vittorio re-emerged from the alcove and headed for the studded door at the end of the passage. The Italian punched a number into the discreet keypad on the door frame and went through, never suspecting that someone was hidden behind him, close enough to make out the code he had used. Sean memorised it, and then moved nearer to the alcove again. Vittorio had left the curtain open a couple of inches, enough to see inside. Claire and MacIntosh were talking quietly together, but he couldn't hear what was being said. He felt a sudden flash of guilt to be intruding on their privacy, and was about to turn away, but stopped himself. She was still his wife! Surely he had a right to know what she was doing, and to whom?

He caught his breath as MacIntosh cupped Claire's crotch with his hand, rubbing it through the velvet, lifting her on to her toes. The Scotsman pushed her against the wall, kissing her mouth below the feathered mask, digging his fingers into the soft space between her legs. Sean's immediate instinct was to burst into the alcove and slam his fist into MacIntosh's jaw. But gradually he mastered it, and his indignation was slowly replaced by a more ambiguous, subtle emotion. He watched as MacIntosh clasped Claire to him by the waist, pressing his lips to her chin, throat and collarbone, before dropping to her cleavage.

Claire moaned as Stuart's tongue darted between her breasts, his hands hard on her waist. Suddenly the desire that had been building in her during the scenes she had watched through the peepholes raged up, threatening to batter everything down before it. She grabbed for her lover's cock, but he pushed her away and reached round to undo her dress, tugging it down so she could feel cool air on her back. She heard him draw breath as she shrugged her dress off and stepped out of it. He stared at her without speaking, drinking in the sight of her in her ruby corset, suspenders and high heeled shoes, her eyes teasing him through her mask. His gaze travelled over her, returning several times to the triangle of curls between her legs, before he groaned and pushed her back against the wall. She closed her eyes as he kissed the exposed tops of her nipples and ran his hands up her legs, stroking the silky stockings, until he reached the inside of her thighs. His fingers found the curls there, and she opened herself to him, spreading her legs wantonly. The sensation of surrender was so delicious that she gasped and opened her eyes.

And gasped again. There was a man standing in the shadows beyond the curtain, watching her. Her body tensed. It was too dark to see much except for the whiteness of his shirt, and his eyes shining through the mask he wore. Stuart's fingers probed deeper, and recklessness swept over her. She had no idea who the mysterious spy was, and found she didn't care. It wasn't likely to be anyone she knew, and even if it was, he wouldn't recognise her. She was still wearing her mask.

'Fuck me,' she said to Stuart, never taking her eyes off the other man.

But Stuart had other ideas. He grabbed her wrists with his free hand and pinned them against the wall over her head, then nipped the fat bud of her clitoris between his thumb and forefinger and started to rub it. Claire tossed her head from side to side as tremors wracked her body. She fought to free her hands, but he refused to let them go, even when he brought her at last to a knee-weakening climax. He gave her no time to recover her breath, however, still keeping her wrists imprisoned above her head, he tugged the cups of her corset down, so that her breasts were bared to him, and took one nipple between his sensuous lips. He flicked it with his tongue, making her moan and squirm even more. Even though she had just orgasmed, her whole body was aching for more, like an addict craving a fix.

'Fuck me, Stuart. Now!'

He released her hands, and she grabbed eagerly for his belt. In a second, she had unbuckled it and pushed down his trousers and shorts to release his erection. She cupped his buttocks and pulled him to her, all the while staring at the man in the shadows, knowing what an erotic sight they must present. Stuart lifted her off her feet and she rubbed herself against him, smearing the wet lips of her sex up and down the shaft of his cock. It was too much for his self control: he dug his fingers into her buttocks and brought her down on to his cock, slamming her against the wall. She cried out and wrapped her stockinged legs around his hips, pushing him deeper, so she could feel his swollen cock fill her up. She dug her nails into his buttocks. Then, her gaze still holding the glittering one behind the curtain, she brought one finger to her lips, sucked it, and dropped it down to the cleft of Stuart's buttocks. Slowly, she pushed it up into the snug crevice between them. Stuart shuddered and slammed into her, again and again, head thrown back, neck muscles straining. She clenched the muscles of her vagina tighter, fighting her own climax as she tormented him with her finger. But she could not hold it off forever. She felt one final spasm, deep inside her, like a protestation, and slumped sobbing on to her lover's shoulder. He stiffened too and gave a last, cataclysmic thrust into her. Then they collapsed together, half-senseless against the wall.

Sean reeled back into the shadows, shaken to the core. Claire had seen him. He knew she had. And yet, even as her eyes had locked with his, she had continued to fuck MacIntosh, taking a delight in the fact she was being watched. He knew that she had changed in the last few months, but he had had no idea how much. Was it the Scotsman's influence, he wondered? Or was it simply that she had matured, and discovered the potential for pleasure that had been there all along? He had no idea. All he knew was that he was bitterly jealous that he hadn't played a part in the transformation. His hands itched to throttle Mac-

Intosh first, and then Claire. Then he changed his mind. Not Claire. His hands were itching to do something quite different to his wife. He saw her again in his mind's eye – her stockinged legs spread beneath the ruby corset, the curls of her sex pearled with moisture. He groaned and ran his hand over his face. He had to talk to her.

But not yet. There was something he had to do first. He waited until his breathing had steadied, before turning to look again towards the door at the end of the passage. Vittorio was involved in something, he was certain of it. He had to find out what it was, if only to satisfy the curiosity that curled like a snake in his guts.

When Claire opened her eyes the man had gone. An absurd feeling of disappointment flooded through her. Stuart lowered her to the ground.

'Come with me, to my room,' he whispered hoarsely. 'Someone could come in here at any minute.'

She smiled wryly: he had no idea just how dangerous it was. She murmured her agreement, and Stuart helped her to dress.

In the darkness of his monastic room, they kissed again, with less urgency than before but more intensity, their breath mingling in the shadows. Then Stuart flipped on the the bedside lamp, and they were bathed in light.

'Do you want a drink?'

Claire saw the ice bucket and champagne and nodded. It was just what she needed to steady herself. After the scenes she had witnessed through the peepholes, and the way Stuart had taken her against the wall in full view of the mysterious voyeur, her heart was still beating unnaturally loud. She jumped as the cork flew out of the bottle.

'Is there anything the matter?' Stuart slanted a glance at her as he poured two glasses of the foaming liquid.

'No.' She hesitated. 'It's just that I'm not used to seeing the kind of things . . .' her voice tailed off.

He handed her a glass. 'I know you're not.' He shrugged. 'I suppose you wouldn't interest me as much if you were.'

She looked at him. 'What do you mean?'

'I know you're not a virgin – far from it. But there's still something pure, something untouched about you. It gives me a lot of pleasure to . . .' he paused, searching for the right word.

'Corrupt me.'

He laughed, but there was an uncomfortable edge to it. 'Is that what I've done?'

Claire took a few rapid sips of the icy champagne, her eyes never leaving his face. He watched her, unnerved by her silence. Then she smiled. 'Not exactly. And even if it is, I wouldn't have it any other way.' She put her glass on the bedside table.

He fingered her diamond earrings.

'You're not wearing the jewellery I gave you.'

'It didn't go with my dress.'

He fixed her with a searching gaze, but said nothing.

Clair realised that in spite of the intimate things they had shared, they were still strangers to each other. As if he had read her mind, he spoke.

'You still don't feel comfortable with me, do you?'

She looked at him, not knowing what to say.

His face twisted. 'It's OK, you don't have to say anything. Your silence is your answer.' He sat on the bed and drew her down beside him. 'Words have never been my strong point, either. I grew up in a family where we never showed each other how we

228

felt. I don't remember my mother ever telling me she loved me, or even hugging me.'

Claire opened her mouth to speak, but he put a finger to her lips.

'I know we haven't known each other very long, but . . .' he halted, his chocolate eyes boring into hers with ferocious intensity. 'Sometimes you seem so distant, as if you're not really with me at all.' He looked away. 'It almost makes me hate you.'

Claire was still silent. She couldn't think what to say. He turned to look at her again, and she met the burning look on his face without flinching.

'Sometimes the way I feel for you grips me so hard it hurts. I've never known anything like it before. I don't know what I can say, what I can do . . .' he began passionately.

This time it was her turn to silence him with her finger on his lips. 'Just show me,' she said. 'Show me the best way you know how.'

He clasped her around the waist and drew her to him. His lips touched hers, warm and meltingly tender, in a kiss that made her light-headed. But the gentleness was unsustainable in the face of the physical need that suddenly swept through them both. His lips forced hers half open. His hot breath and tongue filled her mouth, sending rivulets of pleasure sluicing through her veins. He pushed her back on the bed and, never taking his mouth from hers, began to undress her. His hands found her skin beneath the velvet of her dress, teasing it, stroking it to almost painful sensitivity. Before she knew it, she was lying under him, naked except for her stockings. She looked at him through half-closed lids as he stood up to remove his own clothes, letting her eyes delight in his muscular body, the smooth olive skin that gleamed in the lamplight, and the long cock that reared towards his belly button from the thatch of curls between his legs. She watched him as he rolled a condom over himself. Then, unable to restrain her impatience, she reached for his hand and pulled him down on to her, gasping at the sensation of his hot skin against her own. He kissed her again, while he found her sex with his fingers, and plunged them into her. His fingers twisted and teased in the slippery channel until she was utterly yielding, warm and moaning beneath him. She ran her hands over his back, cupped his buttocks, arching her groin towards his questing hand and cock. He drew back a little and her eyes met his, fever-bright for a moment, before his thumb found her clitoris and she groaned and squeezed her eyes shut. He bit her lips, her chin, as she wrapped her legs around his hips, desperate to feel him inside her. He groaned, unable to resist the invitation, and pushed inside her.

She arched up, pressing her breasts against his chest and he clasped her to him, refusing to let her pull away as he drove himself in and out of her with fierce thrusts of his hips. She didn't want to escape. Her body was engulfed by delicious sensations, that thrilled down to her toes. She wrapped her legs more tightly around him. He stopped, perspiring, and urgently spread her legs again, placing the crook of her knees over his shoulders so she was bent almost double beneath him, as open as a woman can ever be to a man. She gasped as he penetrated her more deeply, and she felt him at the very core of her. At the same time, her orgasm began to well up from the same place, rippling along her limbs, and forcing the breath between her lips in animal gasps. He gave one last, urgent thrust, before his whole body went rigid and his face contorted as if in pain.

'Claire!' He collapsed on top of her, his skin slick against her own.

Her own orgasm trembled through her, leaving her

spent and shivering. She slid her knees down and opened her eyes. Her gaze locked with his and she smiled. He sighed his own satisfaction, and picked up a lock of her hair, idly stroking it along her chin, then against his own cheek. She sighed happily, her whole body saturated with pleasure.

'Claire, if I came to London, to take a break, would you want see me?'

She stroked a bead of sweat from his eyebrow with her thumb. 'Of course I would.'

'Even though I've corrupted you?' The question was half teasing, half serious.

'I was only joking when I said that.' She kissed him. 'I would love to see you in London.'

He relaxed back against the pillows. 'Well, I suppose that's as much as I can ask for, for now.'

'Stuart . . .' Claire began, but she was interrupted by the phone.

'Ignore it,' muttered Stuart.

But the phone rang on.

Finally, he gave in and picked it up with a curse. There was a pause while he listened to the person on the other end, before he said: 'Are you sure? Is he still there? OK, I'll be right with you.' He hung up and turned back to Claire. 'Sorry. I have to go. I shouldn't be long.' He dropped his head to her breast, took her nipple in his mouth, and nipped it between his teeth. Claire squirmed. 'Don't go away. I'll be right back.'

Cherry snuggled up to Quaid's chest, and pulled Harper closer so that she could feel both of their cocks pressing against her as they all moved slowly to the music. She was filled with sweet satisfaction.

'What time is it?' she murmured. There were only a few people left on the dance floor.

The twins bumped wrists as they both looked at their watches. They grinned at each other. 'Three o'clock,' said Harper. 'We should be making our way back to the hotel soon, I guess.' He kissed the cloud of Cherry's hair under his chin.

'I wonder where Claire's got to?' mused Cherry. 'I haven't seen her for ages.'

'I wouldn't worry about it. I'm sure MacIntosh will look after her.' Quaid didn't add that he had seen Sean follow the couple off the dance floor. That was one nest of rattlers he didn't want to get mixed up in.

'Let's have one more dance,' murmured Cherry, 'and then we'll go.'

'Whatever you say, darling.'

Claire towelled herself dry. For a while after Stuart had left she thought she would fall asleep, but the shower had refreshed her. As she rubbed her hair she thought about what he had said. The idea of having him in London, as part of her everyday life, had been strange at first. He seemed so much a part of Venice, and of the fantasy life she had lived for the last week. Although their relationship had started off as purely sexual, it had deepened into something more. But what, exactly? She shied away from analysing her own feelings too closely. She enjoyed his company, in and out of bed. And he had made it clear that he had strong feelings for her. She smiled to herself. Yes, she decided, it would be good to have him with her in London.

She sat on the bed and glanced at the alarm clock on the bedside table. It was three o'clock. Where on earth was Stuart? He had been away for ages. Wrapping her towel around her, she padded to the door and poked her head out into the corridor.

'Claire!' exclaimed Sean, tearing off his mask. 'I've been looking for you everywhere.' In spite of his words, he didn't look pleased to see her. She recoiled at the grim expression on his face.

'What are you doing here?' she asked. 'If you've come to make trouble . . .'

'I haven't. At least not the sort you mean. Put some clothes on, I have something to show you.'

She set her chin stubbornly. She had no intention of letting him tell her what to do.

He sighed. 'Please. It's important.'

She searched his emerald eyes, and found nothing there but honesty. She knew Sean. If he was wanting to cause trouble he would have done it already.

'OK.'

'Hurry up – we don't have much time.'

Claire left him standing in the corridor while she wriggled herself into her basque and dress. She looked at her stockings and decided not to put them on again: her legs were still damp and it would take too long. Her mind was churning with curiosity. What could Sean want to show her? Perhaps it was the alcoves with their peepholes? If he thought he could shock her with that, he was going to get a surprise of his own. She was still furious with him for managing to seduce her again. Part of her brain admitted that she herself was to blame, but another, larger part, couldn't forgive him for having that kind of power over her. She looked at herself in the mirror. Her make-up was almost gone, and her hair clung damply against her cheeks. She tucked it behind her ears, hoping they wouldn't bump into anyone else on their mysterious travels.

When she opened the door, Sean was waiting for her, his long legs stretched out on the carpet.

'At last.' He jumped up and caught her hand. 'Come on.'

She pulled her arm away from him. 'I said I would come with you. I didn't say you could maul me about.'

He shrugged, his eyes instantly icy.

She followed him, retracing the path she and Stuart had taken from the alcoved corridor, and it seemed she had guessed right: Sean had found the peepholes. To her surprise, however, he strode past them, to the door at the end of the passage. She stared as he punched in a number on the keypad.

'What on earth are you doing?' she hissed. 'You'll get us thrown out.'

Sean threw her a glance, and there was a click as the door unlocked. He held it open for her to follow him. She hesitated. Whatever Sean was up to, he was hell-bent on doing it. If he was discovered, there might be less of a fuss if she was there with him. As furious as she was, she didn't want to see him get another black eye.

The corridor beyond was in darkness, but Claire could feel thick carpet under foot and smell incense.

'Please, Sean, let's go back,' she whispered 'These are Vittorio's private apartments.'

She realised she had instinctively reached for his hand, and did not pull away this time. He led her down the corridor, then opened a door on the right, and pulled her inside. The darkness intensified. She heard the click of a light switch, and the room glowed into life. They were in a bedroom, large and sumptuous, dominated by a huge Emperor-sized bed that was covered in a violet satin cover, and hung with crimson hangings. Sean flipped another switch and rows of downlighters illuminated the walls.

Claire gasped.

Chapter Seventeen

She stared at the flushed cheeks, the limbs that were spread wantonly against the velvet, and at the jewellery that gleamed at the throat and wrists. Her eyes skidded over the triangle of pubic hair and the moist flesh folded inside it, to lock with the eyes that smouldered out of the painting at her. Her eyes.

'I don't understand . . .'

Sean said nothing.

Claire walked on. The walls were lined with similar paintings, containing a feast of pouting mouths, breasts and spread-eagled legs. Most of them were a lot less tasteful than the portrait of her. She averted her eyes from one particularly disturbing one, where a slender figure opened itself with jewelled fingers from behind, spreading her buttocks and her sex, her silver hair pooled on the floor beneath her. It was one of the women she had seen with Ewan Jones.

'That's the same one I saw coming out of the palazzo,' said Sean. 'Apparently she's married to the Italian Minister for Transport.'

Claire passed along the gallery. And stopped again.

'Oh, my God,' she whispered.

Cherry looked back at her, an ambiguous smile playing on her painted lips. She was sitting on a flight of ancient stone steps, her arms lifted to capture the mass of her hair on top of her head. She wore only stockings and a transparent shirt, through which her nipples were clearly visible. Her knees were bent, the tails of the shirt pushed aside to reveal her stocking tops and the pink mouth of her sex between them. Claire tore her gaze from the portrait.

'This must have been the commission she wouldn't tell me about.' Claire groped backwards, until she felt the satin coverlet of the bed behind her knees. She sat down heavily and put her face in her hands.

'I'm sorry,' said Sean, his voice low.

'How could he do this? He told me the painting was just for him.' She was scalded with shame for being so gullible, and worse, that Sean of all people should have been witness to it. Hadn't he seen her humiliated enough? She looked up at him through tear-spiked lashes. There was no triumph on his face, just an expression of misery that mirrored her own.

'Are you all right?' he asked. 'I'm really sorry I had to show you this. If I'd told you about it you would never have believed me.'

'I suppose not,' she sniffed. 'I suppose I should thank you.'

He said nothing, but put his hand on her shoulder, warming her chilled skin.

'What are we going to do?' she said, pointing at the portraits of herself and Cherry. 'We can't just leave them here.'

'I know.' Sean's expression hardened. 'We'll have to take them with us. But they're too heavy to lift off the wall by ourselves. Do you know whether Harper and Quaid are still here?'

'I have no idea.'

'I'll go and see if I can find them.' He took her

hands in his. 'Wait for me here – it's less risky than both of us going out through the corridors again. If you hear anybody coming, hide.'

She nodded. 'OK. But don't be long, please.'

'I won't. I promise.'

He slipped out of the room, leaving her alone on the bed.

She let herself fall back on the cover and flung her arm over her eyes. How could Stuart do this to her? She had thought she meant something to him. She had trusted him – physically at least – more than she'd trusted any man before. She gave a laugh of scorn that ended on a sob. And this was how he had repaid her – by selling her to Vittorio, to be ogled at, and probably worse. She lowered her arm to wipe her face, and sat up with a cry of surprise.

Stuart was leaning on one of the posts of the bed, watching her. His face had assumed the same guarded expression he wore whenever he was with Vittorio. She pushed herself away from him, scrambling off the bed, cursing herself for not hearing him come in. She wiped the tears from her cheeks with shaking fingers.

An emotion flickered over his face, and he stretched out his hand towards her. 'Claire.'

'Keep away from me.'

He stepped closer.

'No, I mean it. How could you do this?' She waved her hand around the room. A thought occurred to her. 'Have you fucked all these women, to get them to pose for you? Or should I say for Vittorio? You're no better than a whore, a pimp, a monster, a – a . . .!'

'Go on. I deserve it.'

His response surprised her. She felt some of her fury ebb a little.

'You're right,' he continued. 'I am all of those things. But I have to tell you – '

'Stop! I don't want to hear any more of your lies.' Her eyes slid away from him and came to rest on the portrait hanging above the bed. It was of a black-haired girl, bare-breasted but proud, with melting brown eyes that gleamed with intelligence under her heavy brows. Claire's eyes flew from the painting to the man in front of her.

'My mother,' he confirmed. 'She was young then, no more than a schoolgirl, really.'

Claire stared at him, aghast. 'Surely Vittorio's not – not . . .'

'My father? No. But my mother was his mistress, when she was very young. He drew her into his way of life and she didn't have the experience or the strength to resist him. He can be very persuasive, as you know. Luckily, she met my father. They escaped to Scotland, where Vittorio's influence couldn't reach them. He never forgave either of them.' He looked up at the portrait sadly. 'I think, in his own way, he was in love with her.'

Claire followed his gaze. It was easy to see how Vittorio had fallen for the girl's charm.

Stuart sighed. 'Years later, when I was at college in Florence, I ran into him. Of course, I had no idea about his connection with my family. He discovered who I was, however, and had his revenge by seducing me.' He saw her critical expression. 'Please, try to understand. I was young. When I finally did rebel against him sexually, he found a stronger chain to bind me. He threatened to tell my mother about our relationship. I couldn't hurt her like that. As long as she's alive, I've been prepared to do whatever he asks. Until now.'

'What do you mean? You still betrayed me to him.'

'No, I didn't. Not in the way he wanted me to. He wanted you in his bed. I refused to help him.'

238

'You shouldn't have bothered.' She drew herself up. 'I can look after myself.'

'I doubt it.' He moved closer to her. 'But I don't want to argue. Can't you see what's under your nose, Claire? I love you.'

Her eyes flashed up at him.

'It's true. I've tried to hide it from you, but I can't any more.' He reached out to brush her arm with his thumb. 'I'm so sorry I've hurt you. It was the last thing I wanted to happen. I thought that if I let Vittorio keep the portrait, he would leave us alone. I'll leave him, find a job in London. I'll make it up to you, I promise.' He dropped his face to hers and kissed her. She closed her eyes, feeling the familiar sensations washing over her, robbing her of her strength, her will.

'No.' She pushed him away. Even as her body yearned to be taken into his arms again, her mind rebelled. 'You can't be serious. Do you really think we can be together, after all this?'

'Why not? Aren't we good together?' He imprisoned her hand and pressed it to his lips with a groan. 'What else will you do? Go home to your lonely bed in London?'

'There are other options open to her.' Sean's voice carried across the room from the door. Harper and Quaid stood behind him, their faces stony as they took in the paintings on the walls. Stuart released Claire's hand and turned to face him, his expression suddenly blank and inscrutable.

'We've come for the paintings,' continued Sean. 'And for my wife.'

The other man smiled. 'You're welcome to the portraits. But as for Claire, I think she should make up her own mind.'

'She's not going to stay with a two-faced bastard like you.'

239

'A two-faced bastard? That's rich, coming from you. At least I haven't betrayed her with another woman.'

Claire looked helplessly from Stuart to Sean and back again. Sean's narrow emerald gaze was compelling, but it was the other man's eyes that held her own. Stuart saw her hesitation, and the beginnings of a smile curled around his lips. He reached for her hand. That was his mistake; the whole of her being rebelled at the complacency of the gesture. The spell was broken.

'No.' She ran across the room towards Sean, but stopped just short of his outstretched hand. 'I don't want either of you. You're both arrogant, and selfish. All you can think about is yourselves.'

She saw Stuart's features twist with pain, and then the shutters came down again. He leant against the bedpost and lit a cigarette. The two Americans, embarrassed by the scene they had witnessed, moved towards the portraits of Claire and Cherry. Stuart watched, his eyes narrow through the smoke, as they helped Sean to lift them from the wall and tear the canvasses from the frames.

'We should be getting out of here,' muttered Quaid as he rolled up the canvas of Cherry.

They all moved to the door, Sean tucking the other canvas into his shirt as they did so. Claire looked back.

'Don't do this,' Stuart said. 'You know you'll change your mind.'

Sean took a step towards him, but Claire put a hand on his arm.

'Thanks for the advice,' she said. 'But I have some for you. Get a life, Stuart.' Then she turned and followed the others through the door.

* * *

They found Cherry sitting outside the ballroom. Harper and Quaid took an elbow each and propelled her towards the exit.

'Where on earth have you been?' she asked. 'What have you been doing with Sean? Have you been crying, Claire? And what's that under your arm?'

'We'll tell you later. Come on, we have to get out of here.'

Luckily, nobody followed them down to the jetty, where there were several water taxis waiting for the last guests. It was only when the lights of the Palazzo Giardino disappeared round a bend in the canal, that they all relaxed and began to breathe easier.

'Now will you tell me what all this is about?' muttered Cherry. 'Claire?'

Her friend shook her head and leant back wearily in her seat.

'Sean?'

But Sean was staring out over the water, his back very straight, his face turned away from them all.

'Harper? Quaid? For heaven's sake, will somebody – anybody – tell me what the hell's going on?'

Chapter Eighteen

At the twins' insistence, Cherry said goodbye to Claire and Sean and followed the Americans to their suite.

'I think they could do with some time alone,' said Harper.

His brother nodded. 'I guess so.'

Cherry stamped her foot. 'Will you tell me what's been going on, before I lose my bloody temper? What's this?' She pulled the canvas out from under Quaid's arm. They watched her as she rolled it out.

'Oh!' A furious blush stung her cheeks.

'Isn't that the kind of thing you usually do?'

'It's not the same . . .' she broke off and looked at them. 'How do you know about that?'

'Darling, we're young, free and single. We have no women folk about the place, and read magazines, the same as any man would in our position.'

'You mean you've known right from the beginning?'

'Not exactly. But one of Harper's drawings jogged our memory.'

'It doesn't matter, anyway,' said his brother. 'We haven't been straight with you either.'

'You mean you're not cowboys? You don't have a ranch?'

The men looked at each other.

'We do,' admitted Quaid finally. 'It's just that it happens to have one or two oil wells on it.'

'One or two . . .' Her gaze swept around the expensively furnished suite. She should have guessed. 'But why on earth didn't you tell me?'

'You've no idea how many women start hitting on us when they know we're rich.'

She sighed and let the canvas drop to the floor. 'I can imagine. It must be a bit like me, when I tell a man what I do for a living.'

'Is that why you didn't tell us about it?'

She shrugged. 'Partly, I suppose. But it's also something I'm not particularly proud of these days.'

Harper picked the painting up. 'You shouldn't be earning a living doing something you're not proud of. Money isn't everything.'

'That's easy for you to say,' said Cherry crossly.

Harper was looking at the painting critically. 'Say, this isn't too bad.' He looked at Cherry. 'But all the same . . .' He took a lighter from his pocket and lit the corner of the canvas. When it was burning properly, he tossed it into the empty grate. The three of them watched until the flames had consumed it, and then Quaid stamped on the ashes with his boot.

Cherry found that her eyes were wet, and blinked to clear them. 'It's late,' she said. 'Or, rather, early. My plane leaves at lunchtime, I should get back to the hotel and pack.'

Quaid slapped his forehead. 'Damnation! I forgot. Our plane leaves at ten. We'd better do some packing ourselves.'

'You're leaving too?' Cherry tried to keep the misery out of her voice. 'Where are you going?'

243

'Paris. Harper's always wanted to see the galleries there.'

'I'll leave you to it then.' She moved towards the door.

'No. Don't go.' Harper stepped in front of her. 'At least not yet.'

He kissed her shyly. She closed her eyes, when his mouth left hers again she opened them and looked at Quaid. He was watching them, his expression unreadable.

'Shall we ask her now?' Harper's face was excited and nervous.

Quaid nodded. 'Seems as good a time as any. Why don't you go ahead?'

The thin light of dawn was seeping through the curtains. Claire could hear pigeons cooing on the window ledge, and a medley of church bells calling the faithful to the early morning service. She sat up on the bed and surveyed her crumpled dress. Overcome with exhaustion, she had simply rolled into bed when they had returned to the hotel, not bothering to undress and not even caring whether Sean decided to stay or not.

She glanced around the room and saw that he had stayed.

He lay full stretch on the sofa, his feet dangling over the arm, eyes closed and breathing deeply. His bow tie hung unfastened around his neck and his shirt was pulled out of his trousers. He looked almost angelic in sleep, with his dark blonde lashes sweeping on to his cheeks, and a half-frown between his brows. Only the stubble on his chin and the yellowing bruise over his eye spoiled the impression of innocence. A lock of hair had fallen on to his forehead, filling Claire with the urge to brush it away for him.

She crushed that urge ruthlessly. There was no

chance of a reconciliation with Sean now. He had seen her most basic impulses laid bare, and had witnessed the depth to which her physical infatuation with Stuart had brought her. She sighed. It had been as much her fault as Stuart's. She had been ripe for seduction, and had fallen willingly into his hands. Even now, when she thought about the pleasure he had given her, she couldn't really regret it. All she regretted was that damned portrait. It was too concrete, too obvious a proof of her surrender.

She was straightening her dress, smoothing the crushed velvet with her fingers, when there was a knock at the door. She hurried to open it.

It was Cherry, fully dressed in jeans, a mohair jumper and her usual high heels. Before she could speak, Claire motioned for her to be quiet.

'Sean's still asleep,' she whispered, stepping out into the corridor and closing the door behind her. 'I don't want to wake him.'

'So he's still here? Have you two . . .?'

'No.' Claire cut off the question, and saw that Cherry had her suitcases with her. 'What, are you packed already? The plane doesn't leave until lunchtime.'

'I know. I'm not coming back to London with you.'

Claire raised an eyebrow and smiled. 'You've solved your problems, then? Which one did you go for in the end?'

Cherry blushed. 'Both of them.'

'What?'

'Oh, I know it must sound a bit pervy. But they say they're happy for the three of us to be together.'

'What about you? Is that what you want?'

'Are you kidding? It's the answer to every woman's prayer. I'm so excited. I can't wait to see Paris with them.'

Claire laughed under her breath. 'You're incredible.

245

It doesn't matter what kind of mess you fall into, you always come out smelling of roses.' Her face grew serious again. 'But after Paris, what then? Are you going back to the States with them?'

Cherry shrugged. 'Who knows? We're just going to let things drift along for a while, and see what happens.' She paused. 'I really have to go, they're waiting for me downstairs.'

Claire kissed Cherry's cheek. 'Good luck. You will give me a ring, won't you, to let me know how you're getting on?'

'Of course I will.' Cherry picked up her cases. 'Ta ta, then. And good luck to you, too,' she nodded towards the door, 'with you-know-who.'

Claire watched her friend totter down the corridor and into the lift, then turned with a sigh and went back into her room. Jealousy was a funny thing. She hoped that Quaid and Harper wouldn't let it spoil things for her friend. Was Cherry brave, she wondered, or just naive? She seemed to have an incredible faith in life. She herself would never have had the nerve to plunge into a situation like that, not knowing how it would end. It was in her nature always to want things planned down to the last detail, to have every eventuality catered for. Did that make her a boring person?

As she was heading for the bathroom, her foot nudged the canvas that had fallen out of Sean's shirt. She picked it up, hesitated a moment, then unrolled it and laid it on the floor. She scrutinised it critically. Was it really so bad? It was certainly a flattering portrait. Pietro had captured her firm, high breasts, her slender figure and even the texture of her skin, making it glow with life. Under his knowing hands she had been transformed into something exotic and daring: an adventuress. There was no doubt that if the woman in the portrait wanted something, she would get it. But what about the real Claire Savage?

In Vittorio's bedroom, she had told Stuart and Sean that she didn't want either of them. Was that the truth? Stuart had fascinated her, but he was weak. The seed of contempt had been sown in her feelings for him, and would have eventually grown to smother everything else. As for Sean – was the only reason she said she didn't want him because she doubted she could win him back? Or was it the fear of losing him again that stopped her from admitting she still loved him? Her eyes slid to where he lay, and opened wide. He was watching her.

'I thought you were asleep,' she said.

'I was. But for the last few minutes I've been looking at you, looking at yourself.' He sat up and ran his hand through his hair. 'What do you see there?'

'Nothing.' She looked down and rolled the canvas up again. He took it out of her hands before she realised his intention. She made a grab for it, but he evaded her easily, and unfurled the painting again.

'Shall I tell you what I see?'

Claire chewed her lip, bracing herself for what was coming.

He stroked a long brown finger over the painted cheek and throat, tracing the hollows and curves of her body. 'I see the woman I married you for, when you were twenty-one. The one I thought you would become.'

She stared at him, uncomprehending.

He didn't look at her, but continued to caress the painting with his eyes and finger, until she began to feel almost jealous of it. 'I see a woman who's secure in her own sexuality and beauty, who knows how to give and receive pleasure. Who knows how to take risks.' He looked at her at last. 'I see you, Claire.'

247

She blushed. 'But I . . .'

He silenced her with his mouth on hers. She sat, unable to move as a shimmering pleasure stole through her. Without consciously knowing what she was doing, she raised her hands to his shoulders and felt her fingers dig into the warm flesh beneath his shirt. She didn't know whether she was trying to pull him closer or keep him at a distance. His lips left hers.

'Claire,' he murmured thickly. He was going to say more, but this time she silenced him with a bruising kiss of her own. He groaned and pulled her on to his lap on the floor. She felt his hands undo the zip of her dress, and helped him tug it off over her head, leaving her dressed in nothing but her corset. He looked down at the golden arcs of her breasts above the satin-trimmed cups and sighed. His fingers dug into her bare buttocks as he lifted her up and pressed his face between her breasts, scouring the tender skin with his stubble. He nibbled them, and travelled up her throat with greedy, biting kisses, then he caught her ear between his teeth.

'Do you want to do it here, on the floor?' he whispered. 'Or up against the wall?'

She looked at him.

'I know you like it that way.' He grinned.

All the blood that had risen to her cheeks slowly drained away. 'You!' she gasped at last. 'It was you who spied on me and Stuart through the curtain!'

'Aren't you glad it was me, and not some stranger?' His voice was throaty, teasing.

She remained stubbornly silent, while he kissed and nibbled the delicate shell of her ear. She didn't know what to think, how to react. Sean had seen her fuck Stuart. It was even worse than him seeing the portrait.

She shivered as he pushed his tongue into her ear.

He groaned. 'You've no idea what that did to me.' He took her hand and pulled it to his groin. She felt him, hot and hard under her palm. 'You saw me watching you, and you enjoyed it. Hussy!'

Incredibly, Claire felt laughter bubbling up inside her. She threw her head back and surrendered to the impulse.

'What's so funny?'

'You are. We are.' She pulled his bow tie out of his collar and threw it to one side. Then she began to undo the buttons on his shirt, to reveal the tanned skin underneath. He watched her face, bemused by the smile on it. When she had stripped him of his shirt, she tossed that aside, too, and turned her attention to his trousers. His cock was straining against the fly. She traced the length of it teasingly with one fingernail. He shuddered and pressed her palm to it. Slowly, she unzipped him and released his erection. She clasped it in both of her hands. He closed his eyes at the exquisite sensation, and she kissed him leisurely, feeling him stiffen still further.

He pushed her thighs apart so that she was straddling him. It happened so quickly that she gasped, and then gasped again as his fingers found her sex, slick and aching for him. She felt the tip of his cock seeking entrance. She opened her eyes and looked into his face, dark with desire.

'Can I come home, Claire?' he groaned. 'Let me in.'

She lowered herself on to him. He arched under her, she freed one of her breasts from her corset and pushed the nipple into his panting mouth. He sucked on it desperately as she began to move on him, feeling his cock filling her up, coaxing the familiar pepper-hot tingle of lust from deep inside her. Before she knew it, she was riding him shamelessly, not holding anything back, the sweat sheening her skin as she drove herself towards orgasm. She shuddered as his thumbs spread her labia to find the throbbing button of her clitoris.

Suddenly, he rolled her over, and pinned her beneath him on the carpet. It happened so fast that it took her by surprise. At first she was furious: she had been so close to orgasm. But then he began to move in her, and she forgot her anger. As his movements became more demanding she forgot everything, the carpet under her, her humiliation at Stuart's hands, and even the fact that the man on top of her was Sean. She forgot everything except her own pleasure. Sean's thrusts were urgent, almost violent now, driving her along the carpet with the force of them. She braced herself by clutching at the leg of the bed, and opened herself as wide as she could. A drop of sweat splashed down from his throat on to her breasts, and she felt his muscles bunch, as taut as steel under her fingers. She dug her nails into him cruelly, driving him on, until she felt herself spinning down into the black chasm of orgasm. It sucked her in, and, after what seemed like an eternity, spat her out again, sobbing and shaking. Sean was still moving inside her, his teeth clenched with the effort of holding back his own satisfaction. Then, incredibly, she felt the pleasure she thought had risen to its peak begin to swell again. It crashed over her a second time, and this time Sean was with her. She heard him shout her name, as if from a long way away.

It was quite a while before she opened her eyes. Sean had collapsed on top of her, his skin fiery where it touched hers. She stroked his head where it rested heavily on her breast. He spoke, without moving.

'Can we try again? Will you forgive me?'

She felt tears gather, clamping her throat. She should be asking for his forgiveness too; forgiveness for her obsession with work, and for her unwillingness to give more of herself, both in and out of bed.

Misunderstanding her silence, he raised his head to look at her.

'I love you, you know. I never stopped loving you. Not once.'

She realised she believed him. Slowly, she nodded. 'I love you too.'

'Claire!' As he kissed her, she tasted salt on his lips. It might have been sweat or tears, she couldn't tell, but then as he nuzzled her neck she felt the dampness on his cheeks.

She sighed happily. For the last six months life had buffeted her from the extremes of misery and ecstasy and back again, too many times to count. She was aching all over, mentally and physically. But at last she felt as if she was in control of her own destiny. She shifted and winced as she felt the smart of carpet burns on her buttocks and shoulders. There had been a time when she would have complained about them, but now she found she didn't give a damn. In fact – she admitted incredulously to herself – she even relished their sting.

BLACK LACE NEW BOOKS

Published in March

SILKEN CHAINS
Jodi Nicol

Fleeing her scheming guardian and an arranged marriage, Abbie, an innocent young Victorian woman, is thrown from her horse. She awakens in a lavish interior filled with heavenly perfumes to find that Leon Villiers, the wealthy and attractive master of the house, has virtually imprisoned her with sensual pleasures. Using his knowledge of Eastern philosophy and tantric arts, he introduces her to experiences beyond her imagination. But will her guardian's unerring search for her ruin this taste of liberty?

ISBN 0 352 33143 7

THE HAND OF AMUN
Juliet Hastings

Marked from birth, Naunakhte – daughter of a humble scribe – must enter a life of dark eroticism as the servant of the Egyptian god Amun. She becomes the favourite of the high priestess but is accused of an act of lascivious sacrilege and is forced to flee the temple for the murky labyrinth of the city. There she meets Khonsu, a prince of the underworld, but fate draws her back to the temple and she is forced to choose between two lovers – one mortal and the other a god.

ISBN 0 352 33144 5

Published in April

PALAZZO
Jan Smith

Disenchanted following her divorce, Claire Savage, a successful young advertising executive, finds her sexuality reawakened by the mysterious Stuart MacIntosh, whom she meets on a holiday in Venice. Stuart encourages her to explore the darkest reaches of erotic experience but, at the same time, draws her into a sensual intrigue involving one of his rich clients and Claire's best friend, the feisty Cherry. To complicate matters, Claire's ex-husband appears on the scene, leaving Claire not knowing who to trust.

ISBN 0 352 33156 9

THE GALLERY
Frederica Alleyn

Jaded with her dull but secure relationship, WPC Cressida Farleigh agrees to take part in the undercover investigation of a series of art frauds which will separate her from her long-term boyfriend. The chief suspect is the darkly attractive owner of a London art gallery, and Cressida must use her powers of seduction in order to find out the truth. She encounters a variety of fascinating people, including a charming artist specialising in bizarre, erotic subject matter, and is forced to face up to her innermost desires.

ISBN 0 352 33148 8

To be published in May

AVENGING ANGELS
Roxanne Carr

Disillusioned by the chauvinistic attitude of men in the idyllic summer resort of Tierra del Sol, tour guide Karen puts her fledgling skills as a dominatrix to the test. Pleasantly surprised by the results, Karen opens a bar – Angels – where women can realise their most erotic fantasies. However, the one man Karen really wants – Riccardo Baddeiras – the owner of a rival bar and brother of her business partner Maria, refused to be drawn into her web of submission. Quite clearly, Karen will have to fine tune her skills.

ISBN 0 352 33147 X

THE LION LOVER
Mercedes Kelly

It's the 1920s. When young doctor Mathilda Valentine becomes a medic in a mission in Kenya she soon finds out all is not what it seems. For one thing, McKinnon, the handsome missionary, has been married twice – and both of his wives have mysteriously disappeared. Mathilda falls for a rugged game warden but ignores his warnings that she might be in danger. Abducted and sold into slavery, she finds herself in the weird and wonderful harem of an Arabian sultan and discovers the truth about the two Mrs McKinnons. Will she regain her freedom?

ISBN 0 352 33162 3

If you would like a complete list of plot summaries of Black Lace titles, please fill out the questionnaire overleaf or send a stamped addressed envelope to:-

Black Lace, 332 Ladbroke Grove, London W10 5AH

BLACK LACE BACKLIST

All books are priced £4.99 unless another price is given.

─────✄──────────────

Please send me the books I have ticked above.

Name   ....

Address   ....

              ....

              ....

              .... Post Code ....

Send to: **Cash Sales, Black Lace Books, 332 Ladbroke Grove, London W10 5AH.**

Please enclose a cheque or postal order, made payable to **Virgin Publishing Ltd**, to the value of the books you have ordered plus postage and packing costs as follows:
   UK and BFPO – £1.00 for the first book, 50p for each subsequent book.
   Overseas (including Republic of Ireland) – £2.00 for the first book, £1.00 each subsequent book.

If you would prefer to pay by VISA or ACCESS/ MASTERCARD, please write your card number and expiry date here:

....

Please allow up to 28 days for delivery.

Signature   ....

─────✄──────────────

WE NEED YOUR HELP ...
to plan the future of women's erotic fiction –

– and no stamp required!

Yours are the only opinions that matter.

Black Lace is the first series of books devoted to erotic fiction by women for women.

We intend to keep providing the best-written, sexiest books you can buy. And we'd appreciate your help and valued opinion of the books so far. Tell us what you want to read.

THE BLACK LACE QUESTIONNAIRE

SECTION ONE: ABOUT YOU

1.1 Sex *(we presume you are female, but so as not to discriminate)*
Are you?
Male ☐
Female ☐

1.2 Age
under 21 ☐ 21–30 ☐
31–40 ☐ 41–50 ☐
51–60 ☐ over 60 ☐

1.3 At what age did you leave full-time education?
still in education ☐ 16 or younger ☐
17–19 ☐ 20 or older ☐

1.4 Occupation _____

1.5 Annual household income

under £10,000	☐	£10–£20,000	☐
£20–£30,000	☐	£30–£40,000	☐
over £40,000	☐		

1.6 We are perfectly happy for you to remain anonymous; but if you would like to receive information on other publications available, please insert your name and address

_____

_____

_____

_____

SECTION TWO: ABOUT BUYING BLACK LACE BOOKS

2.1 How did you acquire this copy of *Palazzo*?

I bought it myself ☐   My partner bought it ☐
I borrowed / found it ☐

2.2 How did you find out about Black Lace books?

I saw them in a shop ☐
I saw them advertised in a magazine ☐
I saw the London Underground posters ☐
I read about them in _____
Other _____

2.3 Please tick the following statements you agree with:

I would be less embarrassed about buying Black
Lace books if the cover pictures were less explicit ☐
I think that in general the pictures on Black
Lace books are about right ☐
I think Black Lace cover pictures should be as
explicit as possible ☐

2.4 Would you read a Black Lace book in a public place – on a train for instance?

Yes ☐   No ☐

SECTION THREE: ABOUT THIS BLACK LACE BOOK

3.1 Do you think the sex content in this book is:
      Too much   □   About right   □
      Not enough   □

3.2 Do you think the writing style in this book is:
      Too unreal/escapist   □   About right   □
      Too down to earth   □

3.3 Do you think the story in this book is:
      Too complicated   □   About right   □
      Too boring/simple   □

3.4 Do you think the cover of this book is:
      Too explicit   □   About right   □
      Not explicit enough   □
Here's a space for any other comments:

SECTION FOUR: ABOUT OTHER BLACK LACE BOOKS

4.1 How many Black Lace books have you read?   □

4.2 If more than one, which one did you prefer?

4.3 Why?

SECTION FIVE: ABOUT YOUR IDEAL EROTIC NOVEL

We want to publish the books you want to read – so this is your chance to tell us exactly what your ideal erotic novel would be like.

5.1 Using a scale of 1 to 5 (1 = no interest at all, 5 = your ideal), please rate the following possible settings for an erotic novel:

Medieval/barbarian/sword 'n' sorcery ☐
Renaissance/Elizabethan/Restoration ☐
Victorian/Edwardian ☐
1920s & 1930s – the Jazz Age ☐
Present day ☐
Future/Science Fiction ☐

5.2 Using the same scale of 1 to 5, please rate the following themes you may find in an erotic novel:

Submissive male/dominant female ☐
Submissive female/dominant male ☐
Lesbianism ☐
Bondage/fetishism ☐
Romantic love ☐
Experimental sex e.g. anal/watersports/sex toys ☐
Gay male sex ☐
Group sex ☐

Using the same scale of 1 to 5, please rate the following styles in which an erotic novel could be written:

Realistic, down to earth, set in real life ☐
Escapist fantasy, but just about believable ☐
Completely unreal, impressionistic, dreamlike ☐

5.3 Would you prefer your ideal erotic novel to be written from the viewpoint of the main male characters or the main female characters?

Male ☐   Female ☐
Both ☐

5.4 What would your ideal Black Lace heroine be like? Tick
     as many as you like:

Dominant	☐	Glamorous	☐
Extroverted	☐	Contemporary	☐
Independent	☐	Bisexual	☐
Adventurous	☐	Naïve	☐
Intellectual	☐	Introverted	☐
Professional	☐	Kinky	☐
Submissive	☐	Anything else?	☐
Ordinary	☐	_____	

5.5 What would your ideal male lead character be like?
     Again, tick as many as you like:

Rugged	☐		
Athletic	☐	Caring	☐
Sophisticated	☐	Cruel	☐
Retiring	☐	Debonair	☐
Outdoor-type	☐	Naïve	☐
Executive-type	☐	Intellectual	☐
Ordinary	☐	Professional	☐
Kinky	☐	Romantic	☐
Hunky	☐		
Sexually dominant	☐	Anything else?	☐
Sexually submissive	☐	_____	

5.6 Is there one particular setting or subject matter that your
     ideal erotic novel would contain?

_____

SECTION SIX: LAST WORDS

6.1 What do you like best about Black Lace books?

_____

6.2 What do you most dislike about Black Lace books?

_____

6.3 In what way, if any, would you like to change Black Lace
     covers?

_____

6.4 Here's a space for any other comments:

_____

_____

_____

_____

Thank you for completing this questionnaire. Now tear it out of the book – carefully! – put it in an envelope and send it to:

    Black Lace
    FREEPOST
    London
    W10 5BR

No stamp is required if you are resident in the U.K.